PUBLIC

SAFETY

PUBLIC
SAFETY

A Novel of 1941

Joseph Connolly

iUniverse, Inc.
New York Lincoln Shanghai

PUBLIC SAFETY
A Novel of 1941

iUniverse books may be ordered through booksellers or by contacting:

iUniverse
2021 Pine Lake Road, Suite 100
Lincoln, NE 68512
www.iuniverse.com
1-800-Authors (1-800-288-4677)

Because of the dynamic nature of the Internet, any Web addresses or links contained in this book may have changed since publication and may no longer be valid.

This is a work of fiction. All of the characters, names, incidents, organizations, and dialogue in this novel are either the products of the author's imagination or are used fictitiously.

ISBN: 978-0-595-39886-7 (pbk)
ISBN: 978-0-595-90660-4 (cloth)
ISBN: 978-0-595-84285-8 (ebk)

Printed in the United States of America

For Cindy

One

On a warm April afternoon in 1941, Earl Brady stepped into the office of his boss, the assistant district attorney of Los Angeles County.

"Sit down, Earl. How's the boy?"

Bud Fletcher had a Fort Worth drawl, undiminished by three decades away from Texas. Some suspected, Earl Brady among them, that Fletcher made a deliberate effort to keep his accent. He wasn't much over five feet tall. The son of a domineering oil millionaire, he had been a complete failure at sports and was forever overshadowed by his war-hero brother. He'd left Texas for Harvard Law School and never looked back. *Maybe,* Earl thought, *if you were Bud Fletcher, it was better to be from Texas than in it. All things considered.*

"Fine, Mr. Fletcher, thanks. John's happy to be at Southern Cal. Draft registration isn't until next July for college students. He thinks his lifeguard job might keep him deferred, but that depends on—"

"Well," Fletcher interrupted, "maybe I can put a word in. Let me get to the point here, Earl. I need to give you an assignment. Different. Not a case. It's not an investigation even, really."

"All right," said Earl, wincing at his jittery, overlong reply to the question about his stepson. Small talk with Fletcher was best kept small.

"It's a—" Fletcher jerked his swivel chair into a quarter turn and coughed. It was more like a long, loose, wet growl. "Sorry, it's a committee. You just go to some meetings to start with. They wanted me to be on it, but I thought you could do it, and everyone's agreed."

Fletcher pulled rimless eyeglasses from his face, stuck each lens into his wide-open mouth, and wiped the resulting fog with his necktie. Throughout this process he kept his eyes fixed on Earl.

"I suppose," he said as he replaced the curved wire ear-pieces, "I ought to tell you a little more …"

"That'd be swell, sir."

"… seeing that your first meeting is tomorrow."

"I'm afraid that won't be—" Earl began, before the boss interrupted again.

"Don't worry, I've arranged for a continuance on the Wilson case. Been moved a week. My secretary is calling your witnesses right now."

Irritated, Earl rubbed at the corners of his mouth. He had spent most of the day, and the one before, reviewing exhibits in the Wilson forgery case.

"Here's what I know," Fletcher continued. "This committee is being run by the FBI. There are representatives of the navy, army, LAPD, maybe a couple others. It's to be called 'Public Safety,' or some such … thing. But what it really is, Earl, is this. The government thinks it has discovered Japanese spies around here. Not here in this office, I mean here in California. West Coast."

Fletcher erupted with another coughing fit. This one jackknifed him forward until he disappeared below the top of his desk. As Earl came up out of his chair, he could hear a moist plop hitting the bottom of a steel wastebasket. The boss resurfaced, waved Earl back onto his seat, and continued.

"Anyway, West Coast. Lots of activity, they think. They want to line up cooperation with state and local. We're not getting along well with Japan, I take it. Washington wants us ready to act on sabotage, espionage, et cetera. In case there are hostilities."

"They want us ready to act," Earl repeated softly. "Using state courts?"

"I suppose. At least as far as making arrests, holding suspects until other charges can be filed. I don't know. It's not real obvious to me what our part'll be in this, Earl, to tell you the damn truth. I do know it is deemed"—Fletcher pronounced this with a grimace—"important. That, I have on good authority."

"Time and place, sir?"

Fletcher tapped an index finger twice on his forehead. "Yes," he said, pulling open a desk drawer, "tomorrow morning at eleven, over at the Federal Courthouse. U.S. Attorney's office, Conference Room B." He slid an unmarked envelope to Earl's side of the desk.

"Read this before the meeting. It doesn't say much, but file it in a locked cabinet when you're done. Come see me tomorrow afternoon. I reckon that's it, Earl. Thank you. Say hello to your wife, won't you?"

Fletcher, now standing, clicked off his desk lamp. Earl pushed his chair back, stood, and looked at his watch. Four thirty. The boss was never late for his Wednesday poker game.

Two

As he walked downstairs to his office, Earl Brady tried to look at the bright side. With the Wilson forgery trial delayed, the last two days of tedious preparation were a waste, but his evening had become free. He slid the unopened envelope into a coat pocket.

Earl's own office was about half the size of Bud Fletcher's, but it was all his. He sat on the front edge of his desk, turned the telephone around, and dialed.

On the second ring, "Hello?"

"Sweetheart, it's me."

"I hope so; nobody else is allowed to call me that."

"Good news. I can leave early, and there's no trial tomorrow. Thought I'd take us out for dinner. Maybe the Galley."

"I'll be ready when you get here. Bye, love."

"Bye."

Earl hung up and moved around to his chair, just to take one more look at the next day's calendar. The entire box for April 17 was filled with "Wilson," in large, penciled letters. He turned his head to the right and looked at the photograph of Doris, taken on their honeymoon in Santa Barbara six years earlier.

In the picture she was leaning back against a waist-high wood fence, arms out to the sides, hands loosely gripping the top rail. She wore a tennis dress, her dark hair wet, and her face turned slightly. She was looking down, smiling, embarrassed.

Doris claimed to hate the picture, because "I look like a college brat who just got caught sneaking out of the men's dormitory before breakfast." The day after he'd heard that complaint, Earl had the picture framed.

*   *   *   *

It wasn't yet five o'clock when Earl walked across Temple Street to the parking lot. His pea green 1934 Chrysler, the chrome trim rusting badly at the edges, sat between two LAPD black-and-whites. One was an annoying twelve inches from Earl's driver-side door. After squeezing in, he started up and guided the car onto Temple, then right onto Spring Street.

Passing a red streetcar, he missed being able to travel home to Santa Monica on the Pacific Electric. Service had been discontinued in 1940. More people were getting cars all the time. The Arroyo Seco Parkway had just opened, connecting Pasadena to downtown with a sunken curving track of concrete. Earl had tried the Santa Monica line's bumpy and slow replacement bus but soon began driving to work.

On those trains, he had used his time to read newspapers and maga zines, taking in the words and ideas of unseen others. Driving took that pleasure away. Now, eyes on the road, Earl had to be his own amusement. He usually passed the minutes with memories and speculations.

A few blocks down Spring Street was the Pacific Trust Building, whose tenants included his father's law firm. Brady, Palmer, and Root had a blue-chip roster of real estate, oil, and banking clients. Their businesses had grown up with Los Angeles itself. Earl drove past the PT Building thinking of his father and about his own relief at escaping the place to join the DA's office. *Bless you, Bud Fletcher, for saving me from a lifetime of mineral leases and board minutes. And for having a father who knew my father.*

The DA's office suited him better. Earl Brady, like Bud Fletcher, lived in a state of fraternal eclipse. Simon Brady wasn't merely older than Earl; Simon was the elder brother, more serious, harder working, and far more ambitious. Before Simon was even a teenager, his determination and focus were family legends. Earl had none of these traits, it seemed. What he was blessed with—or cursed with; opinions varied—was curiosity. Earl read books constantly; Simon never looked at one unless it was assigned. Simon never had questions about anything, but Earl would ask until ordered to stop. Earl could never drive past the PT Building without thinking of Simon, who loved the family law firm as much as Earl hated it. Simon, the heir apparent. Simon, who never left anything to chance: meticulous, cautious, thorough, the model business lawyer.

As he drove, it occurred to Earl that his brother would never reminisce or daydream like this. Simon's mind didn't wander; it sorted, organized, and planned. Even his marriage to a dark-haired beauty who was barely out of high school, the daughter of a judge, had seemed utterly practical and calculated. But marriage had relaxed Simon, a little, and fatherhood had softened up some of his formality.

Earl's memory held two lasting images of Simon. One was of Simon behind his desk, dictating a grammatically perfect letter to a scribbling secretary; in the other, Simon stood on Hermosa Beach at the water's edge. He wore rolled-up khaki trousers and held a giggling toddler by both hands, hoisting the boy over the sliding water of a summer evening's low tide. The plane crash that killed Simon, on a windy November afternoon in 1930, had made that little boy fatherless at seven. Doris Grady had suddenly become a twenty-six-year-old widow.

Earl had done the identifying, next morning, at the base of a steep and dry Palos Verdes hillside. He had promised his brother's cold body that the boy would be taken care of; and he would look after Doris, too.

He did. There was monthly paperwork to do for Doris. There were Sunday dinners, movies. Earl took his nephew to sporting events almost every weekend. They spent two weeks attending as many 1932 Olympic competitions as they could, on the law firm's tickets. The idea of marrying Doris, he later told her, first crossed his mind at the 1932 closing ceremonies. The thought embarrassed him. He didn't let himself have it again for a year.

Turning west on Pico now, he remembered a telephone conversation, their turning point.

"Doris, it's me."

"Uncle Earl! Hello there! Let me get Johnny."

"Wait. I'd like to talk to you first."

"Oh. Is everything all right?"

"Ah, fine."

"New job going well?"

"It's great, actually. I prefer it. My father still can't believe I left the firm, but I like it here."

"The gritty world of criminal law," Doris had said with a chuckle. "I can picture you there—if I try hard enough. But I saw big Ed yesterday, and you're right—he can't believe it. Your father thinks you've taken leave of your senses."

Earl laughed, then took a deep breath. "Speaking of that," he said, "I'm calling to invite you out for dinner tomorrow."

"Sure," Doris chirped. "What time will you pick us up?"

"Johnny's not invited."

"Oh?"

"Yeah, I meant 'you,' singular. I want to see you."

"Well," Doris had said, "he'll be disapp … What a nice invitation. Is there something we need to talk about?"

"Not a thing."

✳   ✳   ✳   ✳

Earl arrived in Santa Monica and parked his car.

The legless man who sold the three-cent *Santa Monica Evening Outlook* for a nickel was in his usual place, on the sidewalk outside Tip's Finest Steaks at Fourth and Wilshire. He was plopped on a canvas-covered pillow on a square wood pallet with metal caster wheels. He rested one raw-knuckled hand on his stack of papers, using it only to exchange them for nickels. The other hand was in constant, magician-like motion as it rolled, lit, held, and flicked away cigarettes.

Earl had once tried, while awaiting the jury's verdict in a burglary case, to perform the amputee vendor's trick of rolling a cigarette one-handed. Fifteen minutes of effort had produced a loose pile of tobacco dust and torn paper. The case detective, an amateur cartoonist, later presented Earl with a drawing of the scene, inscribed, "Next time let's not forget the playing cards."

For fear of offending the legless man, Earl had chosen not to tell him about the failed attempt at duplicating his cigarette act. The man never spoke; whether that was by choice or because of his injuries, Earl wasn't sure. They did share one joke, or so Earl believed: in January on the first working day of each year, Earl would point to the date on the paper and say, "This means I'll be forty this year. Getting old, damn it." The man would respond with a faint smile.

*   *   *   *

As he quickly read the lead story before driving away, he promised himself to look at a world atlas.

SANTA MONICA EVENING OUTLOOK
Wednesday, April 16, 1941
BALKAN WAR FRONT AFLAME
Climactic Battle Between Nazis, British Begins

Wide-open battle flamed along the entire British front in Greece today. The Germans acknowledged that Hitler's blitzkrieg invasion was meeting "stubborn" resistance after previously asserting that the Allies were in headlong retreat.

British headquarters in Athens said German Panzer spearheads were executing savage thrusts but declared that nowhere had they overshot the Allied defense line. The apparent collapse of Yugoslavia, coupled with the German break into northern Greece, gave a darker turn to events for the Allies, however, in the eleven-day-old battle for the Balkans.

Hitler's high command reported the capture of Sarajevo, where the assassination of Archduke Franz Ferdinand touched off the 1914–18 World War, and declared that "thousands of Serbs" were surrendering.

Three

The Galley Restaurant on Main Street was decorated in a nautical theme, along the lines of a high school set for *Mutiny on the Bounty*. There were pilot-wheel chandeliers, rope fishnets, brass porthole windows, Polynesian watercolors in bamboo frames. The Bradys settled into a corner table and ordered rum drinks.

"I heard from John today," Doris said.

"He called?"

"No." She laughed. "We got mail from him. He sent a postcard from Balboa Island last week. He said spring vacation is great fun."

"Anything else?"

"Nope. That was a literal quote. I memorized the whole thing, all five words."

"Bud Fletcher asked about John today," said Earl. "Also sends you his best. Cheers."

They clicked glasses. "Whew," said Doris with a grimace and a quick shake of her head after sipping the grog. "How did John's name come up?"

"Just small talk. Although he did say something about helping John with this draft business. Something to keep in mind, I suppose."

"Order me the usual dinner, will you? I'm going to the ladies' room."

He remembered the envelope in his coat pocket. He took out the memo as Doris walked away and held it under the small table lamp.

CONFIDENTIAL MEMORANDUM No. 1

To: Los Angeles Public Safety Committee Members
From: Special Agent T. A. Lindgren, FBI
Date: April 14, 1941

The purpose of this committee will be to share certain information with state and local officials and to begin planning for necessary cooperation and coordination in the event of war between the United States and Japan.

According to a highly reliable source, the Japanese government is working to establish intelligence networks in Southern California (and elsewhere on the West Coast) that could operate to the severe detriment of American interests if our country is forced into a war with Japan.

It is important that the proceedings of the committee, and indeed its existence, should be known only to the smallest possible number of persons at this time. Those within your agency who need to be informed have identified themselves to you. More details will be provided at the first meeting.

*   *   *   *

"It's still warm out," Doris said as they left the Galley. "Let's go look at the moon."

They drove up Ocean Avenue, parked, and walked out to the edge of the grassy bluff overlooking Pacific Coast Highway, the wide sand beach, and the ocean. They sat on a familiar bench, near the railing.

"Nice memories, this place," she said.

He put an arm around her. "Yep. Scene of many past glories."

"The proposition and the proposal," she said. "All that romance on one little wooden bench."

"Know something? I'd do all of it again."

"Me too," said Doris, resting her head on his shoulder. "Me too."

*   *   *   *

The proposition, he remembered, was offered on a cold, windy spring evening in 1934. They had been to the movies. He'd interrupted their kissing and asked when Johnny needed to be picked up from his grandmother's house.

"Tomorrow," Doris answered.

"Tomorrow?"

"That's right."

"I, uh … why is he—"

"'Cause I won't be home tonight."

"And where might you be spending the night?" he asked, catching on. "If you don't mind me asking."

"Let's see," Doris said, reaching into her overcoat pocket. She pulled out a key attached to a brass disk. "Room 210, Del Mar Hotel. Same as you."

*   *   *   *

The proposal came a few months later, at sundown. Same wooden bench.

"What do you want to do tonight?" Doris had asked.

He took a deep breath. "I, ah, I want to ask you to marry me."

"I love you, Earl," she said, throwing her arms around his neck. "And I want to say yes."

"I love you, too. Are you, um, going to say yes?"

She pulled away and answered with a question. "Why do you want to marry me?"

"I'm in love with you."

"I know," she said. "But I have to wonder. I have to ask you something. Is this for Johnny?"

"I … no, it's not. I don't need to marry you to take care of Johnny. Help take care of Johnny, I mean."

She looked out at the ocean, saying nothing. "Listen," he said, grasping her shoulders and turning her toward him. "It would be easier not to. A lot easier, let's face it. You were my brother's wife. There might be some people who think it's odd, or even think it's wrong, for us to be … in this. In love, I mean. But I don't care, see? I'm in love with you; that's what I care about. I didn't plan on this. I'm sure Johnny would be fine if we didn't get married. You would be too, probably. But not me. I wouldn't be fine. I have to ask you. I can't stand not to ask you. I just—"

Doris put a hand over his mouth. "Hey," she said. "I wouldn't be fine either. I love you, and I love what you just said to me. My answer is yes."

He felt himself beginning to cry. "I can't … I … this is …" They started laughing.

"What a fine mess," Doris said.

"What a mess," he agreed. "Should I ask your father? His permission?"

"No," she said. "You just have to ask my son."

Four

After walking the three blocks to the Federal Courthouse, Earl rode an elevator to the sixth floor. The United States Attorney's cheerless receptionist pointed him to Conference Room B. "Hallway behind you, around to the left, second door on the right after you turn the corner." He could have sworn she never looked up.

A short, gray-suited man, probably in his thirties, leaned out of a doorway and nodded in Earl's direction as he rounded the corner.

"Earl Brady?"

"Yes, am I late?"

"No, no. I just heard someone was on the way. I'm Ted Lindgren, FBI."

They shook hands. "Earl Brady, deputy DA, county of L.A. I'm …"

"I know. Pleased to meet you. Come in. Everyone's here, so we might as well get going," said Lindgren. He had turned and was speaking to a larger group. Several men, some in military uniforms, sat around a large, polished wood table. Lindgren moved to one end.

A large, framed photograph of President Roosevelt was the only decoration in the room. Lindgren sat down and clapped his hands together. "Can't finish this until we start it, right?"

Earl had taken a chair next to LAPD Commander Roy Benson.

"Earl."

"Roy."

Earl managed a weak smile as they shook hands. He wasn't surprised to see Benson, just unsettled by the idea of being assigned to the same task. In manner and dress, Benson was fastidious, verging on fussy. When he was out of uniform, like this morning, he favored boldly pinstriped suits garnished with gold coin cufflinks. His pomade-shiny gray hair was combed straight back, away from a puffy, pink face. It was simply not possible to imagine fat Roy Benson doing actual police work; no doubt best for all concerned, he didn't. Bud Fletcher had once described him as LAPD's "full-time space filler, chair sitter, bullshitter, and ass kisser."

Earl had been in Benson's office just once—in his absence, purposely. Earl had wanted to see for himself Benson's "gallery," three walls covered with photographs of Benson, close to fifty by Earl's hasty count. Benson with governors, mayors, movie stars, and assorted others, all smiles and handshakes. According to LAPD legend, the chief himself had gone into Benson's office very early one morning, removed a picture of Benson and Johnny Weismuller, and replaced it with a Hollywood studio shot of Charles Laughton in *The Hunchback of Notre Dame*. The photo, discovered days later by a horrified Benson, was inscribed, "Dearest Roy—We must meet again in Paris! Best wishes—Q."

"… your fellow committee members," the FBI man was saying, "before we proceed, and I'll start with myself. Ted Lindgren. Thirteen years in the FBI. I've worked in Washington, San Francisco, and here in Los Angeles since last summer.

"About two years ago, President Roosevelt expanded the mission of the Bureau, so we now work jointly with the army and the navy on matters of foreign espionage and internal subversion. Since then, my assignment has been counterintelligence.

"You've read my memorandum, I trust. We are positive, gentlemen, that there is now a major effort by the government of Japan to set up spy networks on the West Coast. Nobody knows what'll happen, but we have to be ready for trouble. These people are potential enemies of this country."

Sitting next to Lindgren was a naval officer, who responded to the FBI man's nod.

"Lieutenant William Morrow, ONI, that's Office of Naval Intelligence." Morrow, after some chatter about recent Army-Navy football games, told the group that the Army's Signal Intelligence Service had deciphered the code used for Japanese diplomatic messages. "Captain Reed," Morrow said, turning to the army officer, "is here to take a bow for that. The captain will then return triumphantly to Washington."

There was more bantering, about the California climate and about the nineteen hours of airplane travel Reed faced. There were self-introductions by Benson, Earl Grady, and representatives of the county sheriff and other local agencies. Captain Reed then stood up, gathered his briefcase and his brown-visor army hat, and extended his free arm toward a lanky, tweed-jacketed older man who sat cross-legged in a chair away from the table, against a wall.

"Colonel Walter Jordan taught military history at West Point until his retirement from the army last year," said Reed. "He is now lecturing at the University of Southern California, and I believe writing a book. He is an expert on the Far East. I leave him to represent the army here, for now. I have a plane to catch." Reed directed a small salute to Jordan, and was gone.

The retired colonel was now up and pacing, four or five steps in each direction, arms folded, in front of the three windows overlooking Main Street. He was well over six feet tall. The curly pile of gray on top of his head, much longer than the hair on the sides and back, made him seem even taller and thinner.

He looked familiar. For a moment Earl tried to place him, but he quickly gave up; Earl met a lot of people in his line of work. His job did not require knowing people as much as finding out what they had to say about isolated events. He had forgotten most of the faces, and probably all of the names.

"I am given to understand," Jordan said slowly in a deep, elegant voice, "that my role is to give this group some background information. I am happy to do this. Let me—"

Lindgren interrupted. "Colonel, before you begin, may I? Just briefly."
"Of course."

"Let me just emphasize," said Lindgren, "our sources are highly reliable as to local Japanese activities. Not to beat around the bush, here, gentlemen, our main sources of information are intercepted messages to and from the Japanese government itself. We—the U.S. government, I mean—foresee that we might need the help of local authorities, and we might need it on short notice. So we want you to understand better what it is and who it is we're talking about. That's the background for Colonel Jordan's background, so to speak. All right then. Sorry, sir."

"Well," Jordan said, "I'll start by reminding you that last fall, Japan made a formal alliance with Germany and Italy. You know what Hitler's been doing in Europe: Poland, Czechoslovakia, Holland, Belgium, France. War with England. Have any opinion you want about American soldiers fighting in another European war. I think it's a bad idea myself, but that is not why I'm here. You see, gentlemen, we now have a special problem at this end of our own continent. The ambitions of Japan in the Pacific cannot be wished away."

The colonel sat down and continued. "They are very ambitious indeed, and their new treaty makes matters worse. On their own, left to their own devices? The Japanese might simply mark their calendars, wait five more years, let our forces leave the Philippine Islands as scheduled, and just walk in there. But I believe their new German partners will push for more action, and sooner. That is my opinion. Right now, today, militarily speaking, America is vulnerable. Vulnerable, gentlemen, and not just in the Philippine territories, either. There's Hawaii, where the Pacific Fleet"—he nodded toward Morrow—"recently moved. And even here, on our own western coast. Los Angeles, San Francisco, Seattle, the Alaska territories."

Earl was trying to absorb at least some of this. At Jordan's mention of the coast, however, Earl's thoughts drifted from strategic maps to the moonlit ocean view from a wooden bench on the Santa Monica bluffs.

"Japan," Jordan went on, "is hell-bent on expanding its empire. The Japanese invasion of China, going back ten years now, was a brazen violation of international agreements. The cruelties committed against civilians in China by the Japanese army have been unspeakable. Unspeakable."

Then Earl half-realized why Fletcher had put him on the committee. He made a note on an otherwise blank pad: "Tokyo Club."

Jordan spoke for another ten minutes. About Shintoism, the patriotic code based on worship of the Imperial family. About Japanese immigration to the West Coast and Hawaii. About the solidarity and the separateness of Japanese immigrants. Lindgren of the FBI announced that the group would receive more details about specific Japanese groups at the next gathering. They would meet the first or second Thursday of each month, he said, usually at 4:00 PM.

*   *   *   *

As Earl approached his secretary Maria's desk, she held up a message slip. "See me about Mr. F. as soon as you get in. Betty." Earl ducked into his office only long enough to drop his briefcase onto a chair and scribble a note to Maria. He handed it to her on his way to the stairs, then went quickly up two flights to Fletcher's office. Betty was typing.

"What is it?" asked Earl, still holding the message.

Betty lifted her fingers from the Royal's keys, picked up a pencil, and motioned for Earl to hand her the message slip. She wrote some numbers on the back. "Boss was taken to Good Samaritan Hospital last night," she said. "Straight from the Athletic Club card room. He was having trouble breathing."

"Oh, my God," said Earl. "Have you talked with him?"

"No, sir. His daughter called this morning. Promised she'd call again this afternoon," said Betty, looking past Earl at a wall clock, "but ... not yet."

It was 2:30. Earl looked at the message slip again. It said 9:15 AM. He felt a stab of guilt at the morning's absence. Backing away from the desk, he said, "I'll ... thanks, Betty. I'll call over there. Right away."

A minute later he was at his own desk, waiting to be connected to the third-floor nurses' station.

"Three west, Nurse Evans."

"Yes. This is Deputy District Attorney Brady, calling about Mr. Fletcher." There was no response.

"I was told I should call this number," he added.

"One moment, sir." A full minute passed. Earl sensed a stall and feared the worst.

"Hello, Earl." It was the subdued and muffled, but still unmistakable, voice of Bud Fletcher.

"Sorry not to call sooner, Mr. Fletcher. I just got out—"

"Call me Bud," came the rasping interruption.

"Yes, sir. I went straight to the FBI meeting this morning and didn't get in until after lunch. Are you all right?"

"I've had better days. Better nights, for damn sure. Doctor says my lungs sound like hell. I'm not supposed to talk much. I promised them I'd just listen if you called. Tell me about it."

"Well," said Earl as he tried to gather his thoughts, "it went fine. The FBI agent ran the show, but he didn't go much beyond that memorandum. Benson was there."

"Oh, for Christ's sake," Fletcher sputtered.

"I know, I know. County sheriff's office, highway patrol, a navy officer, an army officer. They told us the 'highly reliable source' is actually the Japanese government itself. Diplomatic messages have been intercepted, somehow. The army has broken their code. There wasn't anything about what the messages are, but we're getting more at the next meeting. Once a month, the agent said. The main speaker today was a retired army man, a West Point history professor at one time. Talked about the Japanese war plans. He was very alarmed about it."

Earl paused to consider his next statement. "I think I know why you sent me to this meeting, sir." He waited again, but Fletcher said nothing.

"Was it the Tokyo Club case that made you think of me?"

"I did recall it," Fletcher admitted. "You might want to send for that file."

"I already have."

"Good. I have to go. I'll call you tomorrow."

"All right, sir. Get better soon."

"My name is Bud."

"Yes, sir. Bud."

✳   ✳   ✳   ✳

Fletcher put the telephone receiver in its cradle and laid back against the starchy pillow.

"He seems like he was listening pretty carefully," he said. "Go on."

Walter Jordan looked at his old friend, shaking his head slowly and smiling faintly. "The way I see it," he said, "Roosevelt agrees with the Brits that we should be in. Public opinion is against it. However this great debate goes, however it turns out, Washington is not going to do what must be done about the Japanese. Not until it's too late."

"All right," Fletcher said. "I'll keep Earl on this."

Five

The Tokyo Club file was retrieved with difficulty from a dusty room in the
Hall of Justice basement, its door marked "Dead Files." The district attorney's office had closed the Tokyo Club investigation in late 1938. The
file's location in the "Dead" room was not determined according to when
it was closed, but instead by the happenstance of when it (and other files)
had been sent downstairs. On Friday afternoon the file was delivered to
Earl's office by a pimpled clerk who had found it, using a ladder, on a shelf
between two cases closed in 1934 and 1940.

The product of the investigation was a cardboard box containing separate folders and envelopes. Earl hoisted the box to the surface of his desk
and pulled out a folder labeled "Correspondence and Memoranda."

His own memorandum to Fletcher about ending the investigation sum-
marized the background. The Tokyo Club, short for "The Little Tokyo
Social Club," was one of a string of suspected gambling houses on the
West Coast. Rumors had persisted for years about corrupt "arrangements"
between LAPD officers and Japanese gambling bosses.

Not that it was generally understood, but there was always tension
between the local Japanese and Chinese. It had gotten worse in the 1930s,
after the Japanese invasions of Manchuria and China. There were sometimes assaults and other crimes alleged between Chinese and Japanese.

None was ever proven, though, usually because of the suspects' quick departures from the country. As more stories circulated about the Japanese army's brutality in China, there were some boycotts of Japanese products. Occasionally, there would be a stinging newspaper editorial.

The local Japanese leaders tried to blunt the criticism. In the summer of 1938, the Tokyo Club had managed to plant a story in the *Los Angeles Times* about hiring a Chinatown restaurant to cater a large banquet. The Tokyo Club spokesman made comments that sounded conciliatory, respectful. He was hopeful that "our two nations' common goals in East Asia" would soon be reached. He was sure that the Golden Dragon's food would be excellent.

The dinner was attended by over two hundred people, club members and prominent guests from the Japanese banking and business communities. Within six hours of the party's conclusion, at least half of them began suffering diarrhea, vomiting, or both. Sixty-eight were seen in medical clinics or emergency rooms, and four spent at least one night in a hospital.

The LAPD had reacted to the victims' complaints with a shrug, perhaps because they truly didn't care. Earl would later believe, though, that the cops had seen immediately what he learned only after investigating for a month: there would be no way to prove anything. There were five different dishes that had been at least tasted by all sixty-eight victims (the "crappers and chuckers," as Fletcher called them). The pots and pans had been promptly washed. The Golden Dragon produced several witnesses who insisted, some in English and some through an interpreter, that they had eaten from the same batches of food just before it was taken to the Tokyo Club. The English-speaking son of the restaurant's owner, in his first interview by the LAPD, blamed the Tokyo Club's own water, silver, glassware, and "too much bad Scotch."

Earl investigated, despite these denials. The restaurant cooperated, making more denials all the while. Earl and his team interviewed every employee, as well as a handful of the restaurant's lunch customers on the date of the Tokyo Club banquet. They consulted two doctors. They took statements from eleven Japanese who had previously eaten at the Golden Dragon. Nothing came of it.

In some cases, a moment arrives when it is plain that the investigation is going nowhere, that nothing will ever come of it. The Tokyo Club was like that, Earl remembered. The investigation had continued, though, for an extra day or two. A few more interviews. One more conference with the medical expert. He remembered why.

At the end of what Earl thought would be his last visit to the Golden Dragon, the owner's son—whose name, Sun, caused much confusion— had asked how much longer the investigation might last.

"We're getting there," Earl told Sun as they both stepped through the door. It was a hot October morning. Earl took off his jacket for the uphill hike to the Hall of Justice.

"You know, Mr. Brady, we did not commit any offense."

"So you have said. We have to look into this. We appreciate your cooperation." It wasn't the first time Earl had recited this to Sun. He began walking up Broadway.

"The Japanese deserved it."

Earl stopped and turned. "Excuse me?"

"They deserved it," said Sun. "I repeat, Mr. Brady, we did not poison them, but they had it coming."

"They had it coming? That's interesting. Who did poison them?"

Sun smiled and shook his head. "No, Mr. Brady, do not misunderstand. I do not think the Japanese were poisoned. Not necessarily so. They might have made it up. They are liars."

It took Earl a few seconds to think of something to say. "So—we're dropping the bad Scotch theory?"

"Mr. Brady, I would like you to have something. Please, come back inside for a moment."

Sun motioned him to a booth, and Earl sat alone, rubbing his eyes. When he looked up, Sun was walking past the empty tables, holding an envelope and a glass of water. He slid into the booth, opposite Earl, and leaned forward.

"Mr. Brady, I am sure you have heard the local Japanese, so politely, refer to their war against China as 'the incident.' You may also know, as it is not any secret, that they all send money home to Japan for their army."

Sun turned the envelope over in his hands, then placed it on the table. He kept an index finger pressed on it, as if signaling that he wasn't quite yet giving it to Earl. It was an odd-sized envelope, about the size of a formal wedding invitation.

"These are photographs," he said in a near whisper, "of the so-called 'incident.' Actually they are photographs of photographs, but they are clear enough. You may keep them. You will see some writing on the back of each. The writing is mine, a translation into English of what is on the back of the originals." Sun lifted his finger from the envelope and folded his hands on the table.

"Please, Mr. Brady."

Earl picked up the envelope and lifted the unsealed flap. The photographs came out face down. There were four, and on the back of each was penciled, "Nanking, December 1937."

The first one Earl turned over was grainy and dark but, as Sun had promised, clear enough. Three severed heads, lined up on some sort of wall or fence. One had a cigarette between its lips. Earl swallowed and looked at Sun, who silently unfolded his hands and extended them toward the pile.

The next photograph showed an open pit, about four feet deep, ringed by standing or squatting spectators. Below them were two figures apparently bound hand and foot, one lying and one sitting, a few yards apart. Standing beside each was a man pointing or swinging—Earl couldn't tell—a large stick. He looked again at Sun and said, "I don't ..."

"Bayonet practice," Sun whispered.

The third picture had been taken closer to its subjects and required no explanation. A blindfolded man was tied, upright, to a leafless tree. A uniformed soldier was plunging the end of a bayonet into the man's chest. Beside the stabbing soldier was another, taller one, wearing glasses. He had one hand on the smaller soldier's lower back, and the other on his leading forearm, as if giving a tennis lesson.

The last photograph showed the front of a young woman, entirely naked, sitting in a chair. Her face appeared swollen. She might have been dead. Her arms were behind the chair. Her feet rested on something, out of the picture, which raised and separated her knees as for giving birth.

Saying nothing, Earl looked up at Sun. "There is your 'incident,' Mr. Brady. There is your brave Japanese army which receives money from the Tokyo Club bar profits."

Earl managed only, "I'll get back to you," as he put down the empty water glass and dropped the envelope into his briefcase.

They closed the investigation a few days later, after Earl had asked the doctor how someone might fake food poisoning, and after Earl had visited Sun again to ask him one obvious question about the photographs.

They were stolen, Sun explained, "or I think the better word is smuggled. At great risk."

✳ ✳ ✳ ✳

The last paragraph of Earl's Tokyo Club memorandum said:

> It is a unique experience for me to have a suspect deny committing the crime and then, without being asked, lay out what his motive would have been. These gruesome photographs, if they are what Mr. Sun claims, would constitute a strong motive. By way of further background, this file contains copies of the July and October 1938 issues of *Reader's Digest*, which ran eyewitness accounts of the "sack" of Nanking. These stories are in line with Sun's suggestion that the pictures were smuggled out of China by missionaries. But motive alone is not enough. We lack evidence that anyone acted on that motive: no confessions or other testimony, no scientific proof. This far-away conflict, between enemies we don't understand well, might or might not be connected to this local episode. Naturally, we could reopen the investigation if something further develops. At this time, however, we have insufficient evidence to charge any person with any crime. Recommend we CLOSE.

Six

CONFIDENTIAL MEMORANDUM No. 2

To: L.A.P.S.C. Members
From: Special Agent T. A. Lindgren, FBI
Date: April 24, 1941

As stated, our next meeting will be at 4:00 PM two weeks from this date, at the same location. It is believed that you will find the following historical and statistical information useful:

a. Background of Japanese Immigration. In 1881, the King of Hawaii and the Emperor of Japan reached an agreement to send Japanese workers to Hawaiian sugar cane fields. The contract labor arrangements were voided in 1898, when Hawaii was annexed to the United States. This had the effect of increasing Japanese immigration, not only to Hawaii but also to the mainland United States. More than 100,000 arrived in the decade of the 1900s. Legislation restricting further Japanese immigration was enacted in 1924, but those already here were allowed to remain.

b. Population Data. An estimated 130,000 Japanese presently reside in the Pacific Coast states, with more than 100,000 of these believed to be in California (constituting almost 2 percent of this state's population). In the Hawaiian Islands, the Japanese are estimated at 160,000. This represents fully 40 percent of that territory's inhabitants.

*   *   *   *

"Welcome back, gentlemen," Lindgren said, "to our second regular meeting. This one should be shorter, but with more specific information. By the way, we will not meet in June. July will be our next one."

"You remember Lieutenant Morrow," Lindgren went on, tilting his head toward the navy officer. "He and I will try to answer questions after I summarize things."

Lindgren paused, tapping the eraser end of a pencil on the arm of his chair. "The Japanese government has almost always used its people here, diplomats and prominent businessmen, for publicity or propaganda work. All of it directed from Tokyo. Usually, pretty ordinary sales pitches: buy our products, visit Japan. Now, with Japan and our government more and more at odds, they are converting this effort to intelligence gathering. It appears they are attempting to set up their network to get information about our factories, military bases, ports, and other transportation facilities."

Lindgren stopped again, frowning. "These people didn't sneak across the border last week," he said. "There are second-generation Japanese who have jobs in the places I just mentioned. A few are even in the U.S. Army. Our intercepts tell us that the Japanese government is trying to recruit these people to make reports. This part of the problem is pretty straightforward. A Japanese airplane factory worker can't hide himself. We're watching them. But there are a couple of other aspects. For one, a Japanese living near Los Angeles Harbor, let's say, can easily keep a watch on shipments of airplanes or other war materials. The other concern is that the Japanese will try to approach different groups they think oppose U.S. policy, or who are just unhappy generally. Our sources mention other foreign immigrants, Negroes, Communists, and labor unions in this category. Lieutenant?"

Morrow leaned back in his chair and rubbed his temples with both hands. "I would add," he began, "that it is not a situation where the Japanese need to organize an intelligence network from scratch. They *are* a network. They have already formed groups, or clubs, or societies, for every imaginable purpose."

Including gambling, Earl recalled. Morrow went on: "They have their religious temples, Japanese language schools and other educational groups, sports clubs, farmers' cooperatives, you name it. The point is, they all belong already to at least one of these organizations. Most of the groups are controlled to some degree by similar ones in Japan. So again I say, these people have in place a highly structured set of channels for communications. Any questions?"

Earl could think of none, but Benson, for once, made himself a little useful. "What should we at the Los Angeles Police Department be doing?" he asked.

"There is no action to be taken now," Lindgren answered. "Although," he added, "you may be interested to know that the Mayor of Vancouver has been campaigning since last fall to close all of the Japanese-language schools there for the duration of the war."

"We're doing certain things, on our end," said Morrow. "The Coast Guard has assigned fifty extra men to the Los Angeles Harbor, to watch for possible sabotage. They are also monitoring the Japanese fishermen. They seem to have a new practice of reregistering their boats under Americans' names while keeping all-Japanese crews."

Morrow turned and nodded at Lindgren, who said, "All we ask you to do at this time is to file away this list of Japanese organizations." He passed around quarter-inch-thick stacks of paper. "These are names and addresses, with some descriptions where it's not self-evident. Just keep this information handy, in case we need your help with some of these groups. Any other questions?"

Earl had one but decided not to ask it. *Why wasn't Colonel Jordan at this meeting?*

*   *   *   *

A woman with a British accent answered the telephone. "History Department."

"Professor Jordan, please."

"One moment. Who is calling?"

"Mr. Brady. From the Public Safety Committee."

"Jordan speaking."

"Colonel, this is Earl Brady with the DA's office. I'm on the committee you spoke to several weeks ago. I was hoping to get an appointment to see you."

"Well, you hardly need an appointment. My schedule is pretty light. I have afternoons open, so pick a day."

"Could you meet me this afternoon, if I come down there about three?"

"All right. Three o'clock it is. My office is on the second floor of the liberal arts building, just inside the Exposition Boulevard gate."

"Thank you."

Earl drove south on Figueroa Street, named for a Mexican-rule governor of California, and parked near the corner at Exposition. Jordan's office had a view of the USC athletic fields. Sweatsuited figures were drifting onto the grassy infield and the red-dirt track, talking and trotting.

"We missed you at the meeting last week," Earl said as he sat down.

"Yes, well … how was it? Anything interesting?"

"It was just more information, some particulars about existing groups and societies and so forth. Is it all right to talk here?"

"Oh, I think so," Jordan said. "May I ask, was your office or the Police Department told to do anything?"

"No, not really. That's just it, sir. I don't quite … I'm frankly not sure what the purpose of this committee is. I was hoping you could shed some light. From the army's standpoint."

Jordan frowned. "Does anybody know you're here, asking me about this?"

"No, sir. I'm just curious, I guess." It occurred to Earl that flattery might help. "I thought your talk at the first meeting was quite interesting. I learned a lot."

Jordan fastened a steady look onto Earl's eyes. After a few seconds Jordan said, "Thank you," and looked down. "It's a bit funny," he said, "that you should ask me for the army's viewpoint on this. My opinions and the army's opinions are different in some important respects. I'm sure I would never be the choice as spokesman."

Earl unfolded a copy of Confidential Memorandum No. 2 and handed it to Jordan, who read it silently, expressionless.

"Interesting," he said. "One fact I would've added. When the U.S. annexed the Hawaiian Islands in '98, one nation in the entire world protested. Japan. The official response of Japan was that it would never—not ever—recognize or acquiesce in American control of the Hawaiian Islands."

"I'd like to go back to what you think," Earl said, "and what the army thinks. How it's different."

Jordan sat back and smiled. "That, Mr. Brady, we haven't enough time for, believe me. Let us say that my strong opinions on the army's lack of readiness for a serious war have caused me problems."

"How so?"

"I should have been more careful," Jordan said. "I ghosted a few editorials, articles for a national magazine in 1939 and '40. My essays argued that our state of readiness was dismal. I cited facts and figures. I said we needed to build forces adequate to defend ourselves before we could even think of rescuing someone else's country again, as we did in 1917. What has it been now? Just over twenty years. Anyway, my language was a little too close to things I'd said in the Faculty Club at West Point. I should've been more careful. Long story short, life became uncomfortable. I worked it out to retire at the end of the spring term last year."

"And now you're here," said Earl.

"Happy to be here. One of the advantages of getting older is knowing more people."

"How is it the army disagrees with you?"

"Soldiers aren't supposed to make policy, or criticize it. Maybe it isn't really the army, it's the government. At least now. The army is getting prepared—heaven's sake, we now have the first peacetime draft in American history."

"I know. My son's a freshman. Here."

"Is he? Question is, getting prepared and drafting boys for what? In my opinion," Jordan said with a brief smile, "Washington is so obsessed with Germany that they're almost completely overlooking Japan. That's our real problem. That's who we're going to have to fight. Personally, I don't want to see us dragged into another European war. We don't have to go over there. Germany is not going to attack America. But Japan," Jordan said, looking out the window, "is coming here. Neither side—not the Roosevelt government, not the isolationists or 'America-Firsters'—understands that. None of them. Partly it's ignorance, but partly it's geography."

"There's ignorance for sure about the geography," said Earl. "Americans don't know much about Asia, myself included."

"Not just that," said Jordan. "The other geography problem is the West Coast, and its distance from the East Coast. Where Washington is. Where all these decisions are going to be made, in other words. Even with air travel, it takes about twenty hours to get out here. There you go, I even said it: 'out here.' That's how the West Coast is regarded. Out here."

Earl thought for a moment. "Getting back to our Public Safety Committee," he said, "wasn't that set up at Washington's direction?"

Jordan shrugged. "It might be a promising sign, I suppose. But I'm not sure how serious they truly are, the FBI, or what they'll do if it comes right down to it."

"Colonel, you don't think … Los Angeles is even farther away from Tokyo. Could Japan possibly try to invade America?"

"Some people think so," Jordan replied.

"How would they ever be able to—"

Jordan interrupted, holding up an open-handed stop signal. "Maybe another time. It's complicated."

"Will you be at the next meeting?"

"If they call me," said the older man. "I'm a part-timer."

Earl stood to leave. "I just wish I could figure out," he said as he pulled open the door, "why I'm on this committee."

He was surprised when Jordan answered.

"I confess, I had something to do with it."

"You? Sir?" Earl closed the door.

"I know Bud Fletcher. I asked him to assign somebody who might take a genuine interest. Somebody who might care. Or at least might be curious."

Somebody not like Roy Benson, Earl thought, with satisfaction. "I do find this interesting, Colonel," he said.

"Good," said Jordan, smiling. "Before you go, tell me your son's name. I'll treat him to lunch over at the Faculty Club."

"Thank you, Colonel. It's John Brady. He lives in the Beta fraternity. That is very kind of you."

Walking back across the campus to his car, Earl was caught in a swarm of students. Singly, and in hand-holding pairs and in chattering groups, all oblivious to Earl. It was about to be a Friday night in springtime on a college campus. Earl considered a surprise visit to John but, seeing himself as an unwelcome dog scattering a flock of birds, he turned his car west onto Exposition Boulevard and drove to Santa Monica.

Seven

Built for the 1932 Olympic Games, the Los Angeles Swimming Stadium was a bicycle ride from the USC campus. A concrete grandstand, although large, was dwarfed by the 105,000-seat coliseum at the pool's northeast corner.

The drive from Santa Monica downtown was faster on weekends. Earl Brady arrived early and parked his car in a vacant lot, where a set of wood bleacher seats had been removed after the games. He remembered sitting there with his nine-year-old nephew to watch water polo and swimming events in 1932. The American "Buster" Crabbe had taken one gold medal for men's swimming. All the other golds—every last one—had been won by Japanese swimmers. Scattered throughout the grandstands had been groups of fluttering white flags with red dots.

He stood under the diving towers and spotted John among the other swimmers. He was halfway through a fifty-meter length, on his back and rolling slightly as his arms reached behind and pulled under, out, up, and behind again.

"He's a swimming machine, Mr. Brady."

The team's coach was walking across the damp concrete deck. Emmett Carson, now in his early thirties, had won a freestyle bronze medal in this pool, then another at the Berlin Olympics of 1936. He was a sometime actor, a summertime beach lifeguard, and the USC swimming coach. Carson's movie roles were limited by the stuttering that had afflicted him since the summer he turned twelve. Embarrassed and frustrated, he had taken refuge in long-distance ocean swims and board surfing. By the time of his graduation from Santa Monica High School, Emmett Carson was the state record-holder at three distances and, owing to the combination of his looks and an endearing speech flaw, he had become irresistible to women.

Like most men, Earl was also charmed by Emmett Carson, who didn't seem to care how he looked: his brown hair was always messy and his choice of clothes indifferent, if they were chosen at all. As usual when coaching, he was wearing a gray sweat suit and black basketball shoes.

"Thanks, Coach," said Earl as he shook Carson's hand. "He does look good. He's improved since joining you, that's for sure."

Carson smiled, fought through the stutterer's grimace, then said, "He was d-dropping … his hips and … swerving a little. He's got … great … potential." Carson arched his eyebrows and nodded. "R-really."

Carson moved to the edge of the pool and then sideways, back and forth, showing two fingers to each of the swimmers as they executed their turns. Saturday practice was almost over.

Soon they climbed out of the water and walked or ran, shivering, through the tall doorway cut into the bottom of the grandstand. A few minutes later they reappeared, dressed. John spotted Earl and waved a maroon canvas bag, his other hand rubbing at his head with a towel.

"Hungry?" Earl asked.

"Starved," said John. "Golondrina?"

"Let's go."

*　　　*　　　*　　　*

La Golondrina Café was the oldest restaurant in the oldest part of Spanish-settled Los Angeles, Olvera Street. The area had become a crime-infested slum by the 1920s but was cleaned up and reopened as "a colorful Mexican market" in 1930. Much of the restoration work had been done by county jail prisoners; the wealthy, civic-minded woman who led the project had famously prayed for the arrest of skilled bricklayers and plumbers. The restaurant had low, beamed ceilings and adobe walls hung with serape blankets, cheaper versions of which could be purchased for a dollar at several *puestos* lining the narrow street outside. Also available in the open-air market were straw sombreros, candles, fresh-blown glass objects, and Catholic decorations for every room in the home.

Mexican food was a favorite of both Bradys, and La Golondrina's was the best. They ate tortillas, alone and in various spicy combinations with cheese, rice, beans, chicken, and beef, with reverent concentration.

"By the way," John eventually mumbled, still chewing, "I went to lunch with that professor you told me about. The colonel."

"So he did call you," Earl said. "I thought maybe he was just talking. You know, being polite."

"No, he … well, he sure is polite. He left a letter in my mailbox. Set up the lunch with the History Department secretary. I felt important."

"Good for him. Not that I know him very well. We've only met a few times, really. Through work. He seemed like an interesting fellow."

"He is," said John. "I was a little nervous, but he said he was new at USC and wanted to know more students. He asked about the team. Nice man."

"What else did he say?"

"Oh, once I relaxed a little I asked him about the army and all. He taught at West Point for twenty years or something. I think he went there just after the war, in 1920 maybe. What's he got to do with the DA's office?"

Earl refilled their water glasses. "He's an expert on Oriental history and culture. He may advise us on some aspects of crime in those areas. China-town, and so forth."

"He was talking about that," said John, "now that you mention it. He asked me about Japanese students at school."

"What did he want to know?"

"Nothing in particular, I don't think. He just wondered if any of them were friends of mine, or friends of my friends. Or whether they just stuck to themselves."

Earl pulled at the check and took out his wallet. Laying bills on the check tray, he asked, "What did you tell him?"

"Not much I could tell him. I talked about my friend on the team. You know him, the one I swam against in high school. Tim Tanaka."

"Sure, I think I do remember him," said Earl. "What school?"

"Inglewood High. He was a year ahead of me."

"What did you tell Colonel Jordan? About Tim."

"I told him what I know," said John. "He was born here, went back to Japan for a year of school when he was nine or ten. Pretty good swimmer, long distance mostly."

"Do you know his parents?"

"No," John replied. "Maybe I met them after a swim meet. Why?"

"Just wondered. Does Tim, ah, speak Japanese?"

"I'm not sure. Why?"

Earl affected a shrug. "Sometimes we need interpreters. If he's interested in making a little money, you know."

The sunshine briefly blinded Earl as they left La Golondrina. His eyes had adjusted by the time they reached the Memorial Plaza at the end of Olvera Street. "I'll ask him, if you want," John said.

"What?"

"Tim. About translating. But he has a summer job, same as mine. Coach got Tim and two other boys on the team into the Santa Monica Lifeguards. We start June 16."

"Well," said Earl as he opened the car door, "how about you bring him over for dinner sometime after work?"

Eight

CONFIDENTIAL MEMORANDUM No. 3

To: L.A.P.S.C. Members
From: Special Agent T. A. Lindgren, FBI
Date: June 26, 1941

Our next meeting will be at 4:00 PM on Wednesday, July 2, at the same location.

For your information, highly reliable sources have it that Japanese authorities are increasing their effort to establish useful contacts with influential Negroes.

* * * *

The History Department secretary put Earl's call through.

"Colonel, it's Earl Brady. Not interrupting, I hope."

"Not at all. I don't know if he told you, but I met your son."

"He did tell me. That was very generous of you."

"Fine young man. I hope I didn't bore him."

"I doubt that," Earl said. "Sir, did you receive the FBI memorandum? About next week's meeting? Mine was delivered today."

"No."

"Are you coming to the meeting?"

"Not that I've been told."

Earl read the memorandum to Jordan.

"That's it?" Jordan asked.

"That's it."

*   *   *   *

An hour later, he was sitting in Jordan's office.

"Horse shit," Jordan sputtered, flipping the memo onto his desk. "It's absolute horse shit. Pardon my language."

"I'd like to know what you think is happening," Earl said.

"This is almost funny," Jordan said, now in a weary tone. "Please don't ask who or what or where, but trust me, I still have a few connections in the army. Men who talk to me occasionally, let's say. Compared to what is truly happening, this alarm about the Japanese persuading a bunch of colored fellows to spy for them is ... I just don't know whether to laugh or cry."

Earl fell back on his training. Keep the witness talking. Nudge him along. "So," he offered, "you don't think it's likely."

"I wish," said Jordan, pausing, "the Japanese were that stupid. I wish they would waste their time on it."

Jordan was up, pacing behind his desk, hands folded at the small of his back. *Parade restless,* Earl thought. He imagined Jordan in uniform: younger, obedient, unquestioning.

"Aren't some of the Negro leaders Communists?" Earl asked.

"I'll be goddamned if I know. But if they are, why would they help the Germans or the Japanese? The Communists want us to *fight* Hitler. The German army has turned East. Hitler is invading Mother Russia, as we speak. And the Japanese generals and admirals are happier than hell about it. They're calling it a 'divine wind.' Japan's last big war was against Russia. The German attack on Russia, don't you see, it eases the pressure on Japan's northern flank. Its Russian front. Japan can look in other directions more easily now."

Jordan looked at Earl. *This is the right one,* he thought. Fletcher had been right.

"I know I have a tendency to be long-winded," he said, "but I suppose that's the one strong suit of history professors. Talking."

"Please," Earl said. "I don't mind. I want to know more about this. Sometimes it's hard to keep up with you, is all."

Jordan appeared to take this as a green light. "Let me put it this way," he said. "Last time you were here, we talked about geography. The West Coast is … well, it's new. California's been a state for about ninety years. Washington, about fifty years as a state. The Panama Canal was opened, what? Twenty-six, twenty-seven years ago? The East and West Coasts weren't even connected by rail until seventy years ago. Certain attitudes die slowly. Assumptions persist. What I mean is, the West Coast is still so new, isolated, so remote in the minds of the East Coast leaders of the country. As a group they've been to London a hell of a lot more times than Los Angeles. Roosevelt himself has been in California—what? Twice in his life."

"So you start," Jordan went on, leaning back and turned sideways from his visitor, the professor lecturing a class of one, "with this combination of unfamiliarity and disregard. Disdain, almost. The West Coast didn't participate much, you see, in the biggest historical events of America: the War of Independence, the Civil War. These places became populated states after all those convulsions, after all that pain and suffering. Or else the Western states were just too far away from the bloodshed to be involved. I'll put it in a lawyer's terms for you, Earl. California is like a new member of the firm. He does good work, and he might be important to the future of the organization, but the founding partners will never, ever consider him equal."

Earl chuckled, prompting Jordan to turn his head. "Sorry," Earl said, "your law firm analogy must have been a good one. It reminded me of someone I know."

"Good," Jordan replied. "So you can see the picture so far. Now, add a couple of things. One, Roosevelt and his advisors, most of them anyway, want to get us involved in the war against Germany. They want that very much. Roosevelt promised the opposite, over and over again, in his reelection campaign last year. That means nothing, except his challenge is to get around that promise. Not that it's a small challenge. The public doesn't want to go to war in Europe again. Lindbergh's 'America First' rally at the Hollywood Bowl last month had an overflow crowd. I know, because I was there. Two, the Japanese alliance with Germany means that if we fight against one, we're also at war with the other. Can we wage war against the Germans in Europe and against the Japanese … somewhere else?"

Jordan stopped and looked again at Earl. "What do you think?"

Earl said nothing, until he saw Jordan reach behind himself to a globe, sitting on a table, and gave it a spin.

"I guess maybe it depends on what you mean by 'somewhere else,'" Earl said.

Jordan moved the globe to the desk top. "It was an unfair question," Jordan apologized. "The War Department is trying to answer it right now. But here's the hell of it. The Roosevelt gang is not, believe me, not going to make defeating Japan the first priority. Again, Asia is remote. People care far less about the fate of Singapore or Manila than they do about Paris and London. So my guess is that the plan will be to hold off Japan, try to contain or limit the Japanese, until Europe has been retaken from the Germans."

"That might be a long time, right?"

Jordan nodded. "Oh yes. Very long. But let's get back to your other question. What do we mean by 'somewhere else?' Where does this defensive stall happen?" Jordan spun the globe again. "It would be damn nice," he said, "if the Japanese offensive were confined to here … or here," he said, pointing to spots on the globe. "The Philippines. Indochina. Just as it'd be nice if the Jap intelligence effort in California were really focused on convincing some colored union organizer that he'd be happier working for the goddamned emperor. I just don't think we can count on such things."

"Well, sir," Earl offered, "that gets back to my question about a Japanese attack on the West Coast."

"Which I don't believe the War Department would deliberately risk, you understand. I just worry that they won't think about it at all. They will simply assume it would never be attempted. Again, it all seems so far away, and the distances in the Pacific are so vast."

Earl looked at the globe. "They are, aren't they?"

Jordan glanced at his watch and took a loud, deep breath.

"The Pacific Ocean is one-third of the Earth. We can talk about this again some other time," he said. "I've got to make a faculty meeting. But let me just show you one more thing. I know, sorry, it's always one more thing. Here is Japan," he said as his finger traced a south-to-north line through pink shapes in a blue field on the globe. Jordan then moved his finger through another string of smaller shapes, just dots, east to west. "These are the Aleutians, part of our Alaskan Territory. From northernmost Japan to westernmost Alaska is a distance of 640 miles. That's all. Less than New York to Chicago, Earl. The Giants travel that far to play against the Cubs. If Japan wanted to, it could seize and occupy the Aleutians. That's my opinion. Then, from the Aleutians it is around two thousand miles to Seattle. That's about the distance from Chicago to Los Angeles. The Cubs travel that far for spring training."

"Maybe," Earl said, "you should be coming to the meeting. What I mean is, I don't think I'm the only one who should be hearing this."

"We'll see," Jordan said as they walked outside, down the brick steps, and onto the concrete path leading away from the liberal arts building. "The arrangement is that I attend by invitation, when asked. Maybe you can suggest to Lindgren that I come next month. I would be interested to hear what the FBI is saying." He paused and smiled. "And I'd promise to be quiet."

"I'll call you next Wednesday, after the meeting," Earl said. "It might be late, though."

Jordan stopped, and they shook hands. "I won't leave until I've heard from you. I'll look forward to your call."

*   *   *   *

SANTA MONICA EVENING OUTLOOK
Monday, June 30, 1941
29 SPIES ARRESTED IN FBI RAIDS

Agents of the Federal Bureau of Investigation arrested twenty-nine suspected German spies yesterday, in a series of raids conducted primarily
in the New York area. One suspect, however, was taken into custody at
a house in Pacific Palisades, according to FBI headquarters.

*   *   *   *

Earl was back in his office before 5:00 PM the following Wednesday.
The July 2 meeting had lasted no more than twenty minutes. He called
Jordan.

"My goodness. That was quick."

"I only took a page of notes," Earl said. "The FBI arrested a Japanese
naval officer last month at the Olympic Hotel, a Lieutenant Commander
... Tachibana? Head spy on the West Coast, they think. I asked where he
was, and Lindgren said he'd been deported already. I asked why they'd let
him go."

"Goddamned good question," Jordan growled.

"It gets even more strange," Earl continued. "Lindgren told us, well, gosh
... really what happened is that Tachibana was *released*.
Fifty-thousand-dollar bond. Then he left the country."

"Oh boy. That's brilliant. Anything else?"

"Lindgren could see I was a little shocked, I think. He muttered some
kind of half-assed explanation—best to keep things quiet—diplomacy—
difficulty of proving anything without turning our cards over. I'm just
reading my notes here."

"I see. Was that it? Anything about the memo?"

"Yes, although he didn't say anything about the Negroes in particular.
Here it is—'Japanese Embassies and Consulates attempting to survey per-

sons and groups openly or secretly opposing U.S. entry into war. Japanese believe such parties might be sources of intelligence information about factories, laboratories, transportation facilities, and government departments.' That was about it for today. For this month, I guess you might say."

"Well," Jordan said, "thank you for calling me. I should let you go home."

Nine

SANTA MONICA EVENING OUTLOOK
Thursday, July 24, 1941
U.S. DENOUNCES JAPAN AS AGGRESSOR
Nipponese Present Themselves as Guardians of
French Indo-China

The United States government strongly denounced Japan today as an aggressor in French Indo-China and declared that the move there menaced American security and interests in the Far East.

Sumner Welles, Acting Secretary of State, issued a formal statement asserting that Japan was preparing for further "movements of conquest in adjacent areas." The statement contained no hint of steps planned by the United States to counter the Japanese move, which was presented by Japan and the French government as "protection" against alleged British-Chinese threats to Indo-China.

"The present unfortunate situation in which the French governments of Vichy and of Indo-China find themselves is, of course, well known," said Welles. "It is only too clear that they are in no position to resist the pressure exercised on them."

＊　　　＊　　　＊　　　＊

The temperature was in the nineties when Earl walked out of the Hall of Justice at four o'clock. July and August in Los Angeles, surprisingly, were not even the hottest months most years. September always took that prize.

He drove through Chinatown and onto the Arroyo Seco Parkway, toward Pasadena. Nonstop and winding, it reminded Earl of a Lionel train set, especially the tunnels under Elysian Park.

Santa Teresa sanatorium was just a mile from the parkway's end. Earl parked the Chrysler under a sycamore tree, near a low hedge bordering the wide, gravel driveway.

"I don't have tuberculosis," Bud Fletcher complained as Earl pulled a chair to the bedside. "I don't belong in this place."

"Maybe they just want to make sure you get rest," Earl said to his boss. "It's quiet here."

"If it was any quieter, I'd lose my mind. I'll be dead of boredom before this lung disease gets me. Thanks for bringing the mail."

"Any word about coming back?"

"Not for a while, they say. I was stupid to try going to work last week. So, I'm back in custody for now. What about the FBI deal?"

"It's a little odd, Bud, I'll tell you. They give us some information about Japanese societies, you know, their groups. Their efforts to gather sensitive information using contacts at aircraft plants, and so on. But nobody ever asks us to do anything."

"What are they doing? FBI, I mean."

"That's the strangest part. They don't seem to be doing much either. Last month they actually arrested some Japanese Navy officer who's supposed to be one of the top spies on the West Coast, but they just let him post bond and leave."

Fletcher rubbed his eyes. "This has been going on for years now, you know. Let me tell you about the *Molino Rojo* case, I call it. The place is a whorehouse in Tijuana. In the *Zona Norte*, where most of 'em are."

He rolled to the edge of his bed and coughed slowly, then spit loudly into a metal pan. "Sorry. Anyway, the *Molino Rojo* is where one Harry Thompson, out-of-luck drifter, ex-navy enlisted man, was recruited to spy by a Japanese navy officer named Miyazaki, I think it was. Miyazaki was supposedly an exchange student at Stanford. The story is, for a hundred bucks a month, and maybe some free Tijuana pussy thrown in, Thompson was delivering whatever information he could still get from his navy buddies in Long Beach and San Diego. The FBI never would've caught him. The navy did, but only because they were lucky. He was convicted in '36 and got fifteen years."

"What happened to the Japanese spy? Miz ..."

"Miyazaki? He left. Just sailed away, like the one last month. The navy actually wanted to nab him, as I heard it, but Washington said no. For Christ's sake, the FBI wasn't even allowed to arrest the American jackass Thompson until after Miyazaki was gone. The diplomats didn't want to upset the Japanese government. They were in talks about Japan backing off in China, as I recall. That was the story of *Molino Rojo*."

"You know, Bud, your friend Colonel Jordan is very worried about all this."

"Oh?" Fletcher seemed to want an explanation.

"We've talked a few times," Earl said. "He took my boy John to lunch at USC one day. How do you know Colonel Jordan?"

Fletcher coughed, slowly and deeply, then sat still with his eyes tightly shut and his jaw clenched. After a moment he opened his eyes. "Never mind that. Walter and I go back pretty far, that's all."

Earl knew that wasn't all. He gave Fletcher his best professional "come on, tell me" look.

He won the stare-down. "I met Walter Jordan in 1918," Fletcher said. "He came to our house to tell my parents that my younger brother had been killed in France. I was home visiting from law school. As Walter was leaving, I asked him to call me if he was ever in Boston. And so he did, about three months later. I wanted to know more than my parents did about how James died, I reckon."

Fletcher paused and closed his eyes again.

"So," Earl said, "you and Jordan became friends?"

"We did. I went to Washington for two years before moving here, and I saw him there occasionally, before he went up to West Point. We've stayed in touch."

"He's an interesting man."

"Oh, he's brilliant. Halfway crazy, sometimes I think, but Walter Jordan is smart as a whip. And you're right, he's always interesting."

Earl wanted to pursue "crazy" but decided it could wait. Fletcher was obviously tired.

"I'll come out again next week, if you're still here."

"There's something else," said Fletcher as Earl got up to leave. "Don't tell Jordan I said this. His son's an army captain, and he's just received orders to go with General MacArthur to the Philippines. Walter's awful proud of his boy, but he's worried."

"He's worried," Earl repeated.

"Thinks our men are just about sitting ducks over there," said Fletcher. "'Bait,' is what he actually said. You go on now. Call me anytime."

Ten

State Beach was teeming, the first Saturday of August 1941. Well before noon, the black-topped parking lot was full of cars as a heat wave drove people to the edge, literally, of the land.

From his canvas chair atop lifeguard station four, John Brady could have counted hundreds of striped beach umbrellas by mid-afternoon, a spreading rash of color that since early morning had crept out from the center of the beach, to the water's edge, to his wood tower and behind it, all the way to the low, gray wall separating the cars from their baking owners. Hours later the field of pastels would be fading, thinning as the umbrellas were taken down and dragged away.

At 6:05 PM the doorless red jeep announced its arrival at station four with a short meow of the siren. John Brady picked up the radio mike from its cradle.

"Station four, closing. Good night."

He grabbed his bag, padlocked the storage box, and jumped onto the soft, warm sand. As John climbed into the jeep, his swimming coach Emmett Carson pointed to the rear with his thumb.

"Th-they want us to bring cans."

A moment later John was tossing the hollow metal torpedo, canvas shoulder strap and towline wrapped around it, into the space behind the seats.

"Where is this place, anyway?" he asked. "I'm tired."

"Gold Coast," said Carson, pointing ahead. "About a half mile before the p-pier." He drove the jeep slowly, over the foot-printed sand, a million tiny dunes, weaving through the remaining beach people. They were on their own now. It was six o'clock. Swim at your own risk.

"Look for a … a pink house, Mexican t-tile roof," said Carson. "Big day out here. Any customers?"

"Three or four," John answered. "Two old ladies, a lost little kid. Some fat clown who got separated from his inner tube. He was furious at me for coming in, of course. But I swear he would've drowned. Oh well. Swam about a thousand on my lunch hour. You?"

"No rescues up there. N-no wind, glassy water. Couple of cut feet on b-broken bottles. Had to break up a fight about two hours ago."

"Let me guess," John said. "You told them you had the police on the way, but you'd let 'em leave. And they were stupid enough to believe it, right?"

"Right-o. Works every time. Th-there it is, I think."

✳   ✳   ✳   ✳

The pink stucco house was the biggest in the group, about a dozen in all. Behind them ran Pacific Coast Highway, where traffic was thick, cars headed back inland to small houses that would feel like ovens, even after the sun dropped. The Gold Coast mansions looked at the ocean across a hundred yards of sand. Even on a near-windless day, when the tall palms barely moved, there was enough salted breeze to keep these houses cool.

Carson parked the jeep opposite a volleyball court in front of the house. Shuffling through the sand in their direction was a sunburned, bald man wearing round sunglasses, a white silk shirt and blue linen trousers. He had a drink in one hand and offered the other to Carson.

"My dear Emmett," said the man with a British accent, "there you are. You're right on time. Good to see you. Welcome," he said, turning to John and shaking hands. "Stuart Green. Please call me Stu."

"I'm John Brady," he replied as Green smiled and turned again to Carson.

"Appreciate this, Emmett, really I do." Green slapped Carson's bare shoulder. "My friends are excited to see your show. Let's relax a little first." Green motioned toward the house. A few dozen people, all holding drinks, stood in the sand or sat on blankets.

"G-get your gear, John," Carson said. "We'll shower and change when we get out of the water."

"Just walk round there and put your things in one of the dressing rooms," said Green, pointing at one side of the house. "Then come back out and find me."

John followed Carson past a group of guests, some of whom smiled or waved at them, up a set of wooden steps with a handrail that was shedding flakes of white paint. A tall plank fence extended from the corner of the house, and a gate, disguised as part of the fence, was ajar. They stepped into a brick courtyard that was a storage area for bicycles, surfboards, beach umbrellas, kites, low canvas chairs, hoses, and other equipment. Attached to the side of the main house was a large wooden shed, divided into three stalls, each with a door that started a foot above the bricks and stopped a foot below the top of its opening. The middle stall was a shower, the other two dressing rooms with slatted benches and rusty wall hooks.

"So, Coach, what do we do?"

Carson explained, as they hung their bags on hooks and surveyed the side of the pink house, that Green was "in the movie business," as were most of his guests. They were interested in a short demonstration and explanation, he said. "You do the talking, just show them how the cans are used, a few safe swimming pointers, we'll hit the water, paddle, swim a couple hundred, that would be it. A free dinner, maybe meet some people, and who knows? M-maybe you get discovered. The next big star."

Back out on the sand, Green appeared to be deep in conversation with another man but, spotting the lifeguards, motioned them to join him. "I want you to meet Billy Rosen," said Green, "before you go on. Best writer in the business. These are my friends, Emmett Carson and Jim ... Brady."

"Pleased to meet you," said John. Green had moved away. "It's John, actually."

"Nice to meet you." Rosen looked over Carson's shoulder, toward the ocean. "I think you're up."

Green had gathered his guests around him and was standing on the driver's seat of the jeep.

"I thought you might enjoy learning about our brave and strong protectors," he shouted, "so we have special guests this evening. Two Santa Monica lifeguards. Let me introduce Emmett Carson, twice an American Olympic swimmer, now the coach at the University of Southern California. In the summer, when school is out, he works, if you can call it that, here at the beach. Emmett Carson, ladies and gentlemen."

There was clapping as Carson hopped up, replacing Green in the jeep. The Gold Coast houses reflected on his sunglasses. "Th-thank you. I'm going to let John Brady, who is one of my swimmers at USC and a lifeguard this summer, tell you a few things and answer questions."

Unprepared, John fumbled through explanations of the short-wave radio communications, the jeeps, and how to recognize a riptide. "I guess we'd like to give you a demonstration, right, Coach?"

"Sh-show them your can," was the reply. The group laughed. "Don't worry, folks, it's ... not what you think," said Carson, laughing, pleased with himself.

John pulled out the three-foot-long metal torpedo. "Couple of reasons for using these," he said. "First of all, it floats. It's hard to hold up and drag someone a long distance in the water, so this gives them something to rest on. Two, because of the towline, we can push the can to them from a safe distance. When someone is panicking, they tend to grab you, almost like they're fighting with you, or maybe they don't want to drown all by themselves. Anyway, it's good to be able to stay a few yards away, at least until they calm down." John looked at Carson, who nodded approvingly.

"C-can we get a volunteer?" Carson asked. "Somebody who can swim?"

Billy Rosen waved his hand. "I'll go," he said.

"I was … hoping for a beautiful woman," Carson said, "but here's what we'll do. Everybody c-come on down to the water."

The group moved thirty or so yards, then partway down the final dampened slope that arrested the sliding waves. Carson stopped.

Rosen would start swimming out, he explained. When he got out fifty yards or so, Carson would "hit the water with a paddleboard, just to show you that … rescue device. I'll c-catch up with him and take him out another hundred. Then J-John will rescue Mr. Rosen using the can."

To applause, Rosen took off his shirt and waded into the water.

"Go when you hear the siren," Carson said. "W-we'll be starting from the jeep. Clear us a path t-to the water."

The group rearranged itself, now lining a short parade route down the wet slope. Rosen, up to his waist, was facing back toward the guests with his hands on top of his head.

"G-great, John." Carson was unfastening the paddleboard from the jeep. "Th-they love it." Carson reached beside the steering wheel, and the siren gave a low, lazy moan. Rosen waved, turned, and began swimming.

Not bad, John thought, as the man negotiated the small surf, over the swells and under the broken waves.

Less than a minute later, Carson hit the siren again and tucked the nose end of the thick, eighty-pound paddleboard under his right armpit. With his left hand gripping a handle on the curved nose, he ran, like a half-naked fullback carrying a huge football. The board dragged on the ground and carved a small trench behind him. Once in the water, the board became weightless, and Carson was quickly lying on it, stroking into the opposing surf. After blasting through the last broken wave, he popped up to his knees and folded himself over, butt on heels and chest on thighs, arms pulling at the water. After no more than five strokes, Carson glided to Rosen's side and stopped by sitting astride the board, legs dangling, then sliding to the rear and turning, the yellow shape angling before him above the surface. Carson waved toward the beach, where the guests clapped and cheered, now joined by a few dozen other people. The size of the audience had doubled and was growing.

Rosen pulled himself onto the front of the paddleboard, lying face down, chin propped on his crossed arms. Carson was now back up on his knees, behind Rosen, paddling farther out.

After a few strokes, he unfolded himself and, kneeling upright, motioned toward shore.

John pressed the siren button, and heads turned in his direction. Holding the three-foot torpedo in one hand, he began his sprint, flying down the slope through the spectators. As soon as his feet hit water, he let go of the metal cylinder, holding the canvas shoulder strap, running with knees high into the deepening water. Just before jumping over the first wave, he looped the strap over his head and left shoulder, diagonally across his chest and back. As soon as the water level reached his crotch, where swimming becomes faster than running, he dove forward and glided underwater. Then kicking, stroking, looking up and ahead, he sought his rhythm.

In about two minutes he reached Carson and Rosen, who held the torpedo in the air like a trophy. The crowd waved back, but any noise was muffled into silence by the surf between them.

"Very impressive, fellows," said Rosen.

"Thanks. You were a g-good sport," Carson replied. "I'll take you back in now."

Carson was already strapping the paddleboard back into its jeep cradle when John reached the shore. The half of the crowd that was still there clapped, including Rosen, who had a towel draped over his shoulders. John rewrapped the cord and strap around the metal can and jogged up to the group. Rosen greeted him and offered his towel. "I'll introduce you to everybody up at the house," he said.

"Thanks. I think I'll use that shower," John said. He saw Carson now sitting in the jeep, with the radio mike at his mouth. He put it down and walked over to John.

"I c-called into to headquarters. M-message for me. I can't stay."

"I'll make sure he gets a ride home," Rosen said.

"I'll see you tomorrow, Coach."

As the jeep wobbled away, Rosen said, "As long as your coach is gone, let me get you a beer."

*   *   *   *

John Brady woke up the next morning with, he assumed, a hangover. He lay in bed, in his parents' house, trying to remember the details. Had all of that really happened?

After the rescue demonstration they had walked to the side gate together, John and Rosen, stopping to pick two brown Pabst bottles out of a metal ice tub.

"Keep that towel," Rosen said. "I'll get myself another one in the house. Come up the steps and inside when you're done. I'll meet you in the living room."

"Thanks," John said, watching Rosen trudge up the stairs. He stood for several minutes under the shower spray, rinsing off the day's salt, sand, and sweat. Then he put on a dry pair of trunks and zipped his red jacket up to the neck. He draped the wet canvas trunks and towel over a surfboard that was leaning against the side of the stairway, then ran up and into the house.

The living room was beyond a kitchen, where two women in black-and-white maids' uniforms were sitting at a table. John gave them a small wave as he passed through then entered the vast picture-windowed space overlooking the beach. The party guests were still outside, standing or sitting in groups, drinking, gesturing, laughing, munching small sandwiches. The sun was still strong, forcing John to shade his eyes as he looked out of the window.

"Some view, huh?" It was Rosen again, combing his wet hair as he stood beside John.

"Sure is," John answered. "Hard to believe we're in a house. It seems like, I don't know, an ocean liner. Can I borrow that comb?"

"Here. Let's get some food."

They went back through the kitchen and made their way out to the front of the house. John was grabbing a sandwich from a buffet table when he heard a woman's voice.

"Good show," she was saying. He turned to see a blond woman, wearing sunglasses and a white dress. She was older than John by several years, he guessed. He instinctively glanced around to see if she was with someone. She seemed alone.

"Thank you," he said. "Glad you were entertained."

"Go ahead, eat your sandwich. My name is Jane."

"Sorry," he said. "John Brady. Happy to meet you. Are you, um—"

"I work for Mr. Green. I wanted to say hello because I went to USC."

"Really? When was that? I've just been there a year and a half, three semesters. I don't know if—"

"No, I finished before you got there. Tell me about your job. Lifeguarding."

They talked, as the sun dropped, sitting on the sand in front of the house. She seemed amused by his stories. As John finished his second and then third beers, the sun was setting and the guests were drifting into the house.

"So, who are all these people?" John asked.

Jane hesitated. "They're … just friends of Mr. Green. Some he's in business with, some old friends from England."

"Special occasion?"

"Not a birthday party, if that's what you mean," she said. "They had a meeting earlier. About the war."

"What about it?"

She smiled, then said, "Lots of questions, for a lifeguard. I thought you were mostly interested in riptides, or whatever they're called." She brushed her fingers across the lifeguard patch on the chest of his jacket.

"Just curious," John said, smiling back. "What about the war?"

"They want America to come in," she said, standing up.

"I wonder if we should go inside," John said. "I'm not sure I'm really supposed to—"

"They're going to watch a movie," she said. "I've already seen it. I'd rather go for a swim."

"Now?"

"Yep. Keep an eye on me?"

"I'm a lifeguard, so I suppose that's my solemn duty."

"Good. I'll go change and see you at the water." She pointed at the ocean. "Go ahead. I'll be down there in a couple of minutes."

He walked out to the end of the flat beach, then partway down the slope. Was this really happening? He sat down, hoping so, then laid back with his head resting on his clasped hands.

"You coming in?" Jane shouted as she dropped two towels beside him, running past. She was wearing a black two-piece bathing suit.

He pulled himself up. She had run into the water and was facing back toward him, waving, knee-deep. Then she turned and dove under a breaking wave.

A minute later they were twenty-five yards out, bouncing off the bottom and treading water.

"Tell me more about this meeting. What did they do?"

"I'm not really part of their meetings," she said. "They talk about trying to persuade people here. Promoting radio and newspaper coverage of the war. They just want the Americans to join the fight against Hitler."

"Meaning me," John said. "I'm the one who gets drafted."

"Oh, stop. Let's change the subject."

She swam away. He let her go about ten strokes, then caught up to her with three of his own.

"So," Jane said, "how do you rescue someone if you don't have that can, or whatever it's called?"

"A few different ways. Put 'em on your hip and sidestroke, with one arm diagonally across. You can use someone's hair, if there's enough of it and if they can float."

"No thanks," she said, stroking her hair.

"You look like a good swimmer anyway," John said. "Water's nice, isn't it?"

"Mmm. Wonderful. Let's get out, though. I guess I won't pretend to drown."

They ran to the towels and wrapped them around their shoulders. "Now what?" John asked.

"To the showers," she answered.

"After you."

It was now dark. As they walked alongside the house, she put a finger to her lips, then cupped her hands around his ear and whispered, "Movie's on."

They were just entering the brick courtyard, faintly lit from the house's windows and a street lamp, when the group inside erupted in laughter.

"It's a cartoon," she whispered. "*Dumbo*, it's called. About a little circus elephant."

She grabbed him by a wrist and pulled him toward the shower stall. Inside, she tossed her towel, then his, over the wood wall into the adjacent dressing booth. Then she turned on the water, which actually felt warm after the night air's chill.

She stood under the shower, turned, then shifted to one side. "Go ahead," she said. John stepped into the spray, closing his eyes as he put his face under the showerhead. He was rubbing his eyes when he felt her arms come around his waist, from the back. He turned. Both parts of her bathing suit were lying at her feet.

Did the rest of it happen? There was kissing, he remembered. Feeling, holding, then she straddled him on the slatted wood bench with the water spraying at their feet. Then they were in her car, talking. She was driving him home. "You're sweet," she was saying.

He got out of bed and dressed. I have all day to think about this, John said to himself as his bicycle glided down the slope to Pacific Coast Highway. A whole day, another summer beach day, lifeguard station four.

Eleven

It was a sweltering Tuesday morning in September. The asphalt surface of the campus parking lot was softening underfoot as Earl Brady approached the liberal arts building.

"I wanted to stop by," he explained, "just to touch base with you. This Public Safety Committee hasn't been doing anything. Hasn't even met for a while."

"That so?" said Walter Jordan, leaning back in his chair while tapping a pencil on a desk blotter. "Any meetings scheduled?"

"No. August and September were cancelled, no explanation. What do you think?"

Jordan dropped his pencil into a leather cup, then rubbed his eyes. "My guess," he said slowly, "is that the government doesn't know what to do. Sure, they've identified the heads of some Japanese clubs and so forth. But that seems to be about it."

"I heard something interesting myself," Earl said, "from my son."

"Oh?"

"John spent the summer as a beach lifeguard. One of his friends is a Japanese kid, also in school here, on the swimming team. They both worked at the beach all day, then bodysurfed until dark."

"Nice life," Jordan interjected.

"Well, the Japanese kid told John something a couple of days ago. Big scandal among the local Japanese, last summer. Some schoolteacher from the Terminal Island neighborhood took forty high school boys to Japan for six weeks, supposedly to learn fencing from a prominent coach there. They've never come back. Word is, they were all drafted into the Japanese army. Dual citizenship."

Jordan was holding his head in his hands, elbows propped on his desk. He looked up. "Have you told anyone else about this?"

"Lindgren, the FBI man."

"And?"

"He said he already knew about it."

✳   ✳   ✳   ✳

It was nearly 2:00 PM when Earl pushed open the red-enameled door of the Golden Dragon. Sun was sharing a table with two men wearing aprons. They scampered to the kitchen as Earl approached. Sun smiled and motioned to a chair.

"Welcome, Mr. Brady. I have ordered lunch for us. I hope you will find it delicious."

"Thanks."

"It will be out here in a few minutes. It is best if final preparation is done just before serving, so they were told to wait until you arrived."

"Very kind of you."

"So, Mr. Brady, you said there were some questions. I am curious to know what you are curious about. More than two years have passed."

"Those photographs," Earl said. "I never asked you exactly where you got them. I'd like to know."

Sun looked at the ceiling, then at his guest. "The photographs were taken in Nanking. Some very courageous people have risked their lives, Mr. Brady, to tell the world what happened there."

"I know. I've seen the stories, and I've seen other pictures. I think I've read every account published in this country about the Japanese army in Nanking."

Sun folded his hands on the table and nodded slowly. "That is interesting." One of the aproned men arrived, holding a tray. He placed two painted ceramic bowls of steaming soup on the table. "Sizzling rice," he said. "Excuse me a moment."

Earl stirred the soup with a white spoon, wondering if he had said too much. Sun quickly returned, holding a large manila envelope, and stood beside the table. "Let me suggest that we spend a moment at a booth near the window. Better light."

Earl followed, and they sat side by side as Sun placed the envelope on the starched white tablecloth. With a figure-eight motion he unraveled a length of string from the round, red cardboard fasteners, then pulled out four glossy photographs. Earl recognized them immediately—clearer versions of the repulsive images he had first seen at the same table, years before.

Sun's chin rested in his cupped hands, his elbows on the table. Earl's fingers poked at the white border of a photograph. Sun broke the silence: "Turn over."

Earl flipped one. On its back were Oriental characters, written in black ink. He looked up at Sun, who turned over the other three photos.

"As I told you before, Mr. Brady, each of these is inscribed with the same words. 'Nanking December 1937.'"

"I remember. So then, these are the originals?"

"Yes. And the writing you are looking at, Mr. Brady, is in the Japanese language."

"I see." Then it hit him. "Wait. What?"

"This is in Japanese."

"But I thought these were smuggled out of China by missionaries."

"Not these pictures, Mr. Brady."

"Where did you get these?"

"They were stolen. From the Tokyo Club."

"When?"

"The night of the banquet. They were left on a shelf in one of the small card rooms, where our boxes—for serving dishes and other items—were being stored during the party. The Tokyo Club members were quite amused by the photographs, I am told, during their cocktail hour."

"Who stole them?"

"It was one of our workers." Earl looked toward the kitchen, but Sun wagged a finger. "Not here any longer."

"Where is he? Who is he?"

"She," Sun replied. He sat back. "Does it matter, Mr. Brady?" Sun looked around, then leaned forward. "Would you arrest her? Did you wish to return the stolen property to its rightful owner?"

Earl looked out the window, at cars and pedestrians. "It could matter. Did she poison the food?"

"No. The food had been eaten before she saw these. That is what she told me. That is what she would tell you. And anyway, Mr. Brady, I think we are not so stupid. My family's restaurant is not to be ruined, just for the fun of having some Japanese bank president shit himself inside out. Please, excuse my language."

They returned to their lunch. Soup and tender steamed rice, spicy kung pao chicken, snow peas, "All very good," Earl said.

"I hope you will recommend the Golden Dragon," said Sun, pouring green tea into small cups.

"I will," Earl said, "but you might get more cops in here than you ever wanted." They both laughed.

"May I tell you, Mr. Brady, for us a place like the Golden Dragon is more than a business. I should say, especially for those like me who were born here. We wish to be less isolated. Chinatown is losing some of its mystery and becoming instead a tourist attraction—this is a step in the right direction. I am quite serious when I speak about our reputation. We would not risk it."

"You do hate the Japanese, though."

"It is a great problem. Most frustrating, especially when most people seem unaware that there is any difference between us."

"I have to admit, I didn't give it very much thought until a couple of years ago," Earl said.

"I admire your honesty."

"Are there Japanese here who agree with you? Who don't want to be so isolated or ... apart?"

Sun hesitated before answering. "I really do not know," he said, "but I hope it is so. And I very much hope your government will find them, if they do exist. You will need them, Mr. Brady. You will need them."

He's right, Earl thought. *He despises the Japanese, but he's telling us we have to work with them. He's right.*

"What will happen in China?"

"If the Japanese have their way," Sun replied, "China will be their colony. Nobody is helping China resist. The British are besieged at home. The Americans want to be left alone, except for some who wish to join the war in Europe. But only in Europe."

Twelve

CONFIDENTIAL MEMORANDUM No. 8

To: L.A.P.S.C. Members
From: Special Agent T. A. Lindgren, FBI
Date: December 1, 1941
   Our next meeting will be at 3:00 PM on Thursday, December 4, at the usual location.

*   *   *   *

Earl drove straight to Colonel Jordan's office after the meeting. It was 4:15 when Jordan's secretary motioned for him to knock on the door.

"Come in."

Jordan was on the telephone. As soon as he saw Earl, he said, "Let me call you later. I have a visitor." Hanging up, he motioned to a chair. "What's new?"

Earl unfolded his notes, a single sheet of paper, and displayed it to Jordan.

Jordan glanced at the wall clock. "Well. That *was* a short meeting."

"Couldn't have been more than fifteen minutes."

"Go on," Jordan said.

"The FBI told us they're monitoring bank accounts of Japanese nationals. Then Lindgren said ... they're preparing for the possibility of detaining anyone whose activities are inimical to the best interests of the United States. The navy officer said some things about Hawaii. Let's see ... here. Out of 198 employees at the U.S. Post Office in Honolulu, fifty-one have dual citizenship. All Japanese."

"Anything else?" Jordan asked.

"Just that the FBI is aware of extra activities going on at the Japanese Consulate. Lindgren didn't say what activities. But it didn't sound good."

Jordan shook his head and faintly smiled. "It isn't."

"Sir?"

"I happen to know," Jordan continued. "Three days ago, the Japanese Consulate offices on the West Coast began destroying records. You're damn right it's not good."

"What's next?"

"We're about to enter the war," Jordan said. "Let me read something to you." He picked up a newspaper from his desk. "This is Premier Tojo addressing a public rally in Japan. He said, 'The fact that Chiang Kai-Shek is dancing to the tune of Britain, America, and Communism in his futile resistance to Japan is only due to the desire of Britain and the United States to fish in the troubled waters of East Asia by pitting the East Asiatic peoples against each other. For the honor and pride of mankind we must purge this sort of practice from East Asia with a vengeance.'"

"Sounds like a rally, all right," Earl said.

"You know," Jordan continued, "there were some in Japan who wanted peace. But the Japanese army would overthrow the government if it tried to comply with American demands to get out of China. They can't do it. No way they can withdraw from China now. The Japanese military clique has prevailed, Earl. They won."

"What will they do?"

"If Roosevelt has anything to say about it, Japan will attack us."

"If Roosevelt ... what?" Earl stood up, bewildered.

Jordan leaned forward onto his desk and sighed. "Our War Department's plans have been obtained by the newspapers. It's all out in the open. They're reading about it in Tokyo right now. And goddamn it, it's just what I figured. The American plan calls for fighting Germany first, then Japan. Which, the War Department hopes, can be held in check while we reconquer Europe."

"How did this plan get out?"

"It was let out, Earl. Let out on purpose. From the top."

"Why would the president let this out?"

Jordan leaned back in his chair with a disgusted frown. "Franklin Roosevelt always told the people he wouldn't lead us into another European conflict. Not everyone believed him, but enough did, and he got reelected on that promise. But don't you see, all bets are off if we're attacked. If the other side shoots first."

"He wants Japan to shoot first?"

"The son of a bitch can't wait, Earl. It's his ticket to enter the war against Germany."

"How do you think this would start?"

"There are three possibilities," Jordan said. "The first shot could be fired at any one of them—or two, or all three. The Philippines is the closest to Japan, of course. That's where the War Department probably assumes the attack will happen. Our forces there have been placed on highest alert, as of today. But then there's Hawaii. And there's Alaska."

Earl looked past Jordan's shoulder, at the globe. "You showed me about Alaska before," he said. "What about Hawaii?"

"Ah," said Jordan in a mocking tone, "the new home of the navy's Pacific Fleet." He shook his head. "People don't know this, but there was a bitter, bitter dispute last summer and fall over that decision. To relocate the fleet to Hawaii. Admiral Richardson, who's a good man, lost his job over it. He tried to point out that the fleet was inadequately supported for such a move, out into the very middle of the Pacific. But there they are, lacking oilers and other supply ships. Stuck in the middle. Neither here nor there."

"Why was the fleet shifted?" Earl recalled, vaguely, reading stories about the move in the summer of 1940. From Long Beach, San Diego, San Francisco.

Jordan shrugged. "Supposedly, Roosevelt and his advisors thought they could scare the Japanese by moving closer. 'A restraining influence,' I think was the phrase. Remember, he was in a reelection campaign and a big, big issue was whether the United States would go to war. Roosevelt needed to buy time. He didn't want that first shot to be fired too soon. Somebody convinced him that this move to Hawaii would slow the Japanese down. They thought the Japanese were poor sailors and crappy pilots and would confine themselves to fighting in China for a while. They still hope so. We'd better all of us hope so."

"How long does this plan say it would take to finish the war in Europe?" Earl asked.

"It doesn't say anything about finishing it," Jordan replied. "But it does say the United States won't be ready to *start* an offensive against Germany until the middle of 1943."

"Jesus. That's a long time."

"A very long time," Jordan said, standing up. "A long time for a short-handed, undersupplied containment strategy in the Pacific. That's right. Let's take a walk outside. Let me talk to my secretary Miss Whitlock, and I'll meet you downstairs."

Five minutes later they were crossing Exposition Boulevard and entering the vast rose garden, in front of the Museum of Science and Industry, without saying a word. The sun had dropped, and a chilly gust of wind had put the palm trees in motion, sounding like the shuffling of cards in an upstairs room.

They walked past a small flatbed truck, engine idling, headlights on. The driver was a Japanese man, wearing a tan-colored jacket and a sweat-stained San Francisco Seals baseball cap. He smiled and nodded. At the rear of the truck, hoisting into its bed a folded canvas tarp filled with brittle brown sycamore leaves and rosebush cuttings, was another Japanese man, younger, unsmiling.

Jordan pointed to a wrought-iron bench. As they sat, the truck drove away. Jordan watched it go and shook his head. "It might be up to you," he said.

"What might be up to me?"

"This committee, the whole 'Public Safety' business has been a farce. The FBI isn't even going to try real counter-espionage. It would never be easy, don't get me wrong. I know the Japanese are close-knit. You and I can't learn the language and then pretend we're Japanese. But I think you'd agree, there is no effort to recruit any of them to work for us. No effort. Have you seen any hint of it?"

"No," Earl agreed. "Just … watching. A few lists. A lot of gossip about who the Japanese are trying to use as sources."

"Right. No doubt a bunch of union organizers and Negroes have been put under surveillance. Hauled in for questioning, perhaps. So what? The FBI is barking up the wrong tree. Like I said before—the Communists don't want to help Japan, they want us to fight Japan."

"And therefore the Nazis?"

"Exactly," Jordan said. "If we're serious about learning what the Japanese are up to, we have to do more than watch. We have to penetrate. Infiltrate. Get some of them working for us. Your office might have to do that."

Earl couldn't quite imagine it. Recruiting Japanese double agents—on what pretext? Vice, gambling? Maybe.

"How would the DA's office do that?" he asked. "And what could we do with the information, if we got any?"

"I know," Jordan said. "It's probably a crazy idea. But then, maybe the navy would take the project over once the shooting started. At least you'd have something for them *to* take over. There's another thing I should tell you, Earl."

"What's that?"

Jordan leaned forward on the bench, elbows on knees. "I'm about to get myself into some trouble again, I expect."

"Oh?"

"*Time* is going to publish an article I'm writing. Next week's issue. I could be burning all my bridges."

"What's it about?"

"The plans. I do think the war plan was deliberately allowed to get out, and into the newspapers. These fellows are baiting Japan into shooting first so Roosevelt can say we were given no choice, and off we go to another European war."

"I can see how some people might be annoyed at you," Earl said.

"It won't have my name on it. I still have people to protect. But, there are those who might recognize my ... voice." Jordan looked into the distance.

"Colonel, why are you telling me this?"

Jordan stood, and they began walking back toward the campus. It was almost dark.

"Because," he said, "this is going to get a lot of good men killed." Jordan closed his eyes. "And it puts the West Coast at risk. Not intentionally, I suppose, but ... I think people could be in for a rude awakening. You—meaning the local authorities, up and down the coast—you may find yourselves in the war business, and soon. Ready or not."

They walked further in silence, out of the rose garden. They parted company on the sidewalk along Exposition, where Earl's car was parked.

"I'll call you tomorrow," he said.

Jordan nodded, then turned and walked through the open campus gate and up the steps to his office. Earl watched for a moment, again imagining Jordan younger and in uniform. Walking not into a brick university building, but into a wood-frame Texas ranch house. "Mr. and Mrs. Fletcher, your son ..."

Earl drove west on Exposition, past the swim stadium, then up Vermont. *This could get a lot of good men killed*, Jordan had said. It struck Earl as he turned west onto Pico, and he almost said it out loud: *Jordan is talking about his own son.*

Thirteen

He had traveled on Pico for about two miles, counting beer billboards—
Lucky Lager, Regal, Pabst Blue Ribbon—when he noticed the black sedan
alongside. The driver was waving, then making a circular stirring motion
with one hand. Earl rolled down his window and recognized the man
immediately. He pointed ahead, to a Richfield gas station. Both cars
pulled in and parked, side by side, away from the pumps. The evening line
was forming, the usual wait for fill-ups ever since the seven-to-seven curfew on gas stations had been declared.

Earl opened his door, but Special Agent Lindgren gestured for him to
stay put.

"I thought you fellows slept in your jackets and ties," Earl said as
Lindgren settled into the passenger seat. The FBI man was wearing a green
sweater over an open-necked white shirt.

"I'm out of uniform, that's right," said Lindgren, drumming his fingers
on the dashboard. "Look, ah, we need to have a talk."

"Shoot."

"I've been ordered back to Washington. I just found out this morning,
and I'm supposed to be there next week. I have to fill you in about some
things before I go. Tonight's really my only chance—I'll be in the office or

packing up my things at home for the next twenty-four hours solid. Then I'm on the train tomorrow night."

"Where should we go?"

"Let's just drive around, if that's all right. Fifteen, twenty minutes is all."

So they drove, as Lindgren talked, for forty-five minutes. Out Pico, up Sepulveda, back to the east on Olympic, down Western, back to the Richfield station, where they sat a few minutes longer, because Lindgren had a lot to say.

*   *   *   *

At six the next morning, Earl was in his car again, driving to Pasadena. Doris had been satisfied—maybe—with his vague account of Thursday evening's meeting with Lindgren.

"Sorry to be late," he had said. "I had a surprise meeting with an FBI agent, the one in charge of this task force I told you about."

She was good-natured about it. "It's all right, I changed the dinner reservation. Sabotage by our nation's enemies?"

"Well, yes, that one. Anyway, the FBI man's being transferred all of a sudden, and he needed to brief me on some investigations we might be brought into. That sort of thing."

She had wrapped her arms around his waist. "I'll get the details later," she said. "Lucky for me, you talk in your sleep."

The sun was rising, almost blinding him through the windshield, as he accelerated onto the Arroyo Seco Parkway. He had been up since four thirty, restless, making notes. Those were now in a loose pile on the seat beside him.

The front door to Santa Teresa was locked, but he could see lights on inside. It was almost seven o'clock. He pressed the small, black doorbell button and heard a weak buzz. Just as he was giving the button a second push, a large, evidently grumpy woman opened the door. "Visiting hours start at eleven," she said, blocking the doorway.

Earl reached into his back pocket and retrieved his wallet. It flopped open in his hand, showing his badge. "I need to see Mr. Fletcher right away. Room eight, I think. Sorry to come so early, ma'am. It's official business."

The woman stepped aside. "Come with me."

Earl followed her, across the empty lobby and down a long corridor. She knocked at a door, and they heard a loud cough in reply. She nodded to Earl. "He's up. Go on in."

He was shocked by what he saw. Fletcher's skin was gray, and he'd lost weight. He was out of bed, though, and sitting in a chair. "Earl," he rasped. "I was thinking I might see you today."

Earl looked down at his old mentor. "So you were expecting me, sir?"

Fletcher coughed again, slowly, loose and deep. "Just tell me what Lindgren said. Then I'll tell you what I know. Promise."

He sat on the edge of the bed, facing Fletcher, and began. "Lindgren said he had mixed feelings about going back to Washington. That he's been frustrated, he thinks it's going to be a mess around here, so in a way he's glad to be getting out. But he also feels guilty."

"I know how he feels," said Fletcher. "Just tell me what he said."

Earl pulled the folded-up notes out of his pocket.

*   *   *   *

Lindgren had started out, the night before as they drove along Pico, by reminding Earl of the Tachibana case.

"Remember the Japanese navy officer we arrested at the Olympic Hotel? Last summer."

Earl remembered. "The one who got bailed out and left? How could I forget?"

"Yep. Embarrassing. I couldn't believe it when the Assistant U.S. Attorney agreed to a cash bond release. Truth is, I don't think he could believe it either, the poor bastard. He gave me one of those looks in the courtroom, you know—'sorry, thanks for trying, I can't do anything about it.' I tried to complain, through proper channels, of course. Nothing. All they can ever talk about is diplomacy, sensitive talks, blah, blah, blah. Office of Navy Intelligence—ONI—they were beside themselves. Morrow was furious. 'Why the fuck are we bothering with these intercepts? Why don't we save time and just give the Philippines to these little shit-bags right now?' And so on. He was raving mad, I'll tell you."

"Are you in trouble for raising a stink?" Earl asked. "Is that why you're being moved?"

"I don't think so. Maybe. I don't know," Lindgren said. "Supposedly my transfer is for a promotion of some kind. We'll see. Tachibana wasn't the first case like this, and not the last, either."

"Really?"

"Sure. Fletcher's told you about the *Molino Rojo* case?"

"Right," Earl said "Right. I heard about that."

"Anyway, let me go on here. At the World's Fair in San Francisco last year—while I was still posted up there—a Japanese agent they called Kono recruited a former sailor who was flat broke and out of work. We got plenty of those around, right? The American, Blake was his name, he didn't quite know what was happening at first. Just to get his hands on a few hundred dollars, he made up the name of a sailor he said he knew. On the *Pennsylvania*, at Pearl Harbor. There was no such person, you see, but Blake wanted the cash. He figured he could just ditch Kono somehow after that. But Kono and another Jap showed up at Blake's place and said they were going to pay for him to go to Hawaii, to meet with his friend to get information about the *Pennsylvania*. So Blake panics. He's bullshitted them, see, and he's not sure how they found him. He's scared, and he comes into our San Francisco office. I'm in Los Angeles by this time, but I go back up there to interview Blake. Then, off I go to Hawaii. To catch a few spies in the act, right?"

"You went with Blake?"

"No, no. I went over there a week before he did. Took another man with me, to pose as Blake's friend on the *Pennsylvania* crew. Set it up with the navy brass over there. So we organized this meeting between 'Blake and the fake,' we were calling them. I then watched the whole thing. More to the point, I watched Kono watching the whole thing. It went perfectly.

Blake was handed this fat envelope of incorrect information—phony repair schedules, training plans, crew rosters, base newsletters, stuff like that—and passed it off to Kono an hour later in the lobby of the Royal Hawaiian."

"You saw all of this?"

"I was fifty feet away from it. Then I followed Kono all the way to Los Angeles."

"Here? Not San Francisco?"

"He came here, all right, and went straight to a doctor's office."

"What for?"

"We didn't know, at least not then. When we arrested Kono—whose real name is Tachibana, that was him—he didn't have the documents any-more. No envelope. Gone. And the only time he was out of my sight, other than while we were at sea, was in the medical clinic."

"But what about the other passengers?"

"We checked. No other Japanese. There were some Germans, so I know that's a possibility—but I had them followed, and I don't think so. They're both high school teachers who left Germany as babies. Anyway, Kono went straight from the gangplank in a taxi, bags and all, to the clinic."

"And this clinic?"

"Doctor Furusawa's clinic," said Lindgren, shaking his head. "I've got Tachibana—or Kono, whatever the hell dead to rights, so off we go to the clinic. It's a house, really, and the assistant lets us in. It looks like a waiting room at your doctor's office—chairs, magazines—but there's nothing to wait for. There's no examination room. I mean, not a single piece of medical equipment, no medicines, no supplies. Not a goddamn cotton ball in the whole building, as far as I can see. If there is anything, it's hidden. Furusawa is very polite, of course, speaks good English. He actually is a doctor, it turns out. Went to Stanford ten years ago and then came to Los Angeles. I show him Kono's picture. 'Upset stomach,' he says. 'From his trip. Bromo seltzer.'"

"What next?"

"Well, I'm ready to rip the place apart," Lindgren said. "But of course, it's decided not to, by the higher-ups. No searches. The envelope from Blake and the fake was full of wrong information anyway, so who cares? Let them have it. I didn't agree with that, but I calmed down a little. So instead we started watching the clinic—at least we were finally doing something that could lead somewhere. I was feeling all right about it, actually. We saw a parade of Japanese go in and out of that place, at all hours. Most of them didn't stay inside long enough to have their temperatures taken or piss in a cup. Walk in, walk out. No way is this a medical clinic. Furusawa was driving to the Japanese Consulate at least once a day. Sometimes twice. Now it looks like we're onto something, after a week or so of this. Actually, we considered bringing you into it—maybe to raid the place for some state or city violation. Just about then, our prize prisoner Kono— Tachibana—sailed over the horizon."

"Did you keep watching the clinic?"

"Oh, yes. Off and on. We were pretty discouraged, though. It seemed like Washington wasn't going to let us accomplish anything. But we watched, and we followed, and we saw the same things. Had a few promising situations. But then it all ended."

"What do you mean?"

"About a month ago, Doctor Furusawa packed up and left. He had to know we were looking at him. He's gone, in any event. I wanted to nab him, but Washington said no. The usual reasons. I watched him board the ship for Osaka. The little bastard stood at the railings and waved good-bye to me. We did tear that clinic apart then, I'll tell you. Not a scrap of paper."

"So now what?" Earl asked.

"Things are about to change. I'm not tooting my own horn, believe me. But I know the new agent coming in for counterintelligence, my replacement. He's a good man, but he's never had an original idea in his life. Does what he's told. No imagination, no initiative. I wouldn't be surprised if the Public Safety Committee were discontinued."

Earl snickered. "Not that it was ever ..."

"I know, I know," Lindgren said. "I tried to make something out of that, but it was the same old business. Watch, wait, and wait some more. I just figured something was better than nothing. At least you're involved, and you have a little running start."

"I'm not sure what you mean," Earl said. "What am I running at?"

"Getting some information from local Japanese who are loyal to America. It's called counterintelligence. The FBI is supposed to do it, but for some reason … we aren't."

"What am I supposed to do?" Earl asked. "Run an ad in the paper?"

"All you have," Lindgren said, "is that list of names and addresses. The clubs, the societies. But I have more on these people, who is really who—from our files. It's on about five sheets of paper, all condensed. You probably won't understand it, just looking. You'll need to have it explained."

"When will you be explaining it?"

"I won't be. I'll probably never see you again, and I'm trusting you not to tell anyone about this. Two exceptions. Bud Fletcher, you can tell him what's up. In fact you should go see him tomorrow morning, first thing. The only other exception is Colonel Jordan."

"I thought you might be getting to him."

"Jordan's got the five pages, and he knows what it all means. I've spent some time with him, and I've told him to work with you. I would have used Bud Fletcher, but he got sick. Anyway, Jordan will take you through it; then you burn the pages after you've taken your own notes."

"Then what will I do," said Earl, "after all this is explained to me?"

"It's your roadmap into the Japanese network," Lindgren replied. "You need to get the ball rolling on this. I can't." They were parked again at the Richfield station.

"Fletcher and Jordan will tell you more tomorrow," Lindgren said. "Good luck." Then he shook Earl's hand, got out of the car, and walked away.

*   *   *   *

"So, Bud," said Earl as he refolded the notes, "here I am. It's first thing tomorrow, and that's what Lindgren told me, and now I would like to hear what you know. If you don't mind."

He was regretting the sarcasm but Fletcher said sympathetically, "Listen, I'm sorry, Earl. You have a right to feel like you've been kept in the dark. Let me tell you what I know, like I promised. Go easy on me, all right? I'm a sick old man, is all."

He had helped Jordan get the USC job, Fletcher explained, after Jordan's army career ended over his vocal support of the "Fortress America" crowd, the America-Firsters. Even then—a year or more ago, in 1940—Jordan was criticizing the War Department's plan for the United States to conduct a "limited defensive war" with Japan while joining forces with Britain to defeat Germany. Jordan thought this was wishful thinking. He was convinced the government was ignoring the real dimension of the Japanese threat.

"He went on and on about the Jap invasion of China," Fletcher said, "and how it could be repeated here. How the civilian Japanese living in China were used as intelligence sources before the invasion. And how vicious the Japanese army was, once it got in there."

"I've seen the pictures, remember?"

"Yeah. Anyway, Walter Jordan and Ted Lindgren first met in Washington in '38 or '39, I guess, when Jordan lectured at the FBI, for the counterintelligence unit they were setting up. Lindgren agrees with Jordan about the Japanese threat. They're both frustrated as hell about Washington's attitude. I gather they were setting up this Public Safety Committee in the hopes that Washington might let us—the locals—actually do something. Maybe Washington wouldn't actively interfere, or maybe it'd be too late to close the drapes if we already had a big arrest and it was out in the newspaper, et cetera. Maybe we'd catch some of these people actually stealing information or trying to buy it from factory workers. That's what they were hoping for."

Fletcher stopped and coughed again. "The other idea is that we might do what the FBI and the army and navy never did, which is infiltrate. Try to recruit some local Japanese to help us, in other words. Find out what *their* plans are."

"Well, I have heard Colonel Jordan mention that," Earl said. "Is he my next appointment?"

Fletcher nodded.

Fourteen

It was 9:30 on that Friday morning, December 5, when Earl arrived at his office in the Hall of Justice. Maria handed him a message slip.

He called Santa Teresa. "Mr. Fletcher, please. Room eight."

"Hello," Fletcher answered, in a rough whisper.

"It's Earl, sir. Are you all right?"

"Yeah. I forgot to tell you something before you left me this morning. Is the Tokyo Club file still in your office?"

"Yes."

"Pull out the medical reports on the food poisoning victims."

"That'd be under crappers and chuckers?"

Fletcher laughed weakly. "Can you find it?"

"Here it is. What do you want from this?"

"I just wondered," said Fletcher, "where the victims went for their treatment."

Earl removed a stack of one-page interview reports from a folder marked, "Medical Records—Victims." He skimmed the top one, concerning "Okita, Tetsu—male, 42," who had reported eating various dishes and drinking various drinks, then suffering nausea and intestinal distress. "Initial medical treatment sought at local Japanese medical clinic."

"Let me look at a few of these, Bud," said Earl as he turned the next report, "and I'll call you back."

An hour later, he reported to Fletcher that all sixty-eight of the victims who sought medical assistance had gone to a "local Japanese medical clinic." Four had been admitted to hospitals on Dr. Furusawa's orders, then released the next day: "recovered, in no apparent distress." Several had proceeded to hospital emergency rooms, where they were "treated and released." The others had been given various remedies at the clinic. It was the same clinic. Dr. Furusawa had seen sixty-eight patients in one night.

* * * *

At three o'clock that afternoon, Earl returned from court to his desk and called Jordan's office.

"He isn't in today," said the secretary. "May I ask who is calling?"

"Earl Brady."

"Oh, yes, Mr. Brady. Colonel Jordan said to give you his home number if you called. Ready? Webster 1852."

"Thank you," Earl said as he wrote the number on a scrap of paper. "Can you give me his address?"

"Well, sir ... I suppose, since he wanted you to have his telephone number. And he did say it was important that he speak to you. Here it is ... 267 Van Ness."

"Thank you again."

There was no answer after six rings. He let it go eleven times when he tried again an hour later. He put the scrap of paper in the pocket of his shirt, then dialed a different number.

"History Department."

"Hello, it's Mr. Brady again. I'm not getting an answer at the number you gave me for Colonel Jordan."

The woman confirmed the number and said she didn't know of any others. "Mr. Brady," she said, "when you do reach him, would you mind giving Colonel Jordan a message? I'm leaving soon. This one person has called twice this afternoon, and I ..."

"Certainly I will. What is it?"

"Mr. Mead, Thomas Mead. From *Time* magazine. Madison 0120."

"Any idea why Mr. Mead is so anxious to speak with Colonel Jordan? Just in case the colonel asks."

"Well, he says that something the colonel was writing is overdue. They expected it by noon today. I know he finished the article, because he called me to say he was ready to have a taxi sent to his house. I thought he would be at the *Time* office by now."

"I'll pass the message along to him," Earl answered her, "don't worry. Have a nice weekend."

"Likewise, Mr. Brady. Good-bye."

*   *   *   *

That was fast, Jordan was thinking as the taxi pulled to a stop in front of his house. It was 11:30. He had made the call to his secretary only about ten minutes earlier.

"For the *Time* magazine office?" the driver asked as Jordan approached.

"Yes, thanks for coming so promptly."

The driver was wearing sunglasses and a straw Panama hat. He nodded and flipped the meter flag as Jordan settled into the backseat. He pulled the article from his coat pocket, unfolded it, and began to proofread it again. He didn't notice the gray Ford sedan turning onto Van Ness behind the taxi.

By the corner of Wilshire and Western, Jordan was content with his article and returned it to his pocket.

He wondered why the driver was turning right off Wilshire, almost a mile from the *Time* office. Then he wondered why the taxi was pulling over to the curb and stopping. He didn't understand why the Mexican-looking young man in a business suit was opening the cab's door and sliding quickly into the backseat. Jordan put his right hand on the driver's shoulder, reaching with his left for the door handle.

"Say, what the hell is—" The pistol grip hit Jordan behind the right ear, and he fell sideways into the younger man's lap. "*Vamanos*," the man said to the driver.

*   *   *   *

Earl Brady's Chrysler angled onto Beverly west of downtown and soon was turning south on Van Ness.

Number 267 was one of the smaller houses on the block, a one-story gray stucco with brick trim around the windows and doorway. At 4:30 he parked at the curb and crossed the sidewalk, then followed a short brick walkway, bordered by a low box hedge, to the concrete front porch. As he stepped up to the door, he heard a slapping sound behind him and turned to see the evening paperboy, on his bicycle, backhanding another folded newspaper onto the neighboring porch. Earl retrieved Jordan's paper, returned to the door, and pressed the buzzer. He barely heard music—classical, from a radio or a phonograph—inside. But there was no answer. He buzzed again, then knocked, then knocked again.

There was a blue Chevrolet in the driveway to the side of the small house. He walked past it toward the rear, popping the folded newspaper on the side of his leg. Behind the house was a small, enclosed yard with dormant Bermuda grass, a few heavily pruned rosebushes, one lemon tree, and a clothesline. The back door to the house, he noticed, was slightly ajar.

He knocked on it. "Colonel Jordan? Are you home? It's Earl Brady." The music was coming from a tabletop radio, he saw as he pulled open the door and leaned into a kitchen. "Colonel Jordan?"

Earl continued to call out the name as he moved through the empty house. He was soon standing beside a desk in one of the two bedrooms, waiting for someone to answer the telephone at LAPD Wilshire Division.

Fifteen

Earl waited in his car. He had gotten through to Lester Smith, a young Wilshire Bureau detective. A football star at Loyola High, Smith had joined the LAPD after knee injuries forced him off the team at Santa Clara. They had worked together once before: Earl remembered asking Smith why their burglary defendant was showing up in court with two black eyes and a swollen lip. Smith was matter-of-fact. "Some people," he explained, "you just gotta hit."

He wasn't Earl's first choice, but on a Friday evening one couldn't be too picky. Smith pulled to a stop and got out of his unmarked car. A black-and-white parked immediately behind Smith. Two uniformed cops emerged, with flashlights. Earl waved at all three to follow him down Colonel Jordan's driveway. "We'll talk inside."

"Thanks for coming," he began as they stood in the kitchen. "Here's the deal. This is the home of a man I was supposed to see today. Official business. He's a retired army officer who teaches at USC and writes newspaper and magazine pieces occasionally. *Time* magazine's been trying to reach him all day, too. No answer, but his phone works. I used it to call you. When I—"

Smith interrupted with a palms-down, piano-playing gesture. "Whoa. What is this person's name, Mr. Brady?"

"Right. Sorry. It's Jordan. Colonel Walter Jordan. He's about sixty, tall, thin, curly gray hair shorter on the sides."

Earl described what he had found, or not found, when he came looking for Jordan. He gave Smith the telephone number and location of Jordan's office at the university. He was embarrassed to know so little about Jordan, to be almost useless in any effort to find him.

"He's an old friend of Bud Fletcher," said Earl. "Bud's at a sanatorium out in Pasadena. Lung disease of some kind. He'll know more personal information about Jordan."

"Let's call Mr. Fletcher from here," Smith suggested. "Where's the phone?"

Earl led them to the smaller bedroom which, he now saw, Jordan used as a study. The bed was covered with books and magazines, and the desk had a typewriter and a lamp on it. Also a cup of pencils, an ink blotter, and a telephone. Earl dialed Santa Teresa.

A woman answered in room eight. "He's about to eat dinner," she said.

"Please tell him it's Earl Brady and it's important."

He quickly explained the situation to Fletcher. "Jesus," he growled. "Put Smith on."

"Right. Here he is. I'll call you later."

While Smith used the telephone, Earl and the officers walked through the house again. As in the study, he was seeing more, noticing more, now that he was no longer looking for Jordan himself. Framed photographs— of family groups, school classes, teams, and a young Jordan with a young woman. *Fletcher will know who she is,* Earl thought.

There was a brick fireplace recessed into a wall of the living room, a varnished wood mantle above it at shoulder level. A couple of small trophies, an empty, cut-glass flower vase. Earl also saw a small, white matchbox and leaned forward to see what was printed on the side. It was a telephone number. Then he stood on his toes to read the top: "Golden Dragon Chinese Restaurant."

*   *   *   *

It was nearly 6:30 when Earl left Jordan's house. He'd given Smith his home address and telephone number. The detective promised to call as soon as he knew anything.

Earl drove south to Pico and turned west. Where would Jordan go? If that was Jordan's car in the driveway—Earl didn't know—why would Jordan need a taxi go anywhere? The questions were obvious ones. Smith would do a good job. Fletcher had provided some information: Jordan was widowed, with one son who was an army captain in the Philippines. *Maybe that was it,* Earl thought: the first shot is coming, Jordan's son is about to be engulfed in a Japanese invasion, and Jordan is off somewhere, in some way trying to communicate with him. *Son, your commander-in-chief has tipped off the Japanese that this would be an opportune moment for them to attack you. The president has his reasons. He hopes you will understand.*

As Earl rolled through the dimly lit stretch between mid-city Los Angeles and Santa Monica, he remembered the scrap of paper in his shirt and pressed on the gas pedal. There was a telephone at the corner of Sepulveda and Pico.

"Operator."

"Hello. Please get me Madison 0120."

"Ten cents, please. Thank you, dialing that number."

He looked at his watch. Maybe they're still there. One ring. It's a magazine. They could have hours like newspapers. Two rings. Three. Four.

"Mead."

Earl jumped. "Oh—hello, Mr. Mead. Sorry to call this late. Calling about Colonel Walter Jordan."

"Really? Who are you?"

"Sorry. Earl Brady. I'm a deputy district attorney. I've been trying to reach the colonel all day, and his secretary told me you were too. She gave me your number, in case I heard from him. So he could return your calls."

"Well, he hasn't."

"That's what I wanted to know," Earl said. "He's missing today. Didn't go to work, didn't call you back, no answer at his house. It isn't like him, I don't think. He was also supposed to see me today, or talk to me anyway. Some important things. And I understand he had a deadline with you. For an article?"

"That's right."

"He told me a little bit about it. Anyway, I've been to Colonel Jordan's house, just a short while ago. Not there, and none of the local hospitals have him. It isn't like him to just disappear this way. I have some of our people on it. Any ideas?"

"Not really," Mead answered. "I don't know him too well. But you're right, it's not like Colonel Jordan to blow a deadline. He's a disciplined man. But to tell you the truth, I had to put him out of my mind as of about two o'clock today. This article was going to be pretty prominent, but at some point we have to give up and go to another layout. Lord, I hope he's …"

"All right," Earl said. "Thanks for talking to me. We'll have Colonel Jordan call you when we find him. If you hear from him, please tell him to call me, at home. Earl Brady, Exeter 3202."

Before leaving the telephone booth, he called the Golden Dragon and made a Saturday lunch date with Mr. Sun.

*   *   *   *

SANTA MONICA EVENING OUTLOOK
Friday, December 5, 1941
SOLDIERS ARRIVE ON MANEUVERS

Soldiers from Uncle Sam's Army rolled into Santa Monica today, assigned the task of defending the vast Cloverfield plant of the Douglas Aircraft Company against a theoretical enemy attack. Over the next ten days, "war games" will test the army's ability to intercept air raids on strategic defense areas.

Captain A. C. Smiley, in command of Battery C, set up headquarters on the abandoned grounds of the school on San Vicente Boulevard at Bristol Avenue, across the street from the Brentwood Golf Course.

*　　*　　*　　*

As he turned into his driveway, Earl reminded himself of the two calls he needed to make and the one he'd be waiting for. To Fletcher, because Earl had promised. To Lindgren, if he could be reached before his train left town. From Smith, if he had any news.

He gave his explanations to Doris and promised dinner out, after his calls. The first was to LAPD headquarters.

"Watch command."

"This is Deputy DA Earl Brady. Let me talk to the WC on duty."

"One moment."

"Earl. Bert Rossi here. What can we do for you?"

"Evening, Bert. Listen, I have a little problem. I need to talk to an FBI agent who's leaving by train for the East Coast tonight. I don't know when, exactly. Probably all you can do is have him paged at Union Station."

"Right. Give me his name, and we'll get someone to see the station manager right away."

"Ted Lindgren. Destination is Washington DC. He should call me at home. Exeter 3202. Thanks, Bert."

"Any time. I'll call you shortly, if he doesn't. Say fifteen minutes."

Earl decided to give it half an hour before tying up the line with a call to Fletcher. Doris was at the end of the sofa in the living room, reading a book, her bare feet curled under her.

"I need to wait and see if Lindgren calls me," he told her. "Drink?"

"Sure, love. Gin and tonic."

The metal ice tray gave up a few cubes after he ran warm water over its frost-whiskered bottom. He mixed her drink and uncapped a Lucky Lager bottle for himself.

Doris placed her open book on the floor, face down, as Earl set the drink on the table. Earl sat and put an arm around her shoulders, kissed her cheek, and took a swig of beer.

"Been a busy few days for you, hmm?"

"Hectic," he said.

"This is rather civilized," Doris said in a mock aristocratic tone, sipping.

She put the glass down and turned. "We don't have to go out," she said, then reached behind his head and pulled it toward her face. They kissed, slowly and deep. Then the phone rang.

He got to it after three rings.

"Hello."

"Mr. Brady? Bert Rossi calling. We paged your man, but there was no answer. The station manager thinks he was probably on the 4:15. They can check the passenger list if you want, then try to get a message to him tomorrow at the first long stop. Albuquerque, I think he said."

"Ah—sure. That'll be fine. Same message, just to call me. Thanks very much, Bert."

"I'll call you if they find his name. Let you know what time it stops."

"Right. Call me either way. Thanks again."

He dialed Fletcher.

"Hope it isn't past your bedtime, Earl."

"Nope. Just checking in with you, Bud. I haven't heard from Smith. I put a call out to Lindgren, but I think he's already on the train. Somewhere in the desert by now, I guess. You want me to call you tomorrow?"

Fletcher coughed. "Yeah. Talk to me in the morning." He coughed again, louder.

"Good night, Bud."

"One more call," he told Doris.

They were on their second drinks when it came. "He's on it," said Rossi. "Due in Albuquerque, New Mexico at 9:30 tomorrow morning. I guess that's 8:30 here. He'll be given your message as soon as they pull in."

Sixteen

He opened his eyes to see Doris, standing beside their bed, wearing a bath-robe, stroking his forehead. "Telephone," she whispered, leaning down to his ear. "Good morning."

Earl focused, with effort, on the bedside alarm clock. Almost nine. He couldn't remember the last time he'd slept so late. Rolling out of the bed, naked, he grabbed his own robe off the door hook.

"Coffee?"

He nodded, shuffling out of the room. His head was throbbing. "Thanks. Who is it?"

"Ted Lindgren. The connection isn't very good."

He picked up the receiver. "Earl Brady here."

"You called," said Lindgren, shouting to be heard. "I'm in New Mex-ico. I have to reboard in fifteen minutes. Everything all right?"

"No," Earl shouted back. "We can't find Colonel Jordan. I tried to call him yesterday, and so did a lot of other people, it seems. I went to his house, and he was gone. Back door unlocked, open, as a matter of fact. Radio left on."

Doris put a steaming coffee mug on the table, next to the phone. He squeezed her hand. Lindgren hadn't said anything.

"So," Earl continued, "I guess there are two questions. One, do you have any idea where Jordan is. Two, should the FBI office be called about it. What do you think?"

"Oh, boy," Lindgren said. "No is the first answer. I need to think about the second one. If they find out he has, uh, information taken from Bureau files …"

"Jesus, I forgot about that. The five pages, right?"

"Right."

After a long ten seconds of silence, Earl had an idea. "How about if I look in his office at the university? That's where you gave him the … your notes, correct?"

"Correct. Yeah. If you find them, put 'em in your pocket, and then go ahead and call our office. The new man is Frank O'Connor. He knows who Colonel Jordan is. He knows Jordan is a consultant to the Public Safety Committee."

"What if I don't find the notes?"

"I have to figure that out. I'll think on it and call you from the next stop, all right? Let me see—just a minute—St. Louis, tonight. About eight, your time."

"Fine, I guess. Any ideas at all about Jordan, in the meantime?"

"I can't think of anything," Lindgren replied. "You've got somebody working on this, right?"

"We do."

"I can't hear you."

"Yes," Earl shouted. "We have someone on it."

"All right, I'd better go. Listen, I'm sorry about this. I feel like I've left you with a big mess to clean up there."

"It's not your fault." *But maybe it is*, he thought. "Ted, is there any way someone else could know about … what you gave Jordan?"

"I don't believe so," Lindgren said, slowly. "Aw, crap. That does give me something to think about between here and St. Louis. I'll speak with you tonight. Good luck."

"Thanks."

Earl took a few gulps of coffee, then dialed for the LAPD.

"Wilshire Bureau Detectives."

"This is Deputy DA Brady, calling for Lester Smith."

"You just missed him," the receptionist said. "He left about an hour ago, maybe forty-five minutes. Something I can do for you?"

Smith, she explained, was on his way to Palm Springs "concerning a robbery investigation." He wasn't expected back until Monday.

Earl finished his coffee, thinking.

"It's important," he continued. "Tell Detective Smith to call me, if you hear from him or if you can get a message to him. Exeter 3202. Got it?"

"Yes, sir," she said.

"Also, see if there's a file Smith left in the office about a missing person named Jordan. Walter Jordan. Or, if there's anyone else there working on it, have him call me. Actually, I'll call you. I'll call you back in about an hour."

"I'll do this now, sir."

Earl thanked her and hung up, silently swearing revenge against Smith for not calling. Palm Springs, on a December weekend? "Robbery investigation, my ass," he muttered.

"What?" It was Doris, walking into the room holding a coffee pot.

"Oh, nothing," he said. "Getting a little runaround from the cop who's supposed to be looking for Colonel Jordan."

"More coffee?"

"Thanks, I will." He held his cup under the spout. "Sorry about all this. I have to go downtown this morning. Want to walk the beach later this afternoon?"

"Sure," she replied. "You're worried about this colonel, aren't you?"

He nodded.

"Hey," she said. "He's a grown man. Maybe he just—I don't know. None of my business. A walk on the beach sounds nice."

He stood up and hugged her. "Might be hard for me to concentrate today," he said, "thinking about last night."

She reached into his bathrobe. "Tonight," she said, "I'll make you forget last night."

*   *   *   *

After showering and eating two pieces of cinnamon toast, he drove toward downtown, trying to organize his thoughts. His head still hurt. It was 9:45 AM on December 6, 1941. The first stop is USC, he decided. I'll badge my way into Jordan's office and look for Lindgren's notes. Maybe I'll have a short visit with John before I go to Chinatown. Then I'll go see Fletcher, if there's time. Remember to call Wilshire Division. Goddamn Smith.

Saturday morning traffic was sparse. At 10:20, he pulled into a parking space at the edge of campus.

"Excuse me," he said to a pair of students walking past, "where is the University Police office?" They both smiled and shook their heads. "Sorry," chirped a short girl. "Try asking at the Union, or the library. They have maps."

At 10:30 he was knocking at a varnished wood door with gold painted lettering that said "Security." A bald, muscular man, wearing a sweatshirt, opened the door and gave Earl an indifferent nod. "Help you?"

"Good morning," Earl said, opening his wallet to display the silver and gold—plated badge. "Earl Brady, deputy district attorney, county of Los Angeles. Sorry to bother you. I could use some help here this morning."

The man looked at the badge, then again at Earl, extending his hand. "Bill Brown. I'm assistant director of security here. Retired from Long Beach PD two years ago."

Earl knew the last item of information was a test, an authenticity check. "Really?" he said. "You must have worked with Leo Barker in our office there."

"Sure did," said Brown, smiling. "Leo was a buddy. So, what can we do for you?"

"One of your faculty members has been absent—well, missing, really— for a couple of days. Walter Jordan, in the History Department. Do you know him?"

"Sure. Well, I know who he is. The army colonel, used to teach at West Point? Come on in. You say … a couple of days?"

"I know, I know," Earl said. "It sounds a little like we're jumping to conclusions here, overreacting. But he didn't show up for some appointments yesterday. Not like him at all. And, his house was empty, but with lights on. One of his appointments was with me. I've got some people working on it, but maybe you have, I don't know … I don't know much about him."

"I'll see what I can find out. You want me to call you?"

"Yeah, please. Here's my card."

Earl extracted a business card from his wallet and handed it to Brown. "Actually," he said, "there's one other thing. I should look in his office."

Brown cocked his head and frowned, closing one eye. Earl added, "I mean, *we* should look there. Maybe there's some clue about where he went. It could all be a mix-up. Let's go see, all right?"

Brown agreed, and they walked through a small grove of camphor and pine trees to the rear of the liberal arts building. Brown tried several keys, then pushed open a door. "After you," he said.

"His office is on the second floor," Earl said. Brown closed the door, then pointed to another.

"Stairway's through there."

Earl led the way to Jordan's office, one of several in the History Department suite.

It didn't look different. There was a wall calendar, but nothing written into any of the day-boxes. The wastebasket was empty. The only piece of paper on the leather desk blotter was a typed sheet of "Messages Friday, December 5."

Earl's own name appeared, as did Mead's from *Time* magazine, and three names Earl didn't recognize.

"I know who Mead is," Earl said to Brown. "Recognize any of these others?"

"This one's an English professor," Brown replied. "Clark—I'll call and see whether he's heard from Colonel Jordan, if you want. I have all of their home numbers back at the office."

"That would be fine."

"The other two, I don't know," said Brown.

Earl placed two calls. One was a tailor shop, the other a laundry. "Let's look around some more," he suggested. Brown frowned again. "I don't have keys to the files," he said, nodding at the olive-green mental cabinets. "And," he added, "I don't think we should touch anything anyway. Procedures, you know."

Earl decided not to argue. He had another idea. "Let's go on back to your office," he said.

The English professor was at home when Brown called. He knew only that he had called Friday to see if Jordan could meet for lunch.

"Well, we tried," said Earl. "Thanks for your help."

"You'll keep me posted?"

"You bet," Earl assured him. "One last thing. Can you give me the number and address of the History Department secretary?"

✳   ✳   ✳   ✳

The secretary lived alone in a ground-level apartment on Orchard Avenue, on the west edge of the university campus. She answered the door with a surprised look, cradling a small, gray cat. The woman was about his own age, he guessed. She was dressed as she was every other time he had seen her: plain, neat, forgettable.

"Already?" she asked.

"I was just around the corner when I called," he explained. "May I come in for a minute?"

"Yes, but I'm afraid it's rather a mess."

It wasn't. Like its tenant, the place was small, tidy, and a little sad. It might have been the cat, obviously the woman's only steady companion— or perhaps it was the shelved collection of porcelain figurines, or maybe even the Bible on the lace doily covering the table—but the dull melancholy was almost too much for Earl.

"It's a lovely place," he said. "Miss Whitlock, isn't it?"

"Yes. Please sit down. Would you like a cup of tea? English custom, you know."

"No, but thank you."

She sat with her hands folded on her lap and gave a sigh. "No word from Colonel Jordan?"

"Nothing yet," Earl replied. "As you know, Miss Whitlock, he was working with our office, with me, on some rather important cases."

"Do you think he's in danger?"

Earl hesitated. "You must be worried," she continued. "I mean, here it is a Saturday and …"

"A little concerned," said Earl, nodding. "He never did contact the man from *Time* magazine. And also, at his house it looked like—maybe he left in a hurry, or something. So, yes, I'm worried."

"Oh, dear."

"You might be able to help. That's why I called you."

"All right. How can I help?"

"I think we should look through his office," Earl said. "Could be something about where he might've gone. Maybe it's all just a misunderstanding, but I think we should look—the two of us, I mean—to see if something's there. I called you because I don't want to make a big scene over there. No need to embarrass the colonel if it's just a mix-up, say if he forgot to tell you something. We can just do it quietly."

"I don't know if I should be …"

"Miss Whitlock, let me assure you that I'll take the blame if anyone is critical, or, you know, upset about this."

She closed her eyes and sat motionless for several seconds.

"Let me get my handbag," Miss Whitlock said.

*   *   *   *

He parked near the eastern entrance to the campus, so they could approach the liberal arts building from the side opposite Brown's office. At the top of the stairway inside, she pulled a ring of keys from her purse and opened the door to the History suite.

After about ten minutes, Miss Whitlock had confirmed that Colonel Jordan's briefcase and appointment book were gone. "But he always takes those home," she said. Nothing else seemed to be missing from the office.

Earl picked up a framed photograph of Jordan standing in a small group of West Point cadets. It was recent enough.

"I'm going to borrow this," he said. "Don't worry, I'll tell Colonel Jordan myself that I took it," he assured her. Then he asked, "Does he keep a file on the Public Safety Committee?"

"Oh, yes. Well, he has me keep it. In fact, he normally asks me to bring it to him whenever you visit. It's in the cabinet."

"Let me have a quick look, and then we can go," Earl said.

Miss Whitlock unlocked and tugged open the green metal filing drawer. She pulled out a manila folder marked, "Col. Jordan—FBI Committee 1941." She handed it to Earl.

He saw copies of some of Lindgren's meeting notices and what looked like Jordan's notes of the first meeting. Just a few pages, no more. No five-page FBI memo. He handed the folder back to Miss Whitlock. "All right, then," he said.

As she was closing the file drawer, Earl asked, "Did Colonel Jordan have any visitors on Wednesday or Thursday?"

"A couple of students, I think. Other faculty members—you know, they visit one another."

"Did he go anywhere during the day, while you were here, I mean?"

She patted her cheek. "Let me see—wait. On Thursday morning, he did have a meeting here with a man I didn't recognize. They talked in the colonel's office for half an hour, I would guess."

From her description, Earl was certain the visitor had been Ted Lindgren. "Did the man give any papers to Colonel Jordan? Anything you were asked to place in the file?"

"No," she said.

"On Thursday," Earl asked, "did you leave first, or did he?"

"Thursday. Didn't you come in that afternoon, Mr. Brady?"

"Right. It was around 4:45, I think. You were here."

"Yes, I was. Then you and Colonel Jordan left. I remember him looking at the clock on his way out, saying he would call me in the morning. It was about ten minutes of five. I left at five, I think, possibly a few minutes later."

"We should go," said Earl, remembering Brown. "I'll drive you back."

"You spoke with him Friday morning, didn't you?" Earl asked after they were in his car. She nodded.

"Did he call you?"

"Well, yes," she replied. "Let me think. Oh, dear. He told me that he wouldn't be coming to the office. He said something about finishing the article for *Time*. He said to give you his number if you called ... oh, and he asked me to call a cab."

"Why?"

"He said his car wouldn't start."

Earl parked at the curb in front of her apartment. "Would you mind if I used your telephone, Miss Whitlock?"

"Of course. Come in."

The receptionist at LAPD Wilshire Bureau answered on the fourth ring. It was now almost noon.

"This is Mr. Brady again. I meant to call earlier. Did you reach Detective Smith?"

"Yes, sir. I spoke to him about, oh, an hour ago. He said he would be trying to call you. He had me take down a message for you, in case I heard from you first."

"Just a moment." He cradled the receiver and made a writing motion to Miss Whitlock. She quickly produced a pencil and a notepad.

"Go ahead, please."

"All right, Mr. Brady, here it is. Detective Smith said he tried to call you twice last night, but the line was busy both times. This other case came up, and he knew he would have to go out to the desert. He said he talked with someone downtown about what to do regarding the Jordan matter and was told to refer it to the FBI. An Agent Gorman met him here early this morning, before Detective Smith left for Palm Springs. He said he asked the FBI man to be sure to call you. That's it, Mr. Brady."

"Do you have a number for Gorman?"

"No, sorry."

"Thank you. Tell Detective Smith I'll see him—no, ask him to call my office Monday, as early as possible."

"Yes, sir."

Earl tore off the sheet on which he had written, "FBI—Gorman." Then he wrote his home and office telephone numbers and handed them to Miss Whitlock. "Call me," he said, "if you happen to hear anything. Otherwise I'll see you on Monday. Thank you for your help."

"Oh, I just hope everything is all right," she said. "Let me give you my telephone number here—if there's anything else I can do."

He pocketed the slip of paper. "Thank you again."

Seventeen

He was greeted at the Golden Dragon by a pretty Chinese teenager. She smiled at Earl and held up a finger. "One?"

"I'm here to see Mr. Sun. He's expecting me. Earl Brady."

The girl smiled. "Wait here, please."

Earl stood by the door as she hurried through the room and into the kitchen. The restaurant was about half-full. After a minute she returned and led him to a table. "Mr. Sun will be right out. Tea?"

"Thank you. Yes."

He was blowing on a cup of green tea when Sun joined him. They shook hands, reaching across the table. "Welcome back, Mr. Brady. Are you hungry?"

Sun ordered food, then turned to his guest. "From your call last night, I expect you are not here merely to have lunch. What can I do for you, Mr. Brady?"

Earl pulled the photograph out of his coat pocket and placed it on the table. "My turn to show pictures to you," he said. "Do you recognize the older man in the center?"

Sun didn't hesitate. "Yes. Colonel Jordan. I know him."

"How do you know him?"

"You could say that he is a family friend."

"Tell me about that."

"May I ask what—"

"Sorry. Let me explain. He's a friend of mine, too. We've been doing some work together. Colonel Jordan seems to have gone someplace without telling me, or telling his office, and—I'm looking for him. I happen to know he's been to the Golden Dragon before, so I'm here to ask you about it. Have you seen him recently?"

"Last weekend, Sunday I am pretty sure. He was in for dinner."

"Alone?"

"No, he had a group. Four or five people. I think it was someone's birthday. There were gifts." Sun stood up. "I can find out which night."

"No, sit down. That's all right. I've seen him since then myself. Tell me how you know Colonel Jordan."

"He first came here perhaps ten years ago," Sun began. "It might have been during the Olympic games. About that time. He was then a teacher at West Point, as you probably know. He was doing research. He wanted to speak with my father and some other people. Older people. I interpreted for him. He came out to Los Angeles almost every summer for at least a few weeks."

"What was he researching?"

"The 'Red Dragon' plot."

"Sorry. The what?" Earl asked.

"Sun Yat-Sen's revolution to overthrow the Empress Dowager's dynasty. You see, Mr. Brady, Chinatown—here in Los Angeles, although it was in a different area of the city then, forty or fifty years ago—Chinatown was an important place for training revolutionary fighters. They were then smuggled back into China for the insurgency. Colonel Jordan was interested in Homer Lea and the other Americans who raised money for the training. My father and—well, my father knew Homer Lea because of attending the Western Military Academy, but he never actually went to fight. Some of his friends did. Colonel Jordan—"

"Wait a second," Earl interrupted, aggravated by this tangent. "Who is Homer Lea?"

"He was an American, from this area in fact. I think he went to Los Angeles High School. He was some kind of adventurer and a military scholar. He actually went to China and acted as an adviser to Dr. Sun Yat-Sen. This was about 1900, or before. Homer Lea had poor health and died rather young. Colonel Jordan is fascinated by him. Ah, the food is here."

Earl was hungry. They ate in silence for several minutes; then he asked Sun, "Is Colonel Jordan still doing this research?"

"I'm not sure. Since he moved to Los Angeles last year, he's been in the restaurant many times, and he's talked with my father some—and I was about to tell you, he called me just a couple of days ago."

"What about?"

"It was on Thursday night. There were just a few customers still here, so it was perhaps nine o'clock. He was calling to tell me that Japan was about to attack American interests, somewhere. He said he just wanted my family to know, and to be careful. He actually mentioned Homer Lea."

"What's Homer Lea got to do with … any of this?"

"Mr. Brady, that was my question also. Colonel Jordan told me that Homer Lea spent time in Japan after escaping from China. When he returned, he wrote a book predicting the Japanese would someday invade the United States, itself, right here on the West Coast. Colonel Jordan said the book was written about thirty years ago and is outdated in some ways. 'Tactically obsolete,' I think he said. But then he said, 'Little Homer had the Japanese figured out. They're coming after us.'"

"Sounds familiar," Earl said. "Colonel Jordan spoke to me about it too. More than once, although I never heard of 'little Homer.' Any ideas about where Colonel Jordan might have gone—without telling his office? You've known him longer than I have."

"I can't think of where he would be. But let me call you if I hear something."

Earl got up to leave. Sun walked with him to the door, where Earl stopped and asked, "Do you think you might hear something?"

"Colonel Jordan is highly respected. He has many friends in China-town," Sun whispered. "Yes, I might hear something. And I will not be the only one listening."

✳   ✳   ✳   ✳

It was almost 2:00 PM when he walked into the Central Library. Earl hadn't been there in years, maybe one or two visits since studying for the 1928 bar exam in the art history section.

He remembered where the reference desk was. A thin, gray-haired woman peered over her spectacles as he approached.

"Help you?"

"Thanks, yes. Are there any books by Homer Lea?"

"Sounds familiar," she whispered. "Look under L, in the card files just around the corner." She handed him a pencil and a small sheet of paper. "Write down the number, and I'll help you find the books, if we have them."

He quickly found an index card saying, "Lea, Homer. *Valor of Igno-rance, The*. 1909. Military history; politics and world affairs." He wrote down the numbers and returned to the desk, where the woman gave him directions.

He passed through the periodicals reading room on his way. His eye caught a large headline, hanging sideways on a rack.

CHICAGO DAILY TRIBUNE
Thursday, December 4, 1941
FDR'S WAR PLANS!
Goal is 10 Million Armed Men;
Half to Fight in Europe
Proposes Land Drive by July 1, 1943,
To Smash Nazis; President Told
of Equipment Shortage

*   *   *   *

He spent an hour and half reading parts of *The Valor of Ignorance*. Thundering, biblical-style denunciations of the evils of luxury and commercialism. The certain disintegration of a lazy country lacking military readiness. Lengthy arguments about the illusion of an ocean barrier. Maps of West Coast cities and surrounding areas, with detailed descriptions of how the Japanese could invade, conquer and occupy America.

He slid the book into its place on the shelf, promising himself to ask Jordan about all of this. Earl drove home thinking about the Japanese Olympic swimming team, and a fluttering sea of white flags with red dots.

Eighteen

He was bent over the sink, scooping and splashing warm water on his face to remove leftover streaks and blobs of shaving cream when Doris knocked. It was just after 7:00 PM on Saturday, December 6.

"Earl?" she said, opening the bathroom door slightly. "Telephone. Mr. Gorman with the FBI?"

"Good. Be right there. We'll leave for dinner in a few minutes, OK?" Earl dried his face and wrapped the towel around his waist.

"Hello, Brady speaking.

"Robert Gorman, FBI. I was told to call you about Walter Jordan."

"Right. Any news?"

"Yes." Earl could hear Gorman muttering something, to someone. Then he spoke to Earl again. "Yes, we found him."

Earl sat down, his heart pounding. "You—found him. Thank goodness. Is he all right?"

"No, sir, he's dead. You may want to come over here. It's a homicide."

"Where?"

"Santa Monica. Palisades bluffs, you know, the park? Up at the end, just north of San Vicente."

"I'll be there in five minutes."

*   *   *   *

He badged his way past the two Santa Monica P.D. officers who were stationed at a curved row of wooden sawhorse barricades. Their patrol car and two unmarked ones were lined up side by side, between the barricades and the railing at the edge of the bluffs that dropped down to Pacific Coast Highway from the manicured grass park. The cars' headlamps were aimed, more or less, at a cluster of men standing twenty yards away around what looked like a low, white pup tent.

"Agent Gorman?" Earl shouted as he duck-walked under a sawhorse.

One of the men turned, nodded, and walked toward Earl, squinting into the headlamps' glare.

"Mr. Brady?"

"Yes." He showed his badge to Gorman, who nodded again. Up close, the FBI agent looked young enough to be one of John's fraternity brothers. "Thanks for calling me."

"Over here," said Gorman. He led Earl to the pup tent, where a photographer was snapping flashes.

"When—"

Gorman interrupted Earl's question. "I think he was found about two hours ago. Some lady walking her dog just down there a ways. The dog went crazy at the smell, I suppose. She says the body was under the sheet, just about like you're seeing it now."

Gorman led Earl around the sheet, which looked like a body covering except that it was elevated in the center, about two feet off the grass, by a vertical pole. Gorman handed him a flashlight, then squatted at the edge of the sheet and lifted it for Earl, who dropped to one knee. Jordan was on his back, dressed in dark pants and a plaid wool shirt. His hands appeared to be clutching the shiny blade of a sword, extending up from his abdomen to a red-and-black, leather-wrapped handle.

"Gunshot wound, looks like, just behind the left ear," Gorman said. Earl moved the flashlight beam to a patch of matted, stained gray hair.

"And this sword—it's clear through him and maybe stuck into the ground. He's impaled."

Earl had seen murder victims before, just never someone he'd known alive. He felt dizzy when he stood up.

Not here, he thought. *You have a job to do. Slow, deep breaths.*

"OK," he said. "Tell me again what the chronology is?"

"Lady found it earlier this evening," Gorman replied, "about five o'clock. She says it was just dark, whatever that means. She lives across the street and around the corner, on Second. She called Santa Monica P.D. They came out and identified him, from his wallet. There was some cash in that, by the way, so probably not a robbery. Anyway, all the local P.D.'s had a bulletin from us about Jordan, so when the Santa Monica cops called it in to their headquarters, we got the word. I got here about half an hour ago, and remembered I was supposed to contact you."

Earl stared at the sheet, then out over the railing at the ocean. "Any ideas? Leads?"

"Well," Gorman said, "I have what LAPD gave me about the victim. Which is mostly what you told them, I think."

"That so?"

"Yeah. Otherwise, not much yet. We're going to let the locals interview the neighbors, finish combing this area. Your county coroner can look at the body. We'll collect all that information and go from there. Right now, well, I guess there's a bullet in his head, maybe that'll tell us something. And then that ceremonial sword."

"The what?"

"Ceremonial. I don't know, that's what one of the local cops told me. He says it's a ceremonial Japanese sword."

The coroner's wagon arrived. One of the Santa Monica officers moved a sawhorse, while the other gave hand signals to the driver, backing up onto the grass. Earl pulled out his wallet and approached the man who stepped from the wagon's passenger side.

"Earl Brady, DA's office." The man nodded.

"Listen," Earl said, "take this card and make sure the examiner calls me on Monday morning. Got it?"

"Yes, sir."

Earl walked around the wagon to Gorman, who was talking to the other white-jacketed man.

"I'll take the sheet with me after you bag it," Gorman was saying. "There's a sword stuck in the victim's midsection, all the way into the ground. I want the Santa Monica men to measure how far in, as you lift the body. You'll want to leave the thing in, right? In the body?"

"Oh, yes," said the small, bespectacled man. "We'll do a couple of things here before we move him, though. That the photographer over there?"

Gorman nodded, then turned to Earl. "So then, anything you can add about Jordan?"

He tried to think. What had he told the LAPD? What had he learned today, and did any of it matter? When in doubt, ask instead of answer.

"You have his office number at the university?"

"Right," Gorman said.

"Widowed, one son in the army."

"Got that. Wheels are in motion to contact the son."

"You been to his house?" Earl asked.

"No. It's locked up, and we've been watching it. My thinking was to have somebody stake it out overnight, then I'll go there tomorrow morning. I have somebody from the Marshall's office on the way there."

"Why not go now? What if—"

Gorman broke in. "My thinking was, the man's dead. We can't save him. If somebody tries to get into his house now, we'll grab 'em."

"Can I meet you there tomorrow?"

Gorman cocked his head and squinted.

"It's just that I might recognize something, you see," Earl explained. "From working with Jordan."

"You just take it easy tomorrow," Gorman said. "You're a lawyer, Mr. Brady. Tomorrow's Sunday. No need for you to root around in the mud. I'll call you when we're done. Or if we find anything interesting. I have your number."

The reverse snobbery irritated. "Just out of curiosity," Earl said, "why is this a federal case?"

"I wondered about that, too," Gorman replied. "I was told that Jordan is classified as a U.S. government agent, on account of that committee. Ted Lindgren's group."

"I'm on that committee."

"I know."

"Do you know the new agent, Lindgren's replacement?"

"I met him yesterday, in fact. He came straight from the airport. Francis Xavier O'Connor. I wanted to call him earlier, too, but nobody seems to know where he is. His first day is officially December 8. Monday."

Earl extended his hand and shook Gorman's. "Thanks for calling me tonight. I'll be around the house tomorrow. Sure would appreciate hearing from you."

"Right. You will."

✳   ✳   ✳   ✳

He drove slowly down Ocean Avenue. It was almost 8:30. Ahead and to his right, he saw the lights on the pier, their reflections making a jagged and sparkling line across the water. He turned left onto California and left again on Fourth and into his driveway.

Doris had heard the car and was standing in the doorway. "Are you all right?" she said as he squeezed her.

They walked inside and dropped onto the sofa. Earl leaned forward, elbows on his knees and head in his hands.

"It was him. Shot in the head and then"—he made a stabbing motion to his stomach—"they ran a big sword through him. It was gruesome. Left his body up at the end of the Palisades, right on the grass."

Doris stroked his neck and shoulders. "Sorry. That's awful."

"I don't know about dinner," he said.

"I cancelled that. There's leftover spaghetti if you're hungry. Let me get you a beer, huh?"

She moved off the sofa and into the kitchen. Earl tried to think. *Who do I need to call? Fletcher. Miss Whitlock. Sun. Brown. No, the FBI will notify the school. Lindgren.*

"Sweetheart, did Lindgren call?"

"Yes," she said, walking back into the room. "About half an hour ago. Lousy connection again, but I told him exactly what you said. FBI is already on it, Special Agent Gorman, and you'd been called out because they think they found Colonel Jordan's body."

"What did Lindgren say?"

"'God,' I think is what he said. He's going to call again from Washington in the morning."

Earl took a long gulp of beer. "I better make a couple of calls myself."

Earlier he had thrown on the shirt he'd worn all day. Miss Whitlock's number was still in the pocket.

"Hello."

"Miss Whitlock, I'm sorry to call so late. This is Mr. Brady. Terrible news, I'm afraid."

"Oh, dear."

"Colonel Jordan is dead. His body was discovered a few hours ago. That's about all I can tell you. There's an investigation. I just wanted you to get the news from me."

"I'm—oh ..." She was crying or gasping, or both.

"I'll call you again Monday."

He had the operator connect him to Santa Teresa. Fletcher was asleep. Earl decided to leave him that way.

Nineteen

"You might feel better," Doris said, "if you talked about it."

Earl turned his back to the ocean and leaned against the wood railing, folding his arms. Doris had pried him out of the house for a Sunday morning walk to the Palisades bluffs. They were no more than half a mile from the spot where Jordan's body had been found.

"Don't know what to say, really. Don't even know what to think."

She persisted. "You knew the man, Earl. You were trying to find him. You were worried about *something*. Who would have—"

He grabbed his wife's hand and motioned toward the street. "Let's start back," he said.

"I didn't know Colonel Jordan too well," Earl told her. "All he ever seemed worried about were political things. Are we ready if there's a war? You know, army things. I never heard a word about personal enemies."

Doris stretched up to kiss his cheek as they waited to cross the street. "I'm sorry you had to see him that way," she said. "The sword ... oh my God ..."

Earl reminded her that he'd seen murder victims before. He'd handled dozens of homicide cases. In most of them, he told her, the killers either hadn't meant for things to go that far—or if they *had* set out to kill somebody, they tried to make the victim disappear. Bodies found in remote desert trash dumps, or bushy mountain gullies.

"This is different," he said, thinking of the sword through Jordan's middle. "Somebody is sending us a message."

"Us?" Doris looked up Ocean Avenue, toward the end of the bluffs. "You mean—"

"No, no. Not *us*. I mean the group. The Public Safety Committee."

They were two blocks from home when a teenage boy they knew darted out of his front door and bounded to the sidewalk. Turn on your radio, he told them. Hawaii has been bombed. It's the Japs.

＊   ＊   ＊   ＊

Earl stopped his car at the curb directly in front of the Beta fraternity house. A small group of students huddled on the lawn. Earl exchanged waves with the boys on his way up the steps to the open front door, above which were gold-painted Greek letters and two broken light fixtures.

John was one of a group gathered around a low table radio, his legs crossed, flipping a tennis ball from hand to hand. A boy wearing flannel pajama bottoms and a sweatshirt was tuning the radio. After much static, buzzing, whining, and scratching, he located a news broadcast. An excited voice described the attack route of the Japanese planes, the same words they had heard several times already that morning. John looked up.

"Dad!" He pulled himself to his feet and walked quickly toward Earl. "Can you believe this?"

"Yeah. Well, no. Not quite."

"Mother all right?"

"Oh, yeah, she's fine. State of shock, like everyone else. Listen, I'm on my way to a meeting downtown. We want you to spend the night at home, so I'll pick you up when I'm finished. Couple of hours, probably."

"There's a student assembly tomorrow, and—"

"That's fine. I can bring you back in the morning."

"But—all right. I'll be around. Either down here or up in my room."

Earl reached for John's arm and squeezed it. "See you in a while."

*   *   *   *

A U.S. Marshal and two soldiers with slung rifles stood at the door to the Federal Courthouse.

"I'm here for the Public Safety Committee meeting," Earl said. The Marshal examined his badge, then looked at a typed list.

"Go on in, Mr. Brady. Sixth floor."

Seven men were in the conference room. Roy Benson nodded silently. The navy officer, Morrow, was intently reading what looked like a long telegram. Earl didn't recognize the army officer or the man at the head of the conference table.

"Earl Brady, county district attorney's office."

The army officer gave a half-salute across the table. "Major David Newton," he said quietly.

The other man stood and offered a hand. "Frank O'Connor, FBI. Pleased to meet you. Have a seat."

"All right, gentlemen," O'Connor said, "here is where we are at this moment. We have agents arresting a number of Japanese living in this district, as we speak. They are classified as dangerous enemy aliens. Again, that is dangerous enemy aliens. More arrests will occur tonight. Most of the subjects have been under surveillance for some time or belong to groups we have been watching."

Earl remembered the list handed out at an earlier meeting. Several hundred names: categories A and B and C, depending on how suspicious they were.

O'Connor described several of the arrests made in the last two hours and the items confiscated: fishing boats, short-wave radios, cameras, maps, high-powered flashlights.

"We expect that certain zones—areas around ports, government buildings, manufacturing plants, power stations, for example—may soon be declared off-limits to Japanese persons. We will need local law enforcement help with this, as well as other surveillance activities. The particular zones will be announced very soon, at any moment, we hope. Lieutenant Morrow?"

The navy man shook his head slowly. "Reports are still coming in. However, it appears the losses to our fleet at Pearl Harbor may be considerable. We are hearing about air attacks also in Thailand, the Philippines, and Singapore." He stopped and rubbed his eyes.

"Um, let me try to focus on this committee," he resumed. "We are all aware of the large Japanese population in and around Honolulu. There is no question that information was gathered—about ships' movements, for example—and then transmitted by radio. We're sure of it. Bastards."

Earl raised his hand. "I assume everyone knows about Colonel Jordan?"

"We talked about it briefly, just before you got here," O'Connor said. "All we know right now is that everyone needs to be careful. Could be Colonel Jordan was the first war casualty. Let's wrap this up. For now, we would request that the LAPD continue to assist us with the arrests and prepare to become involved in surveillance and enforcing these restrictions on movement. Commander Benson, if you could appoint someone as a contact with me on that?"

Benson agreed with an elaborate nod. "Right away," he said, then turned to look directly at Earl. Benson raised his eyebrows slightly and made a quick "you-me" pointing gesture.

The meeting broke up with belligerent mutterings and sputterings. *Bastards ... Slant-eye sons of bitches ... They'll pay for this ...*

Earl waited for Benson in the hallway. *So this is what the committee was for,* he thought. *To decide in advance who gets arrested after the shooting starts. To put the enemy's local branch out of commission.* Benson was walking toward him now, motioning to the elevator. "Let's talk outside," he said.

"You'll tell me what I missed?" Benson nodded.

The Sunday street was quiet. Jordan's murder, Benson explained, had been discussed at the start of the meeting. "FBI thinks it was meant to be timed just so. Coordinated with the attack in Hawaii."

"But it wasn't, really."

"Right," Benson said. "O'Connor guesses that there was a misunderstanding about the exact hour."

Earl noticed an unmarked LAPD sedan gliding to the curb, followed by two black-and-whites. This was more than Benson's usual entourage. "What's all this?" Earl asked.

"You heard O'Connor. Everyone on this committee needs to be careful, now." Benson moved toward the rear of the car, then turned to face Earl again. "Just call me if you want …" He pointed a thumb at the patrol cars.

*   *   *   *

John Brady was sitting on the curb. He stood up as the green Chrysler approached, holding his canvas team swim bag in one hand as he opened the passenger door. It was just before 2:00 PM on Sunday, December 7.

"Can you believe this?" he said as he slid into the seat.

"Not really," Earl replied.

"I thought you'd be coming to pick me up earlier."

"Sorry. I had to make a stop someplace after my meeting."

John seemed to accept that. Earl was relieved that no further explanation was needed. His "stop" had been at Walter Jordan's house.

*   *   *   *

He had expected to see an FBI agent or a U.S. Marshal there, like Gorman had said the night before. There was no one. Earl had walked along Jordan's driveway to the parked blue car. He reached under the radiator grill, pulled a metal lever to the side, and opened the hood. Everything looked normal, at first glance. Then Earl looked closer. The black ignition wire had an inch-wide wrapping of electrician's tape around it. He peeled off the tape. The wire had been cut.

*   *   *   *

"Anyone mind if I turn the radio off?"

Doris was wiping her hands on a faded floral-print apron, standing beside the Philco console. "I need a break from this. Just for a while. We've been hearing this all day."

Earl and John looked up. "Sure," said John, turning back to the encyclopedia opened on the coffee table in front of the two men, both bent forward on the sofa. They were huddled over a map of Hawaii.

Doris announced that dinner was served. "What did Father Kelly have to say?" she asked as they sat down.

John had attended a special Sunday afternoon mass at St. Monica's. He wanted to go, he had explained to Earl in the car, because the father of one of his fraternity brothers was a navy supply officer at Pearl Harbor. There had been no word.

"Mostly telling everybody to pray," John answered, "for the dead and wounded. For courage in the battles ahead, something like that."

"Does he still think that we should stay out of the war in Europe?" Doris asked. Father Kelly was a noisy America-Firster.

"I guess he still does," John replied. "He was raging about the Japanese bombing us instead of attacking Russia, and on the Lord's Day at that. Then he said something about Communism being the 'great godless evil,' and we should applaud the Germans for fighting it."

Earl wondered what Colonel Jordan would have said to all of that but decided to interrupt his own thoughts. "What's the schedule at school tomorrow?" he asked.

"Student body assembly at 9:30. I don't know about classes. Coach Carson is having a team meeting at three."

The telephone rang. "I'll get it," John said.

"Dad, it's for you," he reported, disappointment in his voice. "Detective Smith."

"Hello."

"Mr. Brady. I'm back in town and figured I should call you. I got the word about Jordan."

"How did you hear?"

"On the radio."

"What?"

"Well, partly on the radio. This afternoon, I got back in the office and the news was on, of course. Goddamn Japs. But then there was a local story about a body, murder victim, found in Santa Monica. Something about the FBI at the scene. I called a friend at the Santa Monica P.D. He said it was Colonel Jordan. He also said there was a DA at the scene, which I figured was you."

"It was me."

"So, I assume Gorman called you?"

"Yes, he did. Rough stuff. Shot in the head, looks like, but then this sword rammed through his middle. Your friend say anything about that?"

"Just the same as you've said. I feel bad about this. I wonder if—"

"No, no," Earl interrupted. "What were you supposed to do? But say— who told you to make the FBI referral?"

"I called downtown and gave the basic status to them. They said they were going to call Benson, who's on this committee with you, right?"

"Yes." Earl groaned, silently. One of Benson's guiding principles: never do work, especially on a weekend, if you can toss it off to somebody else. It was painful to think of Benson being told that Earl Brady couldn't be reached.

"So that's how it happened," said Smith. "Gorman showed up here early yesterday morning. Talked to me for about ten minutes—took notes, wrote down the names and telephone numbers, like that."

"Take your file?"

"Nope. He got the information we had, though. The basics, anyhow."

"Do me a favor, Detective Smith?"

"Sure. Anything."

"There was a Santa Monica P.D. photographer at the scene. I didn't get her name, but she was the only one. She rode downtown with the county coroners, I think because they didn't have anyone to take pictures over the weekend. Anyway, here's what I want you to do. Get your friend to have her develop an extra set of all the shots she took. Every one of them. At the scene, at the morgue, or any place else. For me."

"I'll call him tonight."

Twenty

At 9:40 AM on Monday, December 8, the president of the University of Southern California stood behind a microphone on an auditorium stage. The room was packed full of students. A loudspeaker had been connected and placed at the top of the brick steps outside, where a few hundred others had gathered. John Brady sat on his bicycle at the fringes of the outdoor group.

"Our world changed yesterday," the speech began. "Just two short days ago, for many of you, the foremost concern was our football squad's battle with UCLA. How long ago, how very long ago that now seems!"

John coasted on his bike around the silent crowd, half listening. "Our university will adapt itself to the needs of this nation. I am confident that our students are prepared to devote their time less to fun and more to the cause of freedom and justice. Your immediate obligation, I submit, is to complete your education. It is to be expected, and it is understood, however, that some may choose to interrupt this process to serve their country more directly and more immediately. I urge you to deliberate with care about this. I leave you today with a final request: that although the Japanese attack yesterday was treacherous, we treat our individual Japanese students with the respect and kindness they have earned."

*   *   *   *

The first call Earl Brady made, when he arrived at his office on Monday morning, was to Bud Fletcher.

"He was murdered, Bud. I saw the body myself, on Saturday night. FBI is handling it."

"Why is that?" Fletcher rasped.

"It's because Jordan was on the Public Safety Committee. He was deemed a federal agent, or something like that. I'll try to keep abreast."

"Good. Jesus, Earl, who'd kill him?"

"Well, he had a long sword stuck in him, probably after being shot in the head. Somebody thought it looked like a Japanese samurai. That seems to be the idea. The new FBI man, Lindgren's replacement, called a meeting yesterday about all the arrests they're making. Took in hundreds last night, I hear. At one point he said something about Jordan being this war's first casualty."

He could hear Fletcher coughing. "Listen, Earl, you be careful yourself. This is war, now. Think they picked out Jordan because of—what? Hell, I know he wrote magazine articles. And he could almost bore you silly, talking about the Japanese threats. Maybe that's it."

"Maybe," Earl said. "And one other thing, don't forget. He also had that envelope of documents Lindgren gave him, before Lindgren left for Washington. Some information about local Japanese, from the FBI files, is all I was told by Lindgren. You know anything else about that?"

"Well ... only this," Fletcher said. "It was Lindgren's best dope on two things. First, who the real dangerous local Japanese are. And second, who might be the best prospects to work for us, inside some of those groups."

"Sounds like something everybody could use, right about now," said Earl.

"Oh, boy. Yep."

"Except," said Earl, "the envelope is missing now. It isn't in Jordan's file on the Public Safety Committee. I looked. I got into his office at USC."

"You need to talk with Lindgren."

"He's supposed to call me this morning," Earl said, then filled in Fletcher on the surveillance and movement-restriction plans announced by the FBI.

"No more pussyfooting about diplomacy now, I reckon. Doris all right? John?"

"They're fine, thanks. How about your daughter?"

"Scared out of her wits. Her husband's a doctor, you know. Reserves. Probably be called up pretty quick."

"And yourself?"

"Not too good. Short of breath all the time. Don't worry about me—but thanks for asking. I'll let you go, you got work to do."

He was about to call Gorman when Maria stepped into the doorway. "Coroner's office on the line."

"Thanks, Maria. Call the FBI office and ask for Agent Gorman as soon as I'm off, all right?" He picked up the telephone.

"Grady."

"This is Doctor Levy from the coroner's. You wanted me to call you about Walter Jordan."

"Yes, thanks. What can you tell me?"

"Not much. No poisons or drugs. No booze. Signs of a single blow to the head, right side. Cause of death was the shot to the other side of his head. Single bullet, .38. That wound was older—a few hours older, at least—than the sword puncture. That appeared much fresher. In my opinion, they dumped the body on the grass, then ran him through and tossed the sheet over him. I don't think he was there very long before the lady and her dog found him."

"Where are the bullet and sword?"

"FBI agent took them as soon as we were done Saturday night, or—let's see—sorry, 1:25 AM on Sunday."

"Was the photographer there? The girl?"

"Yes. She was. Took lots of pictures."

"All right. You get her name, by the way?"

"Let me see. Here you go—Madison. Ruth Madison."

"I guess that's it. Say, thanks for calling, Doctor."

Maria leaned into the doorway again. "Mr. Gorman's in a meeting. I left word for him to call you."

Before going into the Monday morning staff meeting, Earl stopped at Maria's desk. It was just before ten.

"I'm expecting calls from two different FBI agents now. Lindgren and Gorman. Get me out of the meeting if they call, either one. Umm—you all right?"

She wasn't. "I just heard from my mother in Oakland," Maria said, her lips trembling. "My younger brother is home today because the schools up there are closed. They think there's a Japanese aircraft carrier off the Mendocino Coast."

"I hadn't heard that. Look, ah—we just have to keep doing what we're doing."

"I know."

"I'll be back in a while. Don't forget to—"

"I won't. Anyone from the FBI calls, I'll come get you."

"Right. Actually, I need to make one more call before I go in," said Earl, retreating to his office.

"Golden Dragon Restaurant."

"Mr. Sun, it's Mr. Brady calling."

"Oh, yes. Terrible what has happened. What can I do for you?"

"It's about Colonel Jordan."

"Yes. Is he back?"

"He is dead. It appears to be a murder. An investigation is underway. I thought I should inform you, seeing as how—"

"I would like to help, Mr. Brady. We will continue to seek information about where he might have gone last week."

"That would be fine."

"And, Mr. Brady. If there is anything else you think I can do, you must please tell me."

"Thank you. I will."

*   *   *   *

At 11:15, Earl was back in his office, reading mail and waiting for the telephone to ring. At 11:25, it did.

"Mr. Brady, this is Ruth Madison. I'm a photographer with Santa Monica P.D."

"Yes, I'm glad you called."

"I have the photos for you. Are you sure it's all right?"

He feigned ignorance. Ask, don't answer. "How do you mean?"

"Oh, I don't know. The FBI and all. He was in a big hurry for these pictures. Just like he was in a big hurry for the sword and the bullet after the postmortem. I ducked out of the office when they came to pick up the prints. I didn't want to be grilled about it. And they took my negatives, by the way."

"Good thinking," said Earl. "But don't worry, I'm sure it's all right. They're always in a hurry, the FBI. I'll take care of it."

Glad I'm not still a Catholic, he thought after hanging up. *Bless me, Father, for I have sinned: I just lied three times in five seconds.*

The afternoon passed—meetings, a hearing to set the trial date for an assault case, office gossip.

John called at 4:30.

"Hello, John. How are things on campus?"

"Crazy. Some people are leaving, either to sign up or because their parents want them out of Los Angeles. One girl I know—her parents live in Chicago, and they made her leave last night."

"What did they say at the assembly?"

"He said we should stay in school, but he understood if some didn't, et cetera. He likes to talk."

"Want to come home again this evening? I'm leaving pretty soon."

"No," said John, "I think I'll stay here. I want to try to find Tim."

"Tim?"

"Tanaka. He wasn't there for the team meeting. Everybody else was. The coach was a little—I don't know—vague about why. Said Tim's probably not feeling very comfortable at school right now or something like that."

"What else happened at the meeting?"

"He said we could swim on our own, but no team training for at least a week, so everyone can decide what to do. He pulled me aside afterward."

"Oh?"

Maria handed him a telegram. "From Washington," she whispered.

"… said he was on his way to an emergency meeting at lifeguard headquarters, and he's going to call me tonight after he gets home," said John.

"Well," said Earl, opening the yellow envelope, "you call us tonight after that. Or if you find your Japanese friend. I'd be interested."

"All right. Talk to you later."

The telegram said, "Calling your home tonight eight your time. Lindgren"

∗   ∗   ∗   ∗

It was drizzling. The legless man and his papers were protected by a beach umbrella standing, tilted, inside an empty metal garbage can. After exchanging a nickel for a paper, Earl sat in his parked car and scanned the first page.

SANTA MONICA EVENING OUTLOOK
Monday, December 8, 1941
CONGRESS DECLARES WAR ON JAPAN
Santa Monica 'On Alert' as Army
Guards Douglas Co.

Santa Monica today had moved into a war footing befitting its position on the ringside of the vast Pacific arena of conflict …

Arrangements were perfected to black out the entire city, with the flip of a single switch in case of necessity. The most detailed precautions were taken for the protection of the Douglas Aircraft Co. plant from attack from the sea or air or from sabotage …

As he pulled out into traffic on Fourth Street, it occurred to Earl that he had forgotten one errand. He executed a U-turn and drove a mile south, to Santa Monica Police Headquarters. The large envelope was waiting for him at the reception desk, with his name on it, just as Ruth Madison had promised.

*   *   *   *

"You cannot believe the stories I've been hearing all day on the radio," Doris said after a long, hard embrace. "Three thousand killed in Hawaii. Philippines, Singapore, more air attacks. Everybody and his brother enlisting. Earl, we can't let John do anything stupid."

"He promised to call us tonight," he reassured her. "I don't think he'll jump into anything just yet. Let's have a drink."

They sat down. "What else was on the news?" Earl asked.

"Air raid alarms in New York. Long Island." Doris took a long drink and tilted her head back against the sofa. "Are we safe here?"

Saved by the bell, he thought as the telephone rang. It was John.

"I know Mother wants to talk to you. Did you hear from Coach Carson, or from Tim?" Earl looked at Doris, still on the sofa, legs folded underneath her.

"Both," John replied. "Carson said the summer lifeguards are being asked to report in tomorrow for further instructions."

"What about school?"

"Well, we probably have to make a choice. We can resign from the lifeguard bureau if we want. I'm just going to go see what they say, then ... I don't know."

"All right," said Earl, looking at Doris. "Best not to do anything too hasty. Find out what's what." Doris was vigorously nodding her approval. "How about if you come over here after?"

"Yeah. Fine. Tomorrow afternoon."

"What about Tim?"

"He's at home, in Inglewood. I talked to him earlier."

"So he's all right?"

"Not really. A lot of Japanese people are being arrested, I guess. Nobody in his family, but some people they know. He's upset. He's on our side, Dad, he really is. I told him he might be able to talk to you."

"Talk to me?"

"Yeah, I hope I wasn't out of bounds. He's going to pick me up after the lifeguard meeting, and he'll give me a ride home. He said he wants to help but he isn't sure where to go. He thinks the lifeguards won't want him on the beach, and he said if he walked into a recruiting station they'd probably start shooting at him."

"Let's talk about all that tomorrow. Here's Mother."

*   *   *   *

He was expecting the telephone to ring but jumped when it did. It was exactly 8:00 PM, December 8.

"Earl Brady speaking."

"Hello. How are you?"

"Is this Ted Lindgren?"

"Yes." A long pause. "Right. Sorry I couldn't call sooner. Why don't you tell me what's happened on our … um … case?"

It was Lindgren, for sure, but he wasn't alone, or didn't have privacy, in any event. Didn't want to say his own name, probably didn't want to say much beyond yes and no.

"Jordan's been murdered," Earl said. "But let me go back. FBI Agent Gorman, do you know him?"

"Yes. A little."

"FBI took over the missing person case, because of the Public Safety Committee connection. Gorman got a briefing from the LAPD man on Saturday morning. With me so far?"

"Yes. Go ahead."

"I went to the university on Saturday anyway, after you and I spoke. Jordan's office looked normal—then at my request his secretary pulls out his file on our committee. There was an envelope Jordan had gotten—from you, I think, on Thursday—that right?"

"Yes."

"Envelope contains your notes, correct?"

"Yes."

He gave it to his secretary to file it, correct?"

"I think so," Lindgren said.

"Well, the envelope is gone. Not in the file. I looked."

Earl waited. "Go on," Lindgren said.

"Gorman called me on Saturday night, about 6:30 or so. The body was found just after dark, at a park in Santa Monica. Only about a mile from my house. I saw it, and I've talked to our medical examiner. Jordan was shot in the head then probably transported to this park, where he was fastened to the ground with a long sword, clear through his belly. Sword handle was pointed straight up. There was a white sheet thrown over the whole arrangement. According to Gorman, the sword looks like a ceremonial Japanese—military—what do they call it—samurai."

"That been confirmed?"

"I don't know. Gorman has the sword, and he hasn't returned my call."

"Everyone has been busy, to say the least."

"Right. The committee was called in yesterday, in fact. O'Connor told us about the arrests. Hundreds already, I hear."

"Yes. More tonight. Was anything found?

"His wallet, with money, is all I heard. Should I ask Gorman?"

"No. Not now."

"Can you tell me about the notes?" Earl asked.

"I don't know."

"Sorry. Let me try this. Do they identify … people of special interest?"

"Yes."

"Either because they're bad or good?"

"Yes. That's right."

"Would the notes be … of interest to the enemy?"

"Absolutely."

"Was Jordan authorized to have the information contained in the notes?"

"No."

"What should I do with Gorman?'
"Nothing. Not yet."
"Are you going to call Gorman? Say, just in the normal course of business, because you worked with Jordan?"
"I'm not sure. Maybe he'll call me."
"Is it possible for me to call you? If anything else comes up?"
"Other way around would be better."
"You'll call me?"
"Yes. Same time. Friday."
"One last question," said Earl. "Was it a promotion for you?"
Lindgren chuckled. "I think so. Thanks for the update."

Twenty-One

At 6:30 on the morning of December 9, Earl Brady woke up and swung quietly out of bed. He stepped from the bedroom and slowly closed the door. Doris didn't move.

In the kitchen, he turned on the small tabletop radio, keeping the volume all the way down while the tubes warmed up. He poured himself a glass of grapefruit juice.

Bending down to the radio, he turned the volume knob slightly. A high-pitched male voice was delivering the local news.

"... Army vehicles were seen throughout this area. Various streets in coastal cities have been barricaded, and curious motorists are turned back. Reason: the army has searchlights, sound detectors, and artillery at strategic points. Other troops, equipped with radios, are patrolling the beaches. Last night at 10:30, at the orders of the Army Air Force Interceptor Command, all Pacific Coast radio broadcasters went off the air lest their signals give directions to attackers. A report of unidentified planes over San Francisco led to a forty-five-minute blackout of the Douglas Aircraft Company plant in Santa Monica. The night shift of the large new Douglas plant in Long Beach, California, which was built without windows, hummed as usual. Civilians were evacuated from the area around Fort MacArthur, which protects the vital Los Angeles—Long Beach Harbor. In San Diego …"

Earl clicked off the radio, picked up the envelope that lay beside it, and sat at the kitchen table.

There were several dozen photographs—at least half of them taken at the park on Saturday night. Images of the propped-up sheet, of Jordan's head wound, of his hands loosely grasping the blade where it entered him, of the entire body uncovered. There was one sidelong shot of himself, squatting, head lowered and to the side, arm extended into the tent. The sheet was illuminated from the inside, like a lampshade.

He flipped quickly through the autopsy photos. Near the bottom of the stack were two pictures of the sword. One of its entire length, the other a close-up of its handle and an adjacent portion of blade. Ruth Madison was good. It was easy to see the engraving, several Asian characters, on the blade just below the wrapped handle.

He slipped the photos back into the envelope, which he dropped into his briefcase.

*   *   *   *

John Brady sat on a bus-stop bench, at the corner of Wilshire Boulevard and Ocean Avenue, in front of the Union Oil gas station. A cold afternoon wind had scrubbed away the clouds. Looking across the street, he could see a band of dark sea beyond the cliffs' edge. He thought about the meeting.

"You fellows in school will need to decide within forty-eight hours," the lifeguard captain had said. "We want you, but we need you full time. It's your choice. If you come to work, I am told there is a good chance you will be exempted from the draft. For now, anyway. If you elect to remain at school instead—well, you're on your own. I don't know what will happen regarding college students."

There had been seven of them, now six without Tim Tanaka. That left three from USC, two from UCLA, and one from Loyola. They all exchanged looks. One of them raised a hand.

"Captain?"

"Yes. Grabowski, right?"

"Yes, sir. What did you mean by saying there might be a draft exemption 'for now'?"

"It appears," said the older man, "that we lifeguards may be placed under the command of the U.S. Coast Guard. Could be wrong, but that's what I believe will happen. This job is changing, obviously. As I said earlier, we will be carrying guns beginning tonight. It's not hard for me to imagine that we could all be officially in the Coast Guard before too long. If you're already in, I don't see how they can draft you. So that's what I mean."

Carson had offered John a ride up the hill from headquarters.

"Just a minute, Coach? I need to call home." He had instead called the Tanaka residence and told Tim, "Wilshire and Ocean in twenty minutes. That all right?"

"It might be thirty, but I'm on my way."

Carson wondered why John didn't need a ride back to school.

"My parents want me to spend the night. I guess I should talk to them about all of this."

"D-definitely. Big decisions."

"What about you, Coach?"

"L-lifeguards for now, but it's … possible I'll be leaving soon."

"Oh, really? Army? Navy?"

"I don't know. I have s-some people to see tomorrow about it. Where is your folks' house again?"

"No, you can just drop me off up here at Pico and Ocean. I need to walk and think, stop in and see somebody on my way. Thanks, Coach."

Carson stopped at the curb. John got out and leaned back into the car. "Thanks again."

"*Vaya con Dios*," said Carson.

John laughed. "*Sí, señor. Hasta la vista.*"

*   *   *   *

John heard a whistle. Tim Tanaka was parked, across Wilshire. "How was it?" he asked as John closed the passenger door.

"Where do I start? Tell you this, it isn't the same job now. If you stay in the guards. No more pulling fat old men out of riptides in between meeting girls."

"Yeah, well, it's December, don't forget."

"We'll be carrying guns, by the way. Even if we don't know how to use them."

"What kind?"

"Pistols. Colt. Maybe rifles in the jeeps. Oh, and most likely we'll be part of the U.S. Coast Guard."

John noticed that they were driving east on Wilshire, away from his house.

"Turn left up here at Lincoln."

"Why?"

"We're invited over to my parents' house for dinner. My dad wants to talk to you."

"Right. That's good. I hope that's good, anyway. Thanks." Tim gave a weak laugh.

"Yeah, it's good. Make a left on California and right on Fourth."

"It sounds like the idea is to keep people away from the beaches," Tim said.

"Yeah, I think so. Possible draft exemption, but then you wind up in the Coast Guard anyway. Maybe that's better than the army."

Tim was quiet as they turned onto California. John pointed him into the driveway on Fourth.

"Take it all the way back. My dad'll be home in a while, I suppose. How's your family doing?"

"A little better. The school principal told my father not to worry about his job, and my mother's getting over the shock, I think. What are you going to do?"

"I don't know yet," John said. "Let's go inside."

The side door was locked, so John led Tim out to the front, where he rang the doorbell. They could hear footsteps. Then the small, round, peep-door quickly opened and closed.

"John."

"Hello, Mother," he said as they hugged. As they separated, Doris looked at Tim and jumped, startled. She looked back at John, embarrassed.

"You remember Tim Tanaka, don't you?"

Doris recovered. "Yes, of course. You're John's friend from school."

"And the lifeguards, last summer," Tim added. "Nice to see you again, Mrs. Brady."

"Come in," she said, wiping her palms on the side of her cotton pants. "I'm a little messy. Been working on the kitchen. They say we need to make at least one room in the house, um, light-proof. The Civil Defense Council." She looked at Tim again and winced.

John jumped in, trying to reduce the awkwardness. "Tim is over so Dad and he can talk. He wants some advice on how to help out. Tim and his family want to … help out."

Doris took a deep breath. "Yes," she said. "Good."

"I could start in your kitchen," Tim offered. "Put me to work."

All three of them laughed nervously. "You're both hired," Doris said. "I promised Earl to get this done before dark."

They soon finished the job of taping black oil cloth onto the four kitchen windows. "Let's go sit," Doris said. "You boys hungry, thirsty? Go ahead, and I'll bring something."

They were sipping ginger ale and eating Ritz crackers when Earl walked in. Doris jumped up to meet him at the doorway. "John's Japanese friend from school," she whispered.

Louder, then: "How was your day?"

"Frustrating, a little," Earl replied. "Hello, John. Hello, Tim. Let me change, and I'll be right there."

Frustrating, he thought as he peeled off his tie and dress shirt. *There's an understatement.* He had finally spoken to Gorman, who by his own admission had done almost nothing about the Jordan murder since leaving the coroner's office early Sunday morning.

"I've had Jordan's house locked up tight," Gorman had told him. "I might get over there tomorrow. We're checking out the bullet, although it's a .38, very common. The sheet came from Montgomery Ward sometime in the last two years, also very common. The sword is—well, it's Japanese, is about all we know at this time."

Earl had been bursting with questions and suggestions. *Maybe you should look at Jordan's fucking car*, he'd wanted to say, but remembered Lindgren ("Not yet"), so he thanked Gorman and asked if he'd mind passing along any developments. Gorman said he wouldn't mind at all.

Earl pulled a V-neck sweater over his T-shirt and rejoined the group in the living room. John and Doris were talking about the lifeguard meeting.

"… so I have forty-eight hours to decide," John was saying. "I know what some of the other college boys are going to do. I need to think about it."

"Well, I've thought about it," said Doris. "I think you should stay in school. Anybody can drive a jeep back and forth on the sand."

"Yeah," Earl said. "I didn't hear everything, but I wouldn't leave school either, just to patrol the beach. What about you, Tim?"

Tim looked surprised to be asked. "I, well … I definitely won't be going full time with the lifeguards. I'm not sure what to do, though. I'm a citizen, but … I don't know whether they'll draft me or even let me join up."

"How about your family?" Earl asked.

"My parents aren't citizens, but my sister and I were born here, so we are. My father's a science teacher at Venice High. My sister's almost finished with nursing school. We all just … we're not sure what to do. My sister is trying to reach Mr. Munson."

"Who is Mr. Munson?" Earl asked.

"I think he works for the State Department, in Washington. He and another man were here about a month ago. They were interviewing people for a report about the loyalty of Japanese Americans. They interviewed my family, all four of us, at our house. My sister then made some other introductions and did some translating. They told us the government was look-ing into what should be done if Japan and the United States went to war."

Why haven't I heard of this? Earl wondered. "What should be done, is that how they said it?"

"Yes, sir," Tim replied. "What should be done by the government, and what should be done by us. They said their report was almost finished."

Doris and John had moved into the kitchen, where Doris could be heard again urging John to stay in school. Tim leaned forward and said, "Mr. Brady, one of the things Mr. Munson told us was that my sister and I should take ownership of our parents' property. We followed his advice. I think he was trying to be helpful, because he liked us. I know he did. But still, it worries me a lot, that suggestion. Especially now."

Earl nodded slowly. "You can read Japanese, right?" he asked.

"Pretty well."

"I think John told me that you went to Japan for a year of school, so—"

"Six months. But yes, I did, when I was twelve. Do you need something translated?"

Earl nodded. "Let me show you. Follow me."

They went to the bedroom, and Earl pulled the Santa Monica P.D. envelope out of his briefcase. The photographs of the sword were on the top of the stack. He picked out one of them.

"Take a look at this," he said as he handed the picture to Tim. "Here, move over and put it under the lamp."

Tim studied the photograph, then looked up. "It's Japanese."

"Can you tell me what it says?"

"It's a family name, I think Nakazawa, and a date. A year, that is … 1931."

"All right. Thanks. Let me put this away, and let's get something to eat."

Twenty-Two

On Wednesday, December 10, Earl spent an entire day, for once, doing his normal job. Four preliminary hearings in the morning, a guilty plea (driving while intoxicated), and two meetings with detectives (burglary and vice) in the afternoon. There were three messages waiting for him when he got upstairs at 3:45: Gorman, Miss Whitlock from the university, and Mead from *Time* magazine.

He called Gorman first. The FBI had found "nothing, really" at Jordan's house, and there were no discernable fingerprints, except Jordan's, anywhere on the sword. Gorman was "hoping" to visit Jordan's university office tomorrow. He would call again "if anything breaks."

He placed his next call to the History Department. "Miss Whitlock?"

"Yes."

"Mr. Brady calling, from the district attorney's office."

"Oh, yes, thank you. I called because there's someone coming to see me tomorrow."

"Yes, I've heard. The FBI."

"Have they found out what happened?"

"They're making progress," he lied. "May I ... if you don't mind, may I stop by your place this evening for a few minutes? I can let you know where things stand." They agreed on a 5:30 meeting.

He rubbed his eyes after hanging up. *I can just hear it,* he thought. *That nice Mr. Brady was here last Saturday morning, and we sneaked in to Colonel Jordan's office, and I showed him the file Colonel Jordan had, and*—

One more call.

"Mead."

"Hello, it's Earl Brady returning your call."

"So Colonel Jordan's been killed, huh?"

"Yes. Sorry, I didn't get a chance to call you."

"Don't worry about that. I just wanted to know if there's anything yet ... ah, about the murder. The investigation."

"Well, the FBI is handling it, so we aren't the ones who would know. Special Agent Gorman is the man in charge of it over there."

"I know. I talked to him this morning."

Earl decided to say nothing.

"I tried to tell Gorman about the article Jordan was writing ... the one that was due last Friday. Just in case it might be, ah, pertinent."

"And?" Earl asked.

"I think you told me before that Jordan had mentioned it to you, the article he was doing. Right?"

"Yes, he did tell me about it. Just ... generally."

"All right, so you know it was about the war plans, and so forth?"

"Yeah," Earl said. "He told me that."

"Here's the funny part. The FBI man, Gorman ... he sounded like he already knew about it, too. I can't figure out how."

*   *   *   *

She must have seen him walking up, through the lace-curtained window. Miss Whitlock opened her door before he could knock.

"Come in, please, Mr. Brady. Can I get you a Coke?"

They sat across from each other, a braided oval rug separating her small sofa from his heavily padded chair.

"I thought it would be best if we spoke privately ... or at least not over the telephone. About this," Earl said.

"Such a gentleman," Miss Whitlock said.

"Well, thank you, I—"

"You also, of course, Mr. Brady. Colonel Jordan, though … he was such an impressive man. I just can't believe it, still. And all of the other horrible news. This world of ours …"

"Well, one thing everyone is trying to understand is why anyone would wish to harm the colonel," Earl said.

"So it's true … he was murdered?"

"I'm afraid so. Did you ever hear anyone threaten him, anything like that?"

"Dear me, no. He had arguments, occasionally, with other faculty members. But just, well, scholarly debates you could say."

"Do you remember anything about the article, the *Time* magazine article that man called about last Friday?"

"You mean what was in the article?"

"Right. Did you type it for him, or—"

"Only the very first draft, which he dictated to me. He asked, but I was so busy last week with Professor Dryman's book. Colonel Jordan typed the final version himself. I remember, because he joked about how slow he was."

"Has anyone looked through his office this week?"

"No, just, well, the university security men came in Monday, or maybe even Sunday, I don't know. By the time I arrived on Monday, there was a big 'Keep Out' sign and a little wood barricade in front of his door. We were all told to stay out, that he had died, and it was under investigation."

"So," Earl said, "The FBI will be there tomorrow?"

"Yes. Shall I—"

"Just answer all of their questions, as best you can."

"What if they ask—"

Earl held up his hand. "Let's not worry about it. They already know all about me. They know I was on the Public Safety Committee with Colonel Jordan. Don't worry. Just listen to the questions and answer them truthfully."

"Answer the questions," she repeated.

"Right. You know where to reach me if you need anything."

She watched him drive away from the curb, then went to her telephone and dialed. A man answered on the first ring. "He's just left," Miss Whitlock said, then hung up.

Twenty-Three

CONFIDENTIAL MEMORANDUM NO. 10

To: Public Safety Committee Members
From: Special Agent F. X. O'Connor, FBI
Date: December 12, 1941

By order of 11 December, the Western Defense Command has been designated as a theater of operations. This has the effect of elevating the defense of this area to a priority status. It is assumed that enemy forces cannot mount a full-scale invasion of the West Coast; however, as demonstrated by the attacks at Hawaii and now the Philippines, a single but well-directed assault can inflict devastating harm.

Assaults could be mounted in different ways, not only through the air. As Admiral Nimitz has stated:

"It's relatively safe and simple for a sub to surface near a port and throw a few shells into a city. It is not beyond the bounds of possibility that Japanese submarines operating off the West Coast of the United States may attempt to lay their shells into cities before they leave."

The North American Pacific Coast is dangerously exposed, with a significant percentage of the nation's aircraft manufacturing facilities being concentrated in the region.

We will meet next Thursday, December 18, at 12 noon, at the usual location. In the meantime, I have been asked to convey the Director's gratitude to local police for their excellent assistance since December 7, in locating and detaining dangerous enemy aliens.

*   *   *   *

By Earl's watch, it was 7:55 PM when the telephone rang on Friday, December 12.

"Hello?"

"Yes. Hello." It was Agent Lindgren.

"I'll just start talking, right?" Earl asked.

"Right."

"Got a memo from O'Connor today. All it says is, the committee will meet next week, on the eighteenth. Thursday."

"Yes, I know."

"That's interesting. Did, um, Gorman call you?"

"No ... not exactly."

"O'Connor?"

"Yes."

"Did he say anything about the Jordan investigation?"

"Not much."

"Well," said Earl, "as far as I can tell there isn't much. Not much of an FBI investigation, that is. Did O'Connor ask you any questions about it?"

"No."

"He told you about the meeting, though?"

"Yes. Um, that will be great."

Earl paused. "I said, did he tell you about the meeting."

"I'm looking forward to it," Lindgren said.

"You mean you're coming?"

"Right."

"Flying?"

"Yes."

They agreed to meet for dinner. "The Golden Dragon Restaurant. Chinatown, on Broadway, west side, just north of College Street. Ask for me, if you don't see me. Got that?"

"Right," Lindgren said. "See you there."

Twenty-Four

"Let me get his daughter," said the woman. "She knows you're coming, and she wants to talk to you before you go in the room. Wait here."

Earl was left alone in the Santa Teresa lobby as the woman disappeared into the dark hallway that led to Fletcher's room. The small tabletop RCA was on quietly. *Amazing,* he thought, *how everyone listens now.* He leaned forward, his forearms parallel on the wood countertop. It was Saturday, December 13.

"... Japanese are making thrusts from several directions at the Philippine island of Luzon," said the radio voice. "The Cavite Naval yard, off Manila, was hit yesterday by a Jap air attack. Admiral Thomas C. Hart has acknowledged that a single, direct bomb hit smashed a navy dispensary in Cavite, killing all nurses, doctors, and patients in the building. We pause now for this word from our sponsors ..."

Earl heard footsteps on the linoleum just as the advertising jingle started. He straightened up to see the receptionist walking toward him with a thirty-ish woman in a black raincoat. "Mr. Brady?" she said, forcing a smile. Her eyes were bloodshot.

"Yes, ma'am," he replied. "Earl."

"Eleanor Berkson. I'm Bud's daughter. I've heard so much about you. Daddy is—" She stopped and held a hand to her mouth. "Excuse me ..."

"Shall we sit down?" Earl offered.

She nodded. He led her to a corner of the lobby, where two rattan armchairs with faded yellow cushions were placed at a ninety-degree angle to each other, a floor lamp and small round table between.

"Sorry," she said. "Daddy is not doing well at all. He looks worse every day, and his breathing gets louder and louder. Thank goodness he sleeps most of the time."

"Your husband is a doctor, isn't he?"

"Yes. How did you know?"

"Your father talks about you a lot." This was a slight exaggeration, but Earl couldn't see any harm. "I think he's mentioned it."

"Well, yes, he is. Just completed his surgery training, so … that's another thing to worry about. He might be called up, especially now that Germany's declared war. He doesn't have an established practice yet, so he could be at the top of the list."

"What does he think about your father's condition?"

She shook her head slowly. "He's dying. Maybe a week, maybe a month."

"God, I'm—"

"I know," she interrupted. She sat up straighter in the chair. "Daddy wants to see you, Mr. Brady. It will cheer him up to talk about something besides his lungs or his heart, and all of this. So I'm glad you're here."

"Look, I should give you my home telephone number. Anything else I can do, you just call me. Anytime at all." Earl stood and walked to the reception counter. Fletcher's daughter followed, and they exchanged numbers.

"All right then," he said. "You be on your way. I'll distract your father for a while here." He extended his hand, but she slipped inside his arm and hugged him.

"Thank you," she murmured, then turned quickly and walked to the door.

He looked at the receptionist, who motioned toward the hallway. "Room eight," she said. "Just pick up the telephone and dial zero if you need me."

Fletcher's eyes were closed. The breathing, once Earl closed the door behind him, sounded like a steel rake being pulled through gravel. The old man raised a hand and whispered roughly, "Earl?"

"Yep." He dragged a thinly padded metal chair to the bedside. Fletcher was tilted upward slightly and shook his head when Earl asked if he wanted the angle adjusted.

"I finally met Eleanor," said Earl. "Nice girl." Fletcher's eyes closed tighter, and his mouth quivered slightly. *Wrong subject,* Earl thought. *Distract him. Divert him. Crimes. War. Politics. Anything.*

"I just came from a meeting of the Tournament of Roses Committee," Earl said.

"Tell me about it," Fletcher whispered.

"They were meeting today about the parade and game. Benson, of course, was there as the LAPD representative. How could he pass up a Saturday lunch at the Valley Hunt Club?"

Fletcher managed a weak smile and patted the bed, a symbolic knee-slap. Earl felt better about his choice of topic.

"Anyway," he went on, "the whole event is being moved to North Carolina. Parade, game, the works. General DeWitt officially ordered all sporting events cancelled."

"I heard," Fletcher said.

"Horse racing is off, too. Large concentrations of people are bombing targets, according to DeWitt. So anyway, it'll be a home game for Duke. You been listening to the radio much?"

"Some," Fletcher rasped.

"The blackout business has been a mess. Chaotic. A whole bunch of traffic accidents, and then we had a small riot break out in Santa Monica two nights ago. Couple of businesses left for the day without turning off neon signs—a group of kids broke the things, then smashed out storefront windows along Wilshire, where some inside lights had been left on. Civil Defense vigilantes, I suppose."

Fletcher was drumming his fingers on the bed. Time for a new topic. "Let me bring you up to date about Jordan," Earl said. "Not a top priority with the FBI at the moment. They seem to—well, this is my guess— they've decided it was a Japanese execution."

Earl couldn't remember how much he'd told Fletcher about the murder, so he continued, describing the sword.

"Makes it easy to close the case, I suppose," said Fletcher, who then groaned and coughed slowly. "Act of war."

"So he's put down as killed by … the enemy, agents of the enemy, something like that?"

Fletcher nodded, coughing again.

"Goddamn it," Earl snarled, "I'd still like to know who did it. Wouldn't you?"

Fletcher, still coughing, nodded again.

"Lindgren is coming to town next week," Earl said. "Surprising. He's meeting me for dinner on Wednesday. Maybe he'll have some ideas, but … truth is, I'm not sure how he really feels about it."

Fletcher rotated a hand, from palm down to palm up. A silent question mark.

"What do I mean? I just think Lindgren's worried the most about what he gave Jordan … from the files. Whatever it was, exactly, it wasn't supposed to leave the FBI. All I know so far is that the Japanese would have been very, very interested in it. That's what Lindgren says. So I don't think he wants it to show up now."

Fletcher took in a breath, then forced out a question. "Are they tracing the sword?"

"They couldn't lift any fingerprints from it. I don't know what else they might be doing. There is a name engraved on the blade, in Japanese. I might have a way to look into that. Do you think I should?"

Fletcher nodded, coughing. He closed his eyes and made a writing motion, his finger dragging across his palm. Earl handed him a pad and pencil from the bedside table. Fletcher wrote, "How?" and turned the pad over to show his visitor.

"How will I look into the sword, do you mean?" Earl asked.

Fletcher nodded again.

"I might have a contact. In the, um, Japanese population here."

Fletcher scratched at the notepad again: "About time! But be careful, and don't assume anything."

"I won't," said Earl. "You've taught me well. That's a little sappy, but I mean it."

Fletcher coughed, then underlined "anything."

*   *   *   *

Off the parkway, and down into Chinatown. It was almost three o'clock. Sun was at a table with a stack of papers and an adding machine.

"Mr. Brady, a pleasant surprise. Would you like something?"

"No, thanks. I was driving by ... just have a small favor to ask."

"Of course. Please sit down."

He would be in for dinner on Wednesday at six, Earl explained. Was there a separate room? "It's an FBI agent. Having to do with Colonel Jordan. It would be helpful if we could have some privacy."

"I am happy to help," said Sun. "I will see to it. Of course, of course."

"Thank you. Next Wednesday, then."

*   *   *   *

On the drive home, Earl thought about Tim Tanaka. He definitely would ask Tim to research the sword, but *how much do I tell him?*

"Act of war," Fletcher had said.

"The war's first casualty," the FBI was saying as they rounded up names from a list.

Maybe it doesn't matter, Earl thought. Thousands of men had been killed on that Sunday morning in Hawaii. By Japanese pilots, guided to their targets by Japanese locals. Maybe it didn't matter exactly who killed Jordan.

Then Earl remembered his conversation with Sun. *Find the loyal Japanese*, he was saying. *You will need them.*

As he drove closer to his house, Earl thought about John. To the near-hysteria of Doris, John had withdrawn from the university. This was his second day of full-time work as a pistol-carrying lifeguard. Three hours of hurried firearms instruction, followed by twelve-hour patrol shifts. These were—as his mother had predicted—little more than driving a jeep back and forth on the chilly sand of State Beach. John was living at home again, where he was required to be "reachable" at all times.

"I'll go back to school when it's over," he had promised as they stood in the kitchen. "This gets me off the draft list, for a while anyway. I'll have a chance to wait and see what to do. A lot of my friends have already jumped." He looked at his mother. "Pilot training, things like that. Would you rather—"

"No," Doris said. "I just …"

John wrapped an arm around her shoulders. "Besides, Mother, don't you feel better having a gun in the house?"

Twenty-Five

John Brady yanked the round microphone from its dashboard-mounted cradle. He had a towel wrapped around his neck and tucked inside the red jacket. The winter sun was dropping, and the wind was starting to bite. "Jeep four, Brady to headquarters."

"Go ahead."

"Two individuals at the waterline," John said, "I estimate three hundred yards north of Santa Monica pier. My position is a hundred yards south of them. They appear to be surf fishing, one adult and one child. I will contact. Over."

"Proceed. Standing by for identification. Over."

He parked the jeep in soft sand, twenty yards inland from the fisherman and his companion. John zipped his jacket, covering the holstered pistol on his right hip.

"Hello," he shouted. "Do you speak English?"

"No," said the man, turning and putting a hand on the small boy's head. "No *bueno*."

"*Playa esta cerrada*," John said. "*Muy importante. Muy—*" Suddenly forgetting the word for "dangerous," he continued, "*No se puede—*" It was hopeless. He looked at the little boy. "English?"

"Yeah, I understand," the boy said, looking up. He was squatting next to a small plank of wood, cutting open mussels for bait. "Can we fish?"

"Tell him I'm with the Coast Guard, and the beach is closed because it's dangerous. Enemy boats ..." John extended one arm under the other, attempting to signify a submarine. "Sorry, but no fishing. You must leave."

The boy turned and spoke quickly to the old man. "OK," he said to John.

"I need to have your names and address. You and your father. Then you can go."

"He's my grandfather," said the boy. "He is Esteban Diaz, and I am José Delgado. 215 Hall Avenue."

"Wait here."

John called in the names. "Just a Mexican and his grandson, fishing. Over."

"Roger. Escort them away from the beach. Over."

"Roger. Out."

As he sat watching the pair trudge across the wide beach toward Pacific Coast Highway, John noticed a solitary parked green car. Through binoculars, he saw Earl standing at the front bumper, waving.

He drove over. "Hi, Dad. What brings you down here on a Monday afternoon in December?"

"I was wondering if you could do me a favor."

"Sure."

"I want to see Tim Tanaka about something. The sooner the better."

"Why?"

"Oh, it's a case ... I need some translation help, on a case."

John looked at his watch. "I'm off in about an hour. Can it wait until I get home? I'll try to call him from there."

"Fine. Let me pick you up—main lifeguard office?"

"Right. Six fifteen, say."

*   *   *   *

"Thank you for coming over, Tim," Earl said as the young man followed him into the living room.

"John probably told you I was looking for some translating again," he continued. Tim nodded. "But it's a little more than that. It's about the sword I showed you ... here, this picture, remember?"

"Yes, sir."

"What I'm going to tell you is confidential. I'm trusting you with this. All right?"

"Yes, sir." Tim held the photograph, careful to touch only the edges.

"We think this sword was used in a recent murder," Earl explained. "The victim was someone who ... the Japanese government ... they probably had a motive to kill him. We would like to know where this particular sword came from. If you could find any information about that, you would be doing a great service."

Tim Tanaka stared at the picture. "I'll try. Do I call you if I ... find anything out?"

"Yes. Call me or see me. Don't tell anyone else that I've asked you to do this. Understood?"

"Yes, sir." Tim held up the photograph. "Can I take this?"

"It's better if you don't, I think. If you start getting very close to an answer, I suppose we can talk about it again. But right now, just copy down the writing. I can tell you this, the handle wrapping is red and black."

*   *   *   *

An hour later, Tim Tanaka was sitting at the kitchen table in his own house, across from his sister.

"I just don't see how he expects me to do this," he groaned.

"But we have to try," she said. Alice Tanaka flipped the sheet of paper back across the table. "Our group made a strong statement right after the attack. We're Americans. This is a chance to prove it. Mr. Brady's giving us a chance."

She was referring to a press release by the Japanese American Citizen's League, repudiating the Japanese government and avowing readiness "to assist in every way our fellow Americans and allies to defeat the Axis."

Tim refolded the paper and put it in his shirt pocket, looking at Alice. "What do you mean by 'us,' anyway?" he said. "Mr. Brady asked *me*. As a matter of fact, he made *me* promise not to tell anyone else about it."

"That may be so," she said, "but I'm working on this too. Don't worry; I won't say anything. And if I find something to pursue, I'll let you pursue it. And you can take all the credit, Mr. Detective."

"Haven't you got enough to do?" he asked. Alice was in nursing school. She had classes and clinical rounds at two hospitals.

"Tim," said Alice, rising out of her chair and turning away, "I think you don't completely understand something." She stood still and quiet for a few seconds, then faced her brother, leaning back against a door. "There's a big argument going on in the American government right now—about us." Alice jabbed both of her thumbs into her collarbone. "What to do with us," she continued. "Mr. Munson's report is going to recommend that we be allowed to serve, but there are other opinions out there. Read the newspapers, Tim. Plenty of people—plenty of high-up people—say we should all just be locked up. Right now. All of us. You and me, right into the same prison as whoever sent signals about ships in Pearl Harbor. Right along with whoever murdered this man. If it was somebody Japanese who killed him, let's try to find out who. So all of us don't get blamed. You see?"

He nodded, silently.

✳   ✳   ✳   ✳

In the kitchen of Stuart Green's Gold Coast beach house the next morning, a uniformed butler served tea and coffee to several people seated around a tile-top table. Green read aloud from a single sheet of paper. "Does everybody understand this?" he asked the group. Each nodded.

"This means that Mr. Brady of the District Attorney's office may be a problem. His son is the lifeguard who gave us the rescue demonstration last summer. Mr. Brady appears to be in contact with some Japanese locals. He is being watched, and he may have to be dealt with, but carefully and at an opportune moment. Please avoid contact with Mr. Brady, but report anything you happen to see or hear, in the usual fashion.

Green stood up. "I believe this is our last meeting," he said, then clasped his hands in front of his chest. "So. Wherever events may take each of us, I wish you good luck."

He turned to the woman who stood next to him. "Safe journey, Miss Whitlock."

Twenty-Six

On Wednesday, December 17, Earl Brady arrived at the Golden Dragon early. It was 5:45 when Sun greeted him.

"Mr. Brady, welcome. I have a private room for you in the back. Shall I take you in now, or do you wish to wait?"

He pointed to the rear of the restaurant, then followed Sun past the tables and into the kitchen, which was steamy and noisy with the clinking of dishes and the rapid chatter of Chinese voices. *They always sound like they're arguing,* Earl thought.

Sun led him through a small doorway and into a concrete-floored hall, illuminated from the low ceiling by a bare bulb. He held another door open and motioned for Earl to enter.

"Your office?" Earl asked, seeing a desk pushed against the far wall. A small, linen-draped dinner table sat in the center of the room.

"Yes, Mr. Brady. It is no problem. You may stay as long as you wish, you and your guest. Will he be asking for you?"

"I think so." Earl described Lindgren.

"I will bring him in as soon as he arrives. Shall I send tea, in the meanwhile?"

Earl ordered a beer instead. Nervous, he drained the bottle in about a minute. He dropped it into a wastebasket under Sun's desk, then sat at the table to wait. At 6:10, the door opened, and Lindgren walked in.

"I will send a waiter," said Sun before closing the door.

"Nice place," said Lindgren, raising his eyebrows.

"I thought we'd want some privacy—for once," Earl replied as they shook hands.

"Sorry about that. We can talk here, all right. Good food?"

"I like it, Earl said. "I've been here several times. Actually, Walter Jordan used to eat here once in a while."

"That so? Well, speaking of that—"

There was a knock at the door, and a waiter came in. They ordered, then Lindgren continued. "I finally spoke with Agent Gorman, about an hour ago."

Earl tried to sound nonchalant. *Routine. Just another case.* "And?"

"You were right," Lindgren said. "The Jordan homicide case is all but closed. Maybe that's an overstatement. If something fell into their laps, they'd take it, but ..."

"What do they have?"

"Not the notes, first of all. Unless they're trying to set me up, that is. But I don't have any reason to think so. I did tell Gorman that the colonel was privy to some sensitive information, but Gorman already knew that much. With the sword, and the timing of it ... he's made up his mind, I'd say."

Earl rubbed his temples and sighed. "But is the FBI really going to—drop it? Do they *want* to know who did it?"

Lindgren shrugged. "Yeah ... but just not enough to do the work and find out. Feeling is, they've got more pressing business. I can't tell this field office what to do."

Oh, please, Earl thought. *Washington always told you what to do—or not do—when you were here.* Maybe it was understandable, though, for Lindgren not to be pushing the investigation. His own career could be ruined if it were discovered that he shared secrets with an outsider. But Earl didn't like Lindgren's pretense of being disappointed at the FBI's attitude, the lack of any desire to find Jordan's killers. *I'm on my own with this one.*

"How's the new assignment?" he asked.

"Busy," Lindgren said. "It was a promotion, though," he said with a smile and another shrug. "Lots of meetings—at least one every day with Hoover. And the Attorney General, usually."

"We're arresting a lot of Japanese around here."

Lindgren grimaced. "I tell you. Incredible, isn't it? For three years we weren't allowed to arrest anybody, and now we haul in—Jesus, seems like everybody."

Earl took a sip of tea and looked at Lindgren. "People are quite scared around here," he said.

"Yeah. We get calls every day to make more arrests. Your own bosses— I mean your DA, your mayor, your state attorney general, your governor—you ought to hear them. They tell the people to be calm, that we're all in this together, a citizen is a citizen, and all the rest. Then they write us these frantic letters and telegrams. Demanding that all the Japanese, every one of 'em, U.S. citizens or not, just—disappear. This food is good, you're right."

The good food led to a whispered discussion of that week's *Time* magazine, which included a helpful article on the physical differences between Chinese and Japanese. *How to Tell Your Friends from the Japs* was the caption.

"How long will you be here in town?" Earl asked as the waiter removed the dishes.

"A few days, probably. Doing some background checks."

"What's that about? If you can tell me, of course."

"Oh, I can tell you some of it. In fact, I'll be asking your office about the people we're looking at. Make sure they don't have local arrest records we don't know about, that sort of thing. They're being considered for certain jobs."

"I see. We'll be glad to help, as always."

"I have a copy of the list for you," said Lindgren, patting his chest. "It's only five names. If you could have someone get started on it tomorrow morning, that would be great." He pulled a single sheet of paper from his inside coat pocket and handed it to Earl. He unfolded it and saw, glancing, that it was a typed list of names with dates of birth, physical descriptions, addresses, and a line or two about occupations. He started to refold the page, then quickly opened it again.

"Wait," said Earl, pointing at a name. "I know this one. Emmett Carson?"

"Do you? Problems?"

"No, no. I just know him. Not well, but yes, I know him. My son knows him better. What's Emmett Carson ..."

"Carson's being considered for a very, let's just say a sensitive position. About all I know is that it would be out of the country. I'm told he speaks Spanish fluently. That true?"

"I don't know. I wouldn't know, necessarily. We're not close friends."

"Let me buy dinner," Lindgren said.

"Thank you. Can I drop you off someplace?"

"Sure. Biltmore, if it's on your way."

They said their good-byes and thank-yous to Sun, then settled into the Chrysler for the short drive to the hotel.

"Hell of a thing, this war," Lindgren said as they drove up the hill out of Chinatown.

"I'll say."

Lindgren turned to face Earl. "Look," he said, "this is just between us: listen, my friend, you need to be careful."

"Of course I do. What do you mean?"

"I mean that I know you're interested in Jordan's murder. Other people know it too. Some people might want you to ... to let it go."

"Why should I?" Earl said, annoyed. "Murder is a crime in California. A man seems to have been killed in Los Angeles County."

"I know that," Lindgren replied. "Just be careful, is what I'm saying. Not everything goes by the book these days."

They rolled to a stop in front of the Biltmore Hotel. Lindgren opened his door, then pulled it shut. "I wish I could tell you more," he said.

"Well, maybe someday," Earl replied.

*   *   *   *

SANTA MONICA EVENING OUTLOOK
Wednesday, December 17, 1941
ALASKAN DEFENSES REINFORCED
Evacuation in Sitka

When Alaska was bought from Russia in 1867, this nation had a collective chuckle. The newly-acquired Northern Territory was referred to as "Seward's Icebox" after the U.S. Secretary of State who engineered the purchase.

No one is laughing now. With Japan threatening the entire Pacific, the Territory's delegate to the Congress, Anthony Dimond, is urging that the Alaska front, especially the string of Aleutian Islands which run to within 600 miles of Japan itself, be reinforced with "planes, more planes—lots of planes." At Sitka, a mere 750 miles from Seattle, an evacuation of women and children began yesterday.

*   *   *   *

"This list of restricted areas is under constant review," FBI Agent O'Connor said, "and we will pass along changes to your offices as soon as we can. So far, it has all gone as smoothly as could be expected."

Earl scanned several pages of the document: ports, power plants, airports, factories. *Maybe it would be simpler to tell them where they can go*, he thought. He drummed his fingers on the conference table and wondered if Tim Tanaka was having any success.

"Ted?" O'Connor said.

Lindgren rose and stood behind his chair. "Good to see all of you again," he said, clasping his hands behind his back. "As you know, the official view of the Department of Justice is that American citizens of Japanese descent should not be assumed to be disloyal to this country. Attorney General Biddle and Director Hoover have made several public statements on this subject. However—" Lindgren paused, and there was knowing laughter from several of the men seated around the long conference table.

"It is understood that there may be overriding military considerations. The secure defense of coastal areas, in particular, is imperative. Obviously. The question of how best to achieve this will be decided by the president himself. I am here to alert you to the possibility—and it is only a possibility—of action being taken to remove all persons of Japanese descent away from proximity to the coast. This would be a considerable task, as you can well imagine. Again, please remember that this is only a possibility at this time. And, gentlemen, the very fact it is being considered is highly confidential. It does not leave this room."

The meeting broke up. Earl caught up to Lindgren in the hallway. "I have a progress report for you on those names," he said.

Lindgren checked his watch. "Let's go back in," he said, turning around toward the conference room.

Earl pulled out his notebook as they sat down. "No record on Andrews, nothing on Howell. Still looking on Jansen—there is a William Jansen, but we think it's a different one. Emmett Carson has no record with us. Stephen Weilner shows up with a misdemeanor conviction, public disturbance in 1937. I should have the file on that when I get back to my office. Want me to call you?"

"What service," Lindgren said. "Yes, sure, call me this afternoon. I'll be here, most likely."

Two hours later, Earl was on the telephone with Lindgren. "Your William Jansen is clean," Earl reported. "The one who came up in our records is over sixty now. Different person."

"Good."

"I'm just looking at the Weilner file right now," Earl continued. "A barroom brawl, it looks like. Your man scored a knockout. It was his twenty-first birthday. Probation and a ten-buck fine. Nothing since."

"Much appreciated," Lindgren said. "Big help, getting this so quickly. By the way, I have a change in plans."

"That so?"

"I leave tomorrow morning. I figured I'd be here through the weekend, but I was just told otherwise."

"Short visit."

"I'll say," Lindgren agreed. "I need to ask one more favor."

*   *   *   *

As he traveled on Pico, Earl reviewed the conversation in his mind. The change in plans, Lindgren had explained, left him short on time. He'd be unable to conduct a certain interview concerning Emmett Carson. Could you cover it? One of Carson's ex-girlfriends, in Santa Monica, right near your place. Just a formality, really. Edna Sampson. She's expecting your call. You can tell her Emmett's being considered for a government position. Just ask her about two things. First, can Emmett really speak Spanish? Second, any reason to think he has sympathy for the Axis countries? Lindgren would call Earl on Monday night.

*   *   *   *

His curiosity prompted Earl to call Edna Sampson that evening. As Lindgren had said, she was expecting it.

"Tomorrow is fine," she slurred. "Just don't come before ten."

Twenty-Seven

Edna Sampson had been beautiful, he could see, but years of drinking had puffed and reddened her face. She wore a head scarf, knotted at her forehead, and a quilted robe. "Housecoats," Doris called them. They sat at a card table in the living room of her apartment. She had made some very strong coffee.

"I haven't seen Emmett much the last couple of years," she told Earl. "He calls me once in a while, stops by sometimes. See if I'm all right. You want sugar in that?" The question was squeezed from a corner of her mouth, as she gripped a cigarette between her lips.

"Yes," he said. "Thanks. You were his girlfriend at one time, right?"

She blew smoke over her left shoulder. "Off and on since high school. We were even engaged, once. Believe it or not. So, what do you want to know?"

Earl had a feeling that Carson "stopped by sometimes" to do more than see if Edna was all right. *Not my concern,* he told himself.

"Mr. Carson is being considered for a job," he explained. "A rather big job, I gather, though I don't know exactly what it is. With the United States government. We only need to confirm a couple of things. One is whether he can speak Spanish."

Edna Sampson threw back her head and laughed. "Yes. Oh, yes. Next question."

"Why are you laughing? Just out of curiosity."

"Takes me back, I suppose. Maybe I laugh so I won't cry."

"About what?"

"Emmett, Emmett." She looked away, then back at Earl. "Where do I start?"

"Wherever you want," he said.

"People think he's not too smart, if they don't know him. Some people anyway. That beach-boy image, you know. Sometimes Emmett seems so—carefree, like he never had to grow up. But there's another side, see. Truth is, he's extremely smart. The stammering throws people off, too, I'm sure of that. He's a real worrier, always—what's the word—brooding, that's it. Brooding. Real sensitive about some things. But yeah, Emmett can speak Spanish. Maybe better than English." She laughed again. "You know what? I don't think he stutters as much in Spanish. I could never figure that out."

"How did he learn to—"

"Oh, boy. There's a long story."

"I'm not in a hurry," Earl assured her. "Is there more coffee?"

"We both took Spanish a couple of years in high school," she said, when they returned from her kitchen. "But that's not the story."

"What is?"

Edna took a gulp of coffee. "The '36 Olympics, in Berlin ... no, I'd have to go back even further. There was talk about boycotting the 'Hitler Games,' they called it. Emmett made the team again, and right away he had people pulling at him, one way and the other. Seemed like one day he's going to Berlin, next day he's going to this other event ... I think they called it the 'Freedom Games.' In Spain, it was going to be, but then they started fighting there."

She lit another cigarette and continued, "So anyway, Emmett went to the Berlin Olympics. He won a bronze medal, you know."

"I do know," said Earl. "He was great."

"Oh, yes," Edna continued. "But what he saw there in Berlin shocked him. All the flags, the uniforms, the marching, the shouting. Everything he'd heard about the Nazis was true, or even worse than he expected. I wish I'd kept his letters. Emmett went on and on about it, in those letters. Ended up by saying he was going from Germany to England, then to be a freedom fighter in Spain. Which is what he did. That's what he told me, anyhow."

"He wrote you about this?"

"Yep. Nine or ten times. And I burned all of them, damn it."

"So he went to England?"

"Stayed there a few months. From his letters, it sounded like school almost. Learning Spanish and reading and going to meetings, classes it seemed like, all about politics and the 'struggle' in Spain, they called it. Then he wrote to me from Paris, where he was about to go south on a train. By this time it was the spring of 1937."

"Did he go to Spain?"

"Oh, yes. The last letter was from Marseilles, later that year. It was short, just saying he had gotten out of Spain, and he was coming home."

"When did you see him?"

"Somewhere between Thanksgiving and Christmas. He was the same old Emmett, except when he'd get wound up and talking about the 'struggle' over there and the 'struggle' here. It was tiring to be around him sometimes. Really exhausting, frankly. Some adventures he had, though."

"What were they? His adventures."

"His 'brigade,' Emmett called it. They actually walked over the mountains to get into Spain." Again Edna laughed. "He was so serious about it, but once in a while there would be a funny part, usually about himself. The brigade didn't have real army uniforms, I guess. Emmett's description of his own outfit was a riot. He'd been given some boots, but after that it was dungarees, a sweater from the Hungarian Olympic team, his own blazer, and a wool, tweed golf cap he'd gotten in London. He thought he looked like a lunatic bird-watcher."

"Did he fight?"

"It's odd," Edna replied, "but I never could figure that out. There was a lot of time he sat in bars and restaurants, seems like, but he did talk about being at the 'front,' whatever that was. He wasn't hurt, that I know, but did he fight? With a gun? I don't know. Sounds silly, but I don't."

"Did he say why he came home?"

"He wanted to 'struggle' here, is what he said. 'Try to get my own country into the great battle against fascism.' Emmett had a lot of slogans, you see."

"So he doesn't care for the Nazis, I take it?"

"Oh, boy. Last time I talked to him was a week ago ... whenever it was that Germany declared war against us. Emmett called me with the news. Which I'd already heard, but he wanted to make sure I knew. You know what? He sounded happier than he's been in years, I swear. Happy as a pig in the mud. So if this job has anything to do with fighting against the Nazis, I'd say you got the right man for it."

That answers my assigned questions, Earl thought, as he stood up to leave. *You could mark me down as someone who never, ever figured Emmett Carson was a deep thinker.*

"Thank you for your time, Miss Sampson," he said.

"Sure."

"What happened to ... why did you burn his letters?"

"He asked me to."

"When?"

Edna Sampson tilted her head back and exhaled a cloud of smoke. "Last week," she said.

Twenty-Eight

SANTA MONICA EVENING OUTLOOK
Friday, December 19, 1941
JAP SUB ATTACKS ANOTHER TANKER!
Raiders Hound American Craft
Only Two Miles Off California

A Japanese submarine attacked the Standard Oil tanker H.M. Storey today off Point Arguello, 175 miles north of Los Angeles. It was the fourth submarine attack on U.S. shipping off the California coast in the last forty-eight hours. A Coast Guardsman said the attack could be seen plainly from the shore.

Other attacks were on a Richfield tanker off Monterey; on a General Petroleum tanker off Cape Mendocino, with three crewmen dead, three missing, and five wounded; and on the Hammond Lumber Company freighter Samoa, between Los Angeles and San Diego.

Survivors from the General Petroleum tanker, Emidio, landed at Eureka this morning. They reported that the submarine that torpedoed them also shelled them as they struggled to escape in open lifeboats.

*   *   *   *

The telephone rang at eight.
"Earl Brady speaking."
"Hello."

"Ted Lindgren?"

"Yes," came the stiff reply.

Here we go again, Earl thought. "Do you want to hear about Edna Sampson?"

"Yeah. Just kidding. We can have a real conversation this time. I'm alone. Everything all right there?"

"No, to be honest about it. I was just reading about all the Jap submarine attacks. Within sight of the California coastline, I mean. Christ's sake, Ted, you can stand on the beaches and watch."

"There was a meeting today about that," Lindgren said. "Japanese language radio communications are apparently continuous out there. Constant operation. Western Defense Command is nuts about it."

"They damn well should be."

"Things are starting to happen," Lindgren said. "The Japanese residents, I mean. When every ship sailing from our Pacific ports is attacked, well, measures will be taken. So don't be surprised by it, Earl."

The doorbell rang. He could hear Doris walking to answer it. "Ask who it is, sweetheart," he shouted. "Sorry, Ted. Go on. It's probably our son getting home from work. He's guarding Santa Monica beach with a pistol."

"Oh Jesus. Well, if there's anything I can do for him ..."

"I might take you up on that sometime."

"Yeah. Well, tell me about Edna Sampson."

"She's known Carson since they were kids. Their serious romance ended several years ago, I think, but they seem to be friends. Edna's a drunk. Sad, because I'd say she was probably a real dish before all the whiskey. Anyway ... Carson does speak Spanish, very well according to her."

"All right."

"How he learned to speak it is a surprise. It was to me, anyway."

Doris was knocking on the door frame between the kitchen and living room. Earl looked up to see her with Tim Tanaka, who gave a small wave, then disappeared into the kitchen.

"Oh?" Lindgren said.

"I don't want to repeat things you already know about Carson," said Earl.

Lindgren didn't take the bait. "What did Edna say?"

"That Carson went to Spain after the 1936 Olympics. Studied the language in London for some time before actually entering Spain with one of the brigades. Came back at the end of 1937, talking nonstop about the worldwide struggle against fascism."

"Anything else?"

"Not really. He hates the Nazis. That was the other question, right?"

"Right."

"This was a real surprise to me, all of this," Earl said. Lindgren made no reply.

"I don't think I told you," Earl went on, "I only know Carson as a swimming coach and a beach lifeguard. I didn't think he ever had a serious thought about politics in his life."

"Excellent," Lindgren said "That helps. We're grateful to you for covering this. Edna Sampson was just one more thing—I ran out of time. So, thanks again."

"Planning any more visits?"

"Nothing firm, but I think so. Probably. I'll call you about it. I should buy you another dinner. Mexican food this time. I miss it."

*   *   *   *

Tim Tanaka sat at the kitchen table, alone, drinking a bottle of Coke and looking at the newspaper headlines. He started to jump up, but Earl motioned him to stay.

"Tim. Sorry about the phone calls."

"Hello, Mr. Brady." They shook hands, and Earl sat down. "Mrs. Brady went next door," Tim said. "She said to tell you she'll be back in a few minutes."

"Right. So, how are you?"

Tim extended a hand at the newspaper headlines. "Not so good," he said. "How is John?"

"Bored, most of the time. I guess they've taught him how to shoot a gun. Whether he could hit anything, I don't know. Most of the time I think he just drives around freezing his ass off."

The banter appeared to have a calming effect. Tim smiled and nodded.

"I came over to talk about the sword," he said. I think I have a … I suppose you would call it a lead."

"Good. We like leads."

Tim gave a sigh. "There are a lot of Japanese people living in Mexico."

"Mexico," Earl repeated.

"Yes. A lot of fishermen in Lower California, but really all over. Mexico City, especially." Tim rubbed the tablecloth. "My lead is that the sword might have come from a shop in Tijuana."

"Can you explain this a little more?"

"There's a good chance that the sword's a fake," said Tim. "A reproduction, just to have as a souvenir. There's a place in Tijuana that sells them. It's called *El Sol Naciente*. I can find out for certain, if I can get the sword."

"I don't think that's possible, but I'll check," Earl said. "What's fake about it?"

"It's a real sword," said Tim. "They're big and heavy. Sharp, too. You could hurt somebody with one of them, that's for sure. It's just that they aren't made in Japan, or used by Japanese soldiers. The shop down there in Mexico sells them for souvenirs, or decorations, or gifts, like I said."

"How can you tell this one's a souvenir?"

"All of the Mexican ones I've seen have black and red handles. That could be just a coincidence. But then there's the engraving. The Tijuana shop does that. And also, the date. Real ones don't have dates on them."

Twenty-Nine

To Earl's surprise, Gorman took his call on Monday morning.

"Mr. Brady, good morning. What can I do for you?"

Routine. Just another case. "Just briefly, I wanted to mention something about the Jordan murder."

"Shoot."

"It's about that sword. I only got a quick peek at it, the night Jordan's body was found. But didn't it have some engraving on the blade? Near the handle?"

"Yeah, I think so. Something in Japanese. Not surprising."

"Right," said Earl. "But listen ... stop me if you've already covered any of this. I was talking with some LAPD boys last week; they've helped with arresting Japanese nationals. We were—just small talk, swapping stories. We were talking about items they'd found in the possession of these people. Cameras, radios, explosives, you know what I mean. It turns out they've come across a number of swords. The Samurai weapons, same things. Anyway, it sounds like most of the ones people have in their houses aren't really army swords. A whole lot of them are made to be souvenirs. Decorations, maybe. Point is, there's a shop in Tijuana that sells 'em. It might be worth checking. Or I could do it, if you want. I could have somebody—"

"No," Gorman finally interrupted, "We'll look into it. But thanks. I hadn't heard this. What's the shop called?"

"*El Sol Naciente.* The Rising Sun."

"Clever. Say, thanks again, Mr. Brady. I'll see what we can do."

*   *   *   *

It was just before noon when Earl got out of the elevator and walked toward his office. He had finished a sentencing appearance, spoken to a *Los Angeles Times* reporter about the case (arson in the garment district), and was ready for some lunch. As he rounded the corner and entered the secretaries' area, he saw Detective Lester Smith talking to Maria.

"Smith. Hello there."

"Hello, sir. See you for a minute?"

"Come on in." Earl motioned to his office.

Smith sat in the visitor's chair and extracted a small notebook from his coat. "Mr. Brady," he said, "it's about the Jordan homicide."

"Call me Earl. But I thought you weren't working on that."

"Yes and no." Smith paused. "Want to hear it?"

Earl clasped his hands behind his head and leaned back. "I interrupted, sorry. Please go on."

"I received a message, came in yesterday morning, to call your boss Mr. Fletcher. He didn't sound too good. Talking in a sort of scratchy whisper, worse than the other time, but anyway, he asked me to interview Colonel Jordan's neighbors. Find out if anybody saw him leave, or anything else, on that Friday. He said to tell you about any results."

Earl leaned forward, elbows on the desk. "What about the FBI? It's their case, isn't it?"

"Well," Smith replied, "I reminded Mr. Fletcher of that. He told me to go ahead—these were his instructions. Told me he'd say so, if there was a beef."

"His instructions."

"Yep."

Good, Earl thought. *I've got help. Thanks again, Bud.*

"Go on," he told Smith.

"Well, I went over there yesterday, right around lunchtime. Just me. I talked to …" Smith tapped a finger down a page of his notebook. "Six people. One of them, lady across the street, saw something. Saw Jordan leaving. She said it was about noon, maybe, on Friday. Yellow cab stopped at the curb and honked—that's why she pulled back her curtains and looked. Jordan walked out and got right into the cab."

"Did she see the driver?"

"No. Wasn't paying that much attention. She didn't remember whether Jordan was carrying anything. But she knows him. It was definitely Jordan."

"Goddamn it," Earl said. "I just missed him by a few hours, then."

"There's more," Smith said. "I spent some time last night and this morning with the taxi companies. I got a little help, but don't worry, I didn't explain the story to my people. We called every cab dispatch number in Los Angeles County, all … let's see, forty-one of 'em. I had to visit six personally to get cooperation, but we covered all of these places. If this was a dispatched cab, which it was, there should be a record of the address, right?"

"Right. But there is none?"

"There is none," said Smith, flipping shut his notebook. "What do you want me to do?"

I want you to forgive me for doubting you, Earl thought. Then he asked, "Did the FBI talk to any of these neighbors?"

"Nope. They all told me I was the first. I guess I should have—"

"Don't beat yourself up," Earl interrupted. "You did fine, Lester. We can't roust the neighbors out of their houses every time a grown man misses an appointment. You had a brand-new possible missing person. Possible. The FBI, on the other hand, has a dead body. They're the ones who ought to feel funny about not interviewing the neighbors, for crying out loud." Earl reached for a pencil and wrote his home address on a scrap of paper.

"Pick me up at my house," he said, "tomorrow morning at eight. We're going to go talk to somebody else."

Thirty

Earl was drinking coffee when he saw, through the front window, Lester Smith's unmarked car pull to a stop. It was ten minutes before eight.

"Morning, Lester." Earl pulled the passenger door shut.

"Earl. So, where to?"

"Not far. 1311 Euclid. Just go east on Wilshire. Euclid is where Thirteenth Street would be, if people weren't superstitious. Go slow so I can explain." Smith eased off the gas pedal.

"Edna Sampson," Earl began. "Former girlfriend of Emmett Carson. He's the swimming coach at USC, beach lifeguard, bit parts in a couple of movies, swam in the Olympic Games twice. Also, he's a Communist."

Smith laughed. "Sorry," he said. "Go on."

"I know, I know. Here's the thing. Edna drives a cab. Edna *has* a cab. It was in her parking place when I saw her before, not long ago."

"We're going to go ask *her* about Walter Jordan?"

"Sort of. I'll do the talking."

"Good idea. Tell me, though, how many cabs are there in Los Angeles, do you suppose? Just roughly?"

"I have my suspicions here, Lester. Humor me. This won't take long. Sorry it's so early, but his lady's a drinker. Got to get her first thing if we want her sober. Euclid is the next street. Make a right."

A minute later, Earl was leading Smith down a sloping driveway, two concrete strips with crabgrass along the middle. He pointed to a door marked "C" but motioned at Smith to continue. At the bottom of the driveway, to their left, was a covered carport. A yellow cab was parked in one of the spaces, marked with a white "C" painted on the concrete. Earl nodded at Smith, who looked at his watch. He seemed bored.

They rang and knocked for a full minute, at least, before they heard slippers flapping across a hardwood floor. The door opened a few inches, until a chain stopped it.

"Edna?" said Earl, badge in hand. "Mr. Brady again. DA's office."

The door closed, then reopened. Edna Sampson wore a white cloth bathrobe with a cigarette burn in the lapel. Her bleached hair was flattened to her skull on one side, sticking out in several directions on the other. Her breath smelled like a horse's. "Come on in," she half whispered.

Smith stood in the doorway, holding his badge at shoulder height, as if taking an oath. "Lester Smith, LAPD," he said to the back of Edna's robe. She waved him in without looking.

"Sit down," she said, pointing to the card table. "I'll be out in a minute. Turn on some lights."

Earl looked around the room. On a shelf behind a bamboo-framed brown sofa were several photographs he hadn't noticed before. Kneeling on the cushion, he recognized one as Carson, smiling, waving in his Olympic-team blazer. 1932, Earl guessed; Carson looked about John's age. Two of the pictures included a younger Edna. "Come here," Earl said to Smith. "Look."

Smith leaned close and whistled softly. "Built," he whispered. Hearing the bathroom door open, they quickly sat at the table.

Edna came in wearing khaki pants, a loose cotton sweater, and a knotted scarf. She had brushed her teeth, for which her morning visitors gave silent thanks.

"More questions about our friend?" she asked, sitting on the sofa.

"A few questions, Edna," Earl said. "About you, actually."

She didn't seem to like that. Edna looked at Smith and narrowed her bloodshot eyes, then turned back to Earl.

"How long have you been driving a cab?" he asked.

"Couple of years."

"What'd you do before that?"

"Different things. Waitress, mostly."

"You like driving better?"

"It's fine." Edna stood and walked to a small end table to retrieve a pack of Lucky Strikes and a matchbook.

"How'd you happen to become a ... driver? Don't see too many ladies—"

"Yeah, that's true. I don't drive it at night. Not that anybody does, this last month. I don't take the risk. No sense ... what did you ask me?"

"How did you—"

"Oh yeah. A friend of my father's. My godfather, in fact. It's his company. His cab. He just lets me keep it here." She lit a cigarette and shook the match out.

"How do you get your fares?"

"Dispatcher calls me. Sometimes Joe calls me—that's the owner—he'll call me himself, now and then. They're nice to me. Joe and my daddy were best friends." She looked at Smith again, then blew smoke at the ceiling. "My license is current. It's valid."

"Oh, I know it is," Earl lied. "We were just curious. Anybody else ever drive that cab? The one down in the back here?"

"Well, I—" She stopped and rubbed an index finger back and forth across her lips. Then she folded her arms and turned her head, staring at the door.

"Edna," said Earl softly, "I won't tell Joe. We're not here about company rules, I promise. We don't care what the company rules are. Promise."

She puffed her cheeks and exhaled. "Maybe a couple of times."

Earl nodded slowly, watching her.

"But not for fares," she said, raising a finger and wagging it side to side. "No, sir, I'd never let him do that. He doesn't have that kind of license. I made him swear."

Earl swallowed, then picked his fingernails. It was time to take a chance. Edna had mentioned no names, but he would. *Routine,* he said to himself. "Emmett doesn't have that license?"

"Right," she answered. "But the cab was fine. He didn't go far with it, but even so he put gas in it. Just a couple of times. He had my permission. Emmett wasn't doing anything wrong. Anybody was wrong, it was me."

"Yeah. Edna, don't worry. Like I said, we're not going to let you get in any trouble about this." He looked at Smith, who was staring wide-eyed but recovered and then said, "That's right, ma'am. Don't worry."

"Did he borrow it recently?" Earl asked.

She sniffled, then tucked some stray hair under the scarf. "Few weeks ago, I think."

"During the day?"

"Yeah, just for an afternoon. Maybe three, four hours."

"Remember what day?"

She shook her head slowly and stubbed out her Lucky Strike in a seashell ashtray.

"Was it a Friday?" Earl asked.

She pushed a few more blond strands under the scarf. "I'm not sure. Maybe."

"Was it before the Pearl Harbor attack? That was on a Sunday."

"Yeah," she replied. "I think maybe it was that Friday. Just a day or two before the bombing."

"Did Emmett say why he wanted to borrow it?"

"I think he told me his own car was at the mechanic's," she replied. "Lube, tires, I forget. He just needed it for a little while."

"Bring it back that day?"

"Oh, yes. By around four, I think. I remember that because I called in and got a fare I had to pick up at five, over in Pacific Palisades. I offered to take Emmett to the mechanic's, but he had a ride with somebody else."

"Who was that?"

"Oh, I don't know. Couple of men in another car. I didn't recognize them."

*   *   *   *

SANTA MONICA EVENING OUTLOOK
Tuesday, December 23, 1941
COASTAL TANKER SUNK BY JAP SUB

Japanese submarines sank the Union Oil tanker Montebello and shelled the Richfield tanker Larry Doheny in new attacks on U.S. shipping off the central California Coast during the night, Twelfth Naval District Headquarters announced today. They were the fifth and sixth attacks in California waters since last Thursday.

All thirty-six members of the Montebello's crew survived, escaping to shore in lifeboats. The ship was destroyed by one direct torpedo hit and a shell, one of several fired, that struck the fore section of the vessel.

The battle was observed from the shore by crowds of people at Cambria Pines. The local newspaper's editor said the firing was audible from shore and that flashes of gunfire were visible in the early morning darkness.

*   *   *   *

Earl folded the newspaper and tossed it into the backseat with the Christmas packages. As he started the car, he was startled by a knock on the rear window. John appeared at the passenger door, then slid into the seat.

"Going my way?"

"This is a nice surprise, John. Off early?"

"Yeah. Shifts are shorter now, eight hours usually. More regular Coast Guard or navy, and I think they have more spotter planes around now, too."

Earl shifted the Chrysler's gears as they crossed Wilshire. "Same places?"

"Yeah. State Beach, down to Venice or up to Malibu a few times a day."

They stopped at a red light, and Earl looked at John. "I saw Tim Tanaka last night."

"I know," John said. "I had lunch with him today. He told me he's seen you."

Earl looked quizzically at John, who said, "Don't worry, Dad. I tried, but Tim wouldn't tell me anything. I don't know what he's doing for you."

At home they emptied the backseat, putting the Christmas boxes in the hallway closet. John dropped his knapsack onto the kitchen table with a heavy thud.

"Be careful with that thing," said Earl, reaching into the refrigerator. "Safety on?"

"Yeah, it's fine."

Earl took a drink of beer. "Do you see Coach Carson very much?"

"Most days. I saw him this morning."

"How's he doing?"

"He's on his way to Washington for a few days," John replied. "Flying out tonight."

"Washington?"

"Interviews for a job, he says. He told me before that he might be going out of the country if he gets the job. Whatever the job is. He's not supposed to say. I just know he's gone until the twenty-eighth, and I have a couple of extra shifts."

Thirty-One

Earl was on his way out the door of his office at 2:00 PM on Christmas Eve when Maria's telephone rang. She put a hand over the mouthpiece and whispered, "Gorman. FBI."

He nodded and pointed to his office. "One moment, please, Mr. Gorman," Maria said.

"Brady speaking."

"I did some following up on the Tijuana angle," Gorman said. "Thought I'd fill you in."

"Thanks."

"It's hard to get solid information out of Mexico, sometimes."

"I know," Earl said.

"Even harder now. *El Sol Naciente* closed up in a big hurry on December 8 or December 9, best we can tell. You were right, though, it did sell a lot of Japanese military souvenirs. Including swords. Engraved while you wait. But that's about all we know. They burned their records."

"Did they leave anything behind?"

"Almost nothing. The owners went to Brazil, we think."

Earl remembered a statistic from a Public Safety Committee briefing: there were an estimated 250,000 Japanese nationals living in Brazil.

"We aren't going to find them down there," Earl said. "Any other leads in Tijuana?"

"No. The Mexican government is getting ready to remove all of its Japanese residents from coastal areas. Makes it even harder than usual to pursue something like this."

"Right. Thanks again for the call, though. Merry Christmas."

"Yeah. Same."

Maria stopped him again as he tried to leave. "Somebody else just called. Tim. A friend of John's. He wants you to call him at this number."

Earl took the message slip into his office, closing the door this time. He agreed to meet Tim Tanaka at 3:30.

*   *   *   *

Earl led Tim into the backyard.

Who dropped you off?

My sister, back in fifteen minutes. Thinks I'm talking to John.

Thanks again for looking into the sword. Can I do something for you?

Other way around. I can do more for you on the murder case. I think I can help. That's why I'm here.

Appreciate the offer. But you need to be careful.

That's what my parents have been doing ever since they arrived. But this has always been my home, Mr. Brady. If I have to take some chances to prove I belong here, then I'll take them.

What can I—

You can trust me. Tell me more about this, please. Let me help.

Ten minutes later, a car horn sounded. Earl watched through a window as Tim opened the passenger door. *God help us if I'm wrong about this*, he thought. It was the closest he'd come to praying in a long, long time.

Thirty-Two

SANTA MONICA EVENING OUTLOOK
Thursday, December 25, 1941
JAP SUB SUNK OFF CALIFORNIA COAST

An army bomber sank a Japanese submarine off the California coast today. Three bombs were dropped, and an explosion followed, filling the sea with debris. It was the first reported sinking of an enemy under-sea craft since Japanese subs opened a campaign against California coastal shipping last Thursday. Since then the submarines had attacked nine ships, sunk one, and damaged two others, killing six seamen and injuring nine.

The bomber victory was described in a War Department communiqué issued in Washington. Wartime regulations prevented disclosure of the exact scene of the sinking. The bomber, apparently on coastal patrol, caught the submarine on the surface. The boat attempted to escape by diving. A bomb was dropped, and the submarine rose suddenly to the surface again. "Two more bombs were dropped, apparently scoring direct hits and filling the air with debris," the War Department said.

✳   ✳   ✳   ✳

"I think it's lousy, John," Doris complained. "Midnight to eight on Christmas night?"

John was pulling a sweater on, to be followed by the red lifeguard jacket and wool mittens. A red jeep was coasting to a stop in front of the house.

"There he is," John said. He kissed his mother's forehead. "I thought this would be better than four to midnight. I might have missed the pumpkin pie."

"Be careful," she said. "Got the turkey sandwiches?"

"Yep. Thanks, Mother. Go to bed. See you in the morning."

He jogged out to the jeep, took the passenger seat, and opened his knapsack. "Sandwich, Billy?"

"Yeah, thanks," the other lifeguard said. "I'll take it when you drop me off at the house."

"How was it tonight?"

"Wild. Compared to the other days, anyway. They sank a Jap submarine earlier today, up north a ways."

"I know. It was on the radio. Afternoon paper, too."

"After that there were about a dozen calls, I hear, from people who were sure they sighted other ones. Who knows? No shooting or anything out here, though."

Billy picked up the radio mike. "Jeep three, Thompson to headquarters."

"Go ahead."

"Shift change. I have Brady. He will proceed in after dropping me off. Over."

"Roger. Time estimate, please. Over."

"Say not later than 12:30," John whispered.

"Estimate no later than zero thirty, zero three zero. Out."

The damp air stung John's face as they picked up speed on Pacific Coast Highway.

"You pulled one of these late-night shifts before, Billy?" John shouted over the wind.

"Just once."

"How's it work?"

"Just stay warm, and it isn't so bad. You'll be inside headquarters a lot of the time. People know the beaches are closed. It's not like before."

After leaving Billy at his parents' house in Pacific Palisades, John drove the jeep slowly out Sunset Boulevard to begin his shift.

*   *   *   *

Hours later, Tim Tanaka crouched between the end of a tall hedge and the trunk of a eucalyptus tree. He was wearing the darkest clothes he owned and a borrowed knit cap. He carried a flashlight and a small screwdriver. He had never broken the law in his life, but at 4:30 AM on December 26, 1941, he was trespassing, he was violating the Santa Monica city curfew, and he was about to commit a burglary.

In his Christmas Eve argument with Earl Brady, Tim had insisted on doing it. "I know that house, Mr. Brady. I'm going."

He did know Emmett Carson's house. He had been there during the summer five or six times, for after-work social gatherings. It was a backyard guest cottage, separated from the two-story main house by what seemed half a football field of lawn, in the center of which was a swimming pool.

Tim had waited five minutes, in the space between the hedge and the tree, after scampering down the driveway past the big house. It had occurred to him for the first time, during his driveway dash, that the owners might have a dog, but nothing had moved. No sounds. No lights. No passing traffic on Idaho Street.

Running a flashlight beam along the ground, he could see that he was about thirty yards from the cottage, which sat in a rear corner of the property. He stood and began walking, slowly, along the hedge. He trained the beam just ahead, at the base of the tall bushes' row of trunks. He brushed the leaves with the fingertips of his free hand as he crept forward.

There was just one door, he knew. He ran to it and found it locked, but he also remembered windows at the rear. He moved quietly to the back. He guided the beam up to the bathroom window. Too high to reach, too small to get through. It would have to be the kitchen.

Tim squatted behind the house and waited another few minutes. It would be easier to run away from somebody before he got inside than after, he figured. So Tim waited. Then he took a deep breath and stood up again.

The chest-high kitchen window was almost too easy. He made a small noise ripping the wire screen with his screwdriver, a tear just big enough to allow him to reach in and pop up the latch. He lowered the wood-framed screen onto the ground. The window itself had no lock, and its poor fit was the only obstacle to raising the lower half. The warped and swollen wood groaned as Tim pushed. He waited again. Then he pulled himself up and in.

Tim scanned the kitchen table and counters with his flashlight. He saw only a small stack of newspapers, then moved into the living room and walked through to the bedroom. Carson's lifeguard parka was tossed across the unmade bed. There was an open closet with a few pairs of shoes on its floor.

He stopped his light on a bedside table. There was a lamp and a book. Tim stepped toward it, anxious to see more. It was a volume of English poetry. Some folded onionskin paper protruded from the top and bottom, just inside the back cover. Tim pulled it out. It seemed to be four or five pages, with typing on it. He squatted down and unfolded the paper, putting it on the floor and aiming his flashlight down.

BACK DOOR TO ANOTHER WAR?
By W.J.

This week's publication, in the Chicago Daily Tribune and other leading newspapers, of "FDR'S WAR PLANS" (see illustration) is surely an embarrassment to Mr. Roosevelt, who vowed repeatedly, in his 1940 campaign, that American boys "are not going to be sent into any foreign wars." The War Department's plan reveals otherwise. In fact, it calls for some five million Americans to be fighting on the European continent by mid-1943 with the objective of defeating Hitler and his Italian Axis partner. In the coming year and a half, according to the document, the United States must dedicate its resources not only to raising and training such a force but also overcoming a desperate shortage of equipment.

What does this mean? It means that America's unpreparedness for war has been advertised to the world. According to well-placed sources, the most dire consequence of this publicity is not the president's embarrassment. Nor is it the smile on Adolph Hitler's face. The most immediate and catastrophic reaction may be expected to come—these sources say—from Japan, the newest member of the Axis. The Japanese government has now been informed, by the publication of these plans, that the United States cannot …

Tim heard a key in the door. He quickly stuffed the pages in his back pocket and clicked off the flashlight.

"You wait out here," someone growled, in an accent Tim couldn't identify. He heard footsteps in the living room. He tiptoed to the doorway and stood beside it, pressing his back to the bedroom wall. Another flashlight beam played across Carson's bed as the footsteps approached. Tim breathed as slowly as he could. The man stopped, just short of the bedroom, and trained his flashlight on the bedside table, on the book. Tim held his breath.

As the man walked into the bedroom, toward the table, Tim darted behind him, through the living room and into the kitchen.

"Hey!"

Tim vaulted over the kitchen sink and out of the window in one motion. His flashlight clattered in the porcelain sink as his hands broke the short fall onto the dirt.

"Victor!" shouted the man, now in the kitchen. "In back!"

Tim rounded the corner of the cottage to see another flashlight beam. He turned and ran to the back again, then continued around the other side. Something grabbed the back of his sweater, and he turned to see a light swinging downward at his head. He put a hand up and felt metal hit the side of his wrist. He grabbed onto the man's long flashlight, spun hard, and fell to the grass, now holding the flashlight. He rolled away from an attempted kick, then swung the flashlight at the man's knee. His first try missed, but then he connected with a loud crack against a shinbone. The man groaned and fell onto his side. Tim got up and ran toward the main house, followed by the footsteps and puffing of his pursuers.

When he reached the street he saw their car, facing east. *I can buy a few seconds by going the other way,* he thought. He was almost a full block ahead when he heard the car start. By the time he sensed it gaining on him, he was crossing Ocean Avenue. The road down to Pacific Coast Highway and the water was a hundred yards away. He turned for it.

The car's headlights switched off as it drew even with Tim, who was running parallel to the low fence at the edge of the steep bluffs. The passenger cupped his hands around his mouth and shouted, "Stop! You cannot get away!"

Tim kept running. He couldn't see the man's face, but he did see the shotgun barrel come out of the window. The man brandished the weapon, holding it vertically to the ground. "You want this? Stop now!" he screamed.

Tim ran on, watching too, as the shotgun was pulled back into the car. They were almost at the turnoff down to the shoreline. The gun barrel came out again. Tim saw a flash and felt a glancing slap at the back of his left leg. He veered right and kept running, now moving sharply downhill. He knew this stretch. They had nearly reached a spot where he could lose the car.

First, though, he had to cross the road. The car was about to pull even with him again, and the shotgun would be reloaded by now. Tim broke to his left, crossing in front of the car, which now sped up and passed him, then stopped. The passenger had jumped out and was leveling the gun's barrel at Tim as he slipped under the wood rail and rolled out of sight.

He could hear the car coming back up the hill, and the men shouting at each other, as he slid feet-first down the rough hillside toward Pacific Coast Highway, a hundred feet below. *This part slopes,* he thought, *but I'll have to jump the last—what? Ten feet? Twenty?*

Tim reached the edge and skidded to a stop. The flashlight beam was about fifty feet to his right. His wrist was throbbing. He reached into his pocket and removed the paper wad. Then he stuffed it into a crevice at the base of a small bush and put a rock over it. He grabbed the edge of the concrete retaining wall and lowered himself over the side.

His right ankle collapsed under him as he landed. He started running—it hurt, but it worked. He crossed the highway and reached the sand. He pulled off his shoes and was halfway to the water before he heard the tires screeching in the parking lot behind him.

He tore off his clothes when he felt wet sand. Pants, sweater. Socks could wait. Keep the shorts on. He hit the water, which was even colder than he'd expected. He swam hard, about fifty yards on six breaths, then stopped and looked back. He thought he heard voices, so he slipped under water and started out again, swimming another twenty-five yards, by his stroke count, from shore. He could see the pier outlined against the night sky, a half mile to the south. He floated on his back for a minute then swam there, slowly, rhythmically. *Just a long, easy warm up,* he told himself. It calmed his nerves, the familiar tempo of reaching, rolling, pulling, kicking.

They had the goods on Carson, Tim knew. He hadn't found everything he'd gone looking for, but Jordan's article was enough. All he had to do was get out of the water and find it.

*   *   *   *

John Brady was struggling to stay awake as he cruised along the wind-blown winter sand of State Beach. The dawn sunlight was in his eyes. He fumbled through his knapsack for sunglasses. They weren't there.

Squinting, he approached the long shadow of the pier. He stopped the jeep a hundred yards short and clicked on the radio. It was 6:50 AM.

"Jeep three, Brady to headquarters."

"Go ahead."

"I am southbound, a hundred yards north of Santa Monica pier. All is well from here. Over."

"Roger. Call again when you reach the south side. Over."

"Roger, will do. Out."

The jeep was not quite under the pier when John heard his own name. A voice was coming from the direction of the water.

"Over here! John, it's me!"

He turned the jeep toward the water's edge and saw arms, waving from the small surf that was slapping and sloshing against the round, wooden pier pilings. He stopped on the wet sand and jumped out of the jeep.

"Tim? Jesus, what are you doing?"

Tim was now knee-deep, walking out of the water. John grabbed a blanket from the rear of the jeep and met his shivering, underwear-clad friend. He pulled the towel from around his neck. "Here. Jesus, Tim, you're almost blue. You all right?"

Tim rubbed himself with the towel, then wrapped the blanket around his shoulders. "Cold, but I'm all right. My wrist—never mind. I'll explain this. Can we find a telephone where you can call my sister?"

John radioed to headquarters and falsely reported nothing, then drove the jeep up to the coffee shop at Pico and Ocean. Tim sat with a towel covering his head and most of his face. John went inside and called Alice Tanaka, then bought four doughnuts.

"Breakfast," he said to Tim as they drove away. "A warm shower is next. Alice will meet us at my house."

Tim was still shivering as he ate. "Thanks, John."

"Yeah, well, you're welcome, but maybe you should tell me what the fuck is going on."

"I will, I promise. Can't tell you the whole story yet. It has to do with the work I've been doing for your dad. I think I found what he needed, but there was a problem getting away from somebody."

"That's it? You found something and there was a problem with somebody?"

"No, that's not it. That's part of it. I promise to tell you the rest."

"When?"

"Maybe in a couple of hours. I need to see Alice, and I need to see your dad, maybe."

"Maybe, huh?"

"I have to find something," Tim said.

"This is killing me."

"I'm sorry. I don't blame you. Just bear with me, all right?"

They parked the jeep at the curb. Doris was in the kitchen.

"John, hello … my God, is that Tim?"

"Hello, Mrs. Brady," Tim said, shuddering. "Sorry about this."

They had agreed on a story. "Tim got roughed up by some jerks. His sister's going to come pick him up here. He just needs a shower and some clothes."

"Well, sure, we—"

"Is Dad up yet?"

"He already left. You just missed him."

"I have to go sign out," John said. "Tim, how about if you and Alice pick me up in front of HQ at eight?"

"Least I can do," Tim said as Doris led him, limping, to the shower.

"Jeep three, Brady to Headquarters."

"Go ahead. Where have you been? Over."

It was almost 7:30, and he was still parked in front of his house. "Sorry, had radio problems for a few minutes there. On my way in. Over."

"Roger. Out."

He started the jeep and drove away. Remembering the blanket, he turned a block later and went back.

"John," his mother said as he walked in.

"I forgot the blanket," he explained, hurrying past her. He reached into the steamy bathroom and grabbed the green blanket off the floor. Tim didn't seem to hear him.

"Coast Guard property, Mother. I don't want to be court-martialed."

"Is he hurt?" Doris asked.

"Nothing serious," John said. "His sister is a nurse, so she'll know. I think he just twisted an ankle."

"Who—"

"I have to hurry, mother. I'll be back in a little while."

Thirty-Three

He had decided to wait for Alice and Tim at the side of Pacific Coast Highway, across the parking lot from the Lifeguard Headquarters Building. He was eating orange wedges from a paper bag. It was almost 8:30 when he saw Tim waving from the passenger window of a blue Ford sedan.

John tossed his knapsack into the backseat and climbed in. "Morning, Alice."

She smiled into the rearview. "Hi, John. Thank you for rescuing my baby brother here."

Tim was staring ahead. "What's the medical report?" John asked.

"I don't think he broke anything. Contusion, big tender bruise, on his wrist. A mild ankle sprain. I taped that up, and your mother gave him aspirin. Some scratches on the back of his leg. He still won't say what happened, exactly, the little bum."

"I told you both, I have to find something." Tim was wearing one of John's sweatshirts.

"Then find it!" Alice demanded. "Start looking, at least."

"No—I know right where it is," Tim said. "As long as nobody stole it, I'll have it in ten minutes. Fifteen, tops."

Alice looked at John in the mirror again, shaking her head.

"This better be good," she muttered.

"Where are we going?" John asked. Alice was stopped, waiting to turn left into Santa Monica Canyon.

"Up to Ocean Avenue," she said. "Then Sherlock Holmes is going to tell me what to do next."

"Just drive the car," Tim groaned.

He had Alice park at the curb on Ocean, just south of the California Avenue incline, where he'd slid down the hill a few hours earlier, in the dark, being chased by two strangers with a shotgun. He'd tell them everything, he promised, whether the paper wad was still there or not. It would just seem more—what? Worth it, he thought, if he could just retrieve this thing.

"Wait here. I'll be back in about five minutes."

"Where are you going?" John asked.

"Not far. Just wait here," Tim said, closing the car door. They watched him hobble quickly to the top of the incline, then continue down, disappearing.

Alice turned. "Do you have any idea, John—"

"He says it has to do with something he's helping my dad investigate. I knew he was doing work for my dad, but I thought it was just translating. I don't see how that gets you beat up and halfway drowned. You should've seen him, Alice. It was like a movie. Shipwreck survivor, crawling ashore. Now what's he doing?"

Tim had reminded Alice, on their way to pick up John, that she wasn't supposed to know anything. About swords, about murders, investigations, or anything else.

"I don't know," she said. "He keeps talking about clues, and leads, and checking things out. Maybe he's just gone nuts. He wouldn't be the only one. He's lucky you were there this morning, that's for sure."

That wasn't altogether true either, Alice knew. Tim had asked John about his schedule and knew he'd be working midnight to eight. The break-in at Carson's cottage had been timed to give Tim a chance to find John patrolling the beach.

After a few minutes Tim reappeared, limping up the incline and toward the car. Alice started the engine. Tim opened the door and sat down. He said nothing. Alice again looked at John in the mirror, frowning.

John grabbed the back of the passenger seat and shook it.

"Well?"

"I found it," Tim said.

"Found *what*?" John shook the seatback again..

"I have to talk to your dad, remember? I'm sorry, both of you. But I really have to talk to Mr. Brady first. Can I call him from your house?"

John fell back. "Let's go," he moaned.

* * * *

"He's in court," Maria said. "He expected to be out by now, but ... shall I have him call home?"

"Yes, Maria," John replied. "Thanks. Soon as possible."

He hung up the telephone and looked at Alice. "No class today?"

"Christmas vacation. Remember Christmas vacations? You haven't been away from school *that* long."

"It does seem like a while," said John. He was relieved, actually, that Doris was out, volunteering at the Civil Defense office. It would all be too hard to explain. "Anybody want some of the famous Brady cinnamon toast?"

He was sprinkling the buttered slices when the telephone rang.

"Hello?"

"John. You called. Everything all right?"

"Yeah. Sorry, Dad, I didn't mean to scare you. Listen, ah, Tim Tanaka is here, and he says he needs to speak with you."

"Sure."

He put the phone receiver on the table and nodded at Tim.

Tim said, "You two mind going outside?"

Alice rolled her eyes. "Fine," John said. "Yeah. Here we go, Alice. Breakfast in the backyard."

They had been sitting in the garden for about two minutes when Tim opened the door and leaned over the steel pipe railing at the top of the concrete steps. "I'm finished. He's on his way here, he says."

Tim walked down the steps to Alice, passing John as he took the plates into the kitchen. "You better go," he whispered to his sister.

She nodded, and they went up into the house. "John," she shouted in the direction of the kitchen. "I need to go, or I'll be late for something. Red Cross interview."

John came into the doorway. "All right. I guess you'll have to get the whole truth and nothing but the truth later," he said, looking at Tim.

"I will," she said. "Thanks again, John. I'll call here when I'm finished in case he needs a ride. I'd be tempted to make him swim home in his underwear, myself."

*   *   *   *

Downtown, Earl Brady had one call to make before leaving. He found the number written on a calendar page, December 19.

A sleepy voice answered, "'Lo?" after five rings.

"Edna?"

"Yes." She sniffled loudly, then cleared her throat even more loudly. "Who is this?"

"Mr. Brady from the district attorney's office."

"Mmm," she groaned. "What now?"

"Listen carefully, Edna. Do you have somewhere … a different place you could go and stay for a few days?"

"Why?"

"For your safety."

"My … huh? Is this about Emmett again?"

"Yes. There's a … problem. You need to go someplace else. Someplace he doesn't know. Where he won't look. Edna, please think fast. I'm trying to help you."

Another sniffle, then, "Yeah, I have an aunt who just remarried. Emmett doesn't know him. My aunt's new husband, I mean. They live up off Mulholland, sort of near that—"

"Don't tell me all this yet. How far away is it, just tell me that."

"About forty-five minutes or an hour, in the car, if that's what you mean."

"Good. Pack some things, Edna, right now. Maybe three days' worth. My son will pick you up in one hour. John Brady. He'll be wearing a red lifeguard jacket and driving a green Chrysler."

"Do I really—"

"Yes. You really do, Edna. Be ready in one hour, please. And don't go anyplace or talk to anybody in the meantime."

"All right."

At Pico and Western, Earl looked in his rearview for about the tenth time, saw the same car, and decided he was being followed. He detoured onto La Brea, and the gray sedan kept following. As he turned left on Olympic, he spotted an LAPD car just ahead. Earl stomped on the gas pedal and swerved into the right lane. Soon he was traveling at almost sixty and passing the police car. He looked in the mirror again and saw the cop motioning him to the curb.

He removed his wallet while rolling to a stop, then got out of the car, holding the open billfold to show his badge. The young cop took the wallet and looked at the silver and gold-plated shield.

"You were going awful fast, Mr. Brady. Is there a problem? I can give you an escort someplace if you need it."

Earl looked around but didn't see the other car. "There is a problem," he said. "I'm pretty sure I was being followed."

"See the car?"

"No, but I'm going to ask you to stay with me to Santa Monica. It was a gray sedan. Ford, I think."

"Yes sir. I'll stay near you until you say otherwise."

"Thanks. And send a message to Commander Roy Benson at headquarters. Tell him you're with me and I'll call him from my house."

*   *   *   *

"Tim. John," he said as he closed the door. "Is your mother here?"

"No," John answered. "She's at the Civil Defense office until three, remember? What's all this about?" He looked at Tim, sitting at the kitchen table, then back at Earl.

Earl excused himself and called Benson. I do need some protection now, he explained. I was being followed, sure of it. Benson seemed flattered to be asked, and approved.

"I can only give you the short version right now," Earl said to John. "Then I need you to do something for me."

John sighed. He was, suddenly, exhausted. He collapsed into a chair next to Tim. "I'll take the short version," he said. "Better than the runaround I've been getting so far this morning."

Earl looked at the wall clock. "We've got just a few minutes; then I have to send you on your way. Tim has found something—a document—that connects Emmett Carson to a murder."

John's mouth dropped open. "Coach Carson? That's—"

"We think," Earl said. "Somebody tried to get the document away from Tim. Again, that's what we think. What we know is they caught him in Carson's house at about 4:30 this morning. He ran away, they shot at him, and they chased him all the way into the ocean. Where you found him."

"Or he found me. Shit, Tim, I—Carson's out of town, though."

"Yeah, we know," Earl said. "When's he due back?"

"Let me think. He's written down for a shift on Monday, so I guess he must be coming back this weekend. Dad, what's that police car doing out front?"

"Not much. Let's say he's acting as a scarecrow."

"All right," Earl continued, "here's what I need you to do. Take my car and pick up a woman named Edna Sampson, 1311 Euclid Avenue, apartment C. She's expecting you. You're driving her to her aunt's house someplace off Mulholland, where she's going to stay for a few days. It's for her safety. She's an ex-girlfriend of Carson's, and she … well, she talked to us.

There's plenty of gas in the car, but here ..."—he reached into his jacket—"here are some coupons. There's a map in the glove compartment, if you get lost."

John stuffed the coupons into his jeans. "1311 Euclid, apartment C. Should I—"

"She's expecting you," Earl repeated, motioning to the door with his thumb. "I said you'd wear your lifeguard jacket and show her your ID. Take your gun, now that I'm thinking about it. If she wants to talk to you on the ride, fine. But don't tell her anything about Tim. She's never heard of Tim and she doesn't know what happened this morning."

"Here I go," John said, getting up from the table.

"Call home when you get to the aunt's house."

"Yeah." John zipped his jacket and held out a hand. "Key?"

"You'll have to admit that you know Carson, I suppose," Earl said. "If she asks. But try not to tell her anything else. Don't answer a lot of questions. Best thing is to be the asker yourself. Understand?"

John grinned at Earl. "Why wouldn't I?"

"Very funny. Drive carefully."

As John walked to the car, Earl went across the street to the waiting cop. Benson's approved this, he explained. That's my son, who is going to pick up a key witness in a big case and take her to a safer place. The cop agreed to follow John at a distance. The green Chrysler pulled away from the curb, and Earl walked back into his house. Tim had pulled the wad of paper from the pocket of his trousers—borrowed from John—and was unfolding it.

"Let's see it," Earl said. Tim handed him the paper. Earl read the first few paragraphs, then scanned the rest quickly, pausing over the concluding sentences.

> U.S. Forces in the Philippines have been placed on high alert, in antic-
> ipation of a Japanese attack. The message to American commanders
> reportedly states that the U.S. government "desires that Japan commit
> the first overt act." With Japan on notice of this country's utter lack of
> readiness for a global war, the question is not *whether* the Emperor's
> forces will soon fire the first shot. The only question is *where*.

"That's it, all right," Earl said. "Let's go into the living room and talk about your … recent experiences."

When he was finished with his account, Tim said, "Can I ask a question?"

"Of course."

"Is Edna Sampson the one who told you—whatever she told you?" Tim realized at once that his question was nonsensical and said, "I mean, is she the—"

Earl interrupted. "Yeah, I know what you mean. Yes, she's the one. I'll explain, but first I need to make another call."

He dialed the FBI. "This is Special Agent Gorman."

My luck is holding. It's about five past noon, and I got him on the first try. "Earl Brady here. Listen, I should meet with you about the Jordan case. I have a development for you. This afternoon all right?"

"Not really. Can you talk now, on the telephone?"

"It's a little complicated," Earl said. "I don't mind coming over there. I think I've found something solid."

"That so?"

"Yeah," Earl said, as slowly as he could, fighting to stay calm. To sound nonchalant. Bored, better yet. "I think you might find it interesting. This might not be what we thought it was."

"What do you mean?"

"It might not have happened the way we thought."

"Hmm." Gorman paused. "Let me call you right back about this."

Shit. Do I want him to know I'm at home? "Sure, we can talk later. I'm about to go out for a couple of hours, though. Branch office meeting. Can I call you when I get there? Half an hour?"

"Yeah," said Gorman. "Do that."

Earl put the phone down slowly, thinking.

"Tim," he said after a minute, "you're absolutely sure those men didn't get a good look at you?"

"Couldn't have been too good," he replied. "I had a wool cap pulled down, and I sure couldn't see their faces."

"And you didn't leave anything in your pockets?"

"Nothing that could tell anybody it was me. Lost my flashlight in the house, but my keys are in the ocean."

"Let's take a ride. Down to your house."

Tim followed to the front door. Earl opened it but hesitated. Tim almost bumped into him from the rear.

"Goddamn it," Earl muttered, closing the door. "John's got my car."

Maybe it's time to ruin Detective Lester Smith's Christmas vacation, he was thinking, when Tim said, "My sister should be calling here soon. She was going to see if I needed a ride."

Earl nodded. "Good. That'd be fine. I'm going to try to reach someone else, too. Whoever calls us first ... the lucky winner gets to drive you and me around for a while."

He left a message for Smith, but Alice's call came in first. She would be there, she said, in fifteen or twenty minutes.

Smith called five minutes later.

"Carson was in on it," Earl told him. "Definitely. We have enough to arrest him."

"Just tell me where," Smith said.

"See if you can find out when Carson is coming back from Washington. Lifeguard schedule has him back at work on Monday, so look at tomorrow or Sunday. Traveling by plane. Be careful, though, he's got some nasty friends around here."

"Got it. Where is ... Miss Sampson?"

"Out of the way. With relatives for a few days. Carson doesn't know them."

"Good. I'll get back to you later about the airplane timetable."

"Also, send a black-and-white to an address my friend here will give you. Right now. It's near Loyola University. Just have it sit on the opposite side of the street, one or two houses away."

*   *   *   *

Alice Tanaka arrived at 12:30. She had changed into a nurse's uniform. "Good idea, that outfit," Tim whispered as he opened the door.

Earl was on the telephone, fighting the urge to scream obscenities at Robert Gorman, Special Agent, FBI.

Maybe, he thought, *Gorman can be baited into a meeting.*

"I fail to see why you don't simply tell me what it is you're talking about," Gorman huffed.

"It isn't simple, is why. I need to meet with you. I don't want to see this get cold."

"Impossible until Tuesday morning, like I told you," Gorman said.

Something about the way Gorman said "impossible" told Earl there was more to it than one man's busy schedule. "What time Tuesday?" he asked.

"Ten thirty. Here."

"I'll see you then."

"Mr. Brady?" said Tim, standing in the doorway between the kitchen and living room. There was a short-haired, bespectacled, uniformed young Japanese woman behind him. Earl stood, still thinking about the FBI. Gorman was stalling. *Why?*

"This is my sister Alice, Mr. Brady."

"Pleased to meet you. Sorry to impose like this." He looked at her uniform. "Are we taking you away from—"

"No," she said. "Don't mention it, especially after what John did for Tim this morning. I'm happy to help. Not that I understand what is happening," she added, smiling and looking at Tim.

The telephone rang. Earl was glad to hear John's voice.

"Where are you?" he asked, looking at his watch. It was 12:40.

"We're at the aunt's house. Closer than she thought. Is that cop supposed to be following me?"

"Yes. Don't lose him."

"Anyway, Edna is all set. What should I do?"

"Get their names. The telephone number and address, too. Tell Edna I'll call her tonight. No, make that tomorrow morning. Has she been drinking?"

"Roger."

"Come on back home, then. No, wait. Drive the car to Tim's house. That's where I'm headed right now."

"Tim's? The Tanakas' house?"
"Yeah. Meet me there."

Thirty-Four

Alice drove them down Lincoln Boulevard, through Venice and the foggy wetlands, past Loyola University, and to the small, stucco house Mr. and Mrs. Tanaka owned from 1923 until transferring it, recently, to their children. Earl apologized for his inability to explain the situation fully to Alice. "It's an ongoing investigation," he told her. "We didn't mean for Tim to get so directly involved, you understand. But here we are. He's been very helpful, I can say that."

She stopped the car in the driveway beside the white house, which was bordered by low azalea bushes and taller camellias. Tall palm trees lined the street. A police car was parked under one of them. Alice saw it. "What is—"

"It's OK," Earl said.

They got out of the car. "We'll come inside in just a minute," Earl said. "I need to have a word with Tim."

Alice nodded, then went to the door and let herself in. Earl held up his badge for the parked cop to see, then turned back to face Tim.

"For some reason we're stuck waiting until Tuesday morning to take this to the FBI," Earl told him. "We need to hold everything together for a few days. I'll explain more on the way back to Santa Monica."

"Back to—"

"We're going back as soon as John gets here. I need to keep you out of sight for a while. I never should have let you go into Carson's house, and I'll be damned if I'm letting anything happen to you now. Or your family."

"But Mr. Brady, I—"

"Tim, here's what you need to do now. I need individual photographs—head and shoulders, you see, like a school yearbook—all four of you. Your parents, Alice, and you. Also, get your deed to the house. Find it and copy down what it says, the property description. Lot number this, parcel number that, tract such-and-such. Copy it all down. Can you do all that while I'm talking to your parents and Alice?"

"Yeah, I think so," Tim replied. "Just ask them to show you the backyard. Keep them outside for five minutes, and I can do it for sure. I'm an experienced burglar, remember."

Earl grimaced, patting Tim on the shoulder. "Never should've let you do that. Now, one last thing. The story is, you're invited to spend the weekend at our house. Say John's having a couple of friends from school. So you need an overnight bag, something like that. Got it?"

"Yeah. Yes, sir."

"Let's go in."

There was small talk, everyone fidgeting. An excruciating tour of the backyard, and an explanation of Tim's weekend plans at the Bradys' house. Tim excused himself to pack a bag, returning a few minutes later with his maroon USC duffel.

"Got everything you need?" Earl asked.

Tim patted the bag. "It's all in here."

There was more small talk. Mr. Tanaka's teaching, Mrs. Tanaka's job at a florist, Venice High School, Santa Monica High School. *Where is John?* Ted Williams. Joe DiMaggio. USC. Nursing school. *Where is he?* Earl squinted, looking out through the living room window.

The green Chrysler finally came into view. John got out and stretched, yawned, and stretched again. Earl looked at Tim and gave him a slight turn of the head. Tim jumped up. "He's here," he said, running out the door.

He met John between the car and house. "I'm spending the weekend at your place. I don't know why; ask your dad later. Me and a couple of other teammates, supposedly, if my parents ask."

"Right," John said. "Toss your bag in. I'm going to say hello to your folks."

Earl was thanking the Tanakas for their hospitality. "Hello, Mr. and Mrs. Tanaka," John said. They bowed slightly. "Alice," he added.

"Hi, John," said Alice. "Save anybody today?"

✳   ✳   ✳   ✳

Earl introduced one of the cops to Alice. The officer seemed bewildered at first, but Alice looked even more so when Earl said, "Miss Tanaka and her family are working for the United States government. We're giving them protection for that reason, so you need to watch the house. Just drive past every hour or so." Earl handed the officer a business card. "Call me or Detective Lester Smith if you see anything." Then he instructed the other car to follow his.

"You drive, John," Earl said, opening a rear door and waving good-bye to Alice and her parents. "Tim, up front. I'll sit back here and talk."

"First of all," Earl said as they drove away, "how was Edna?"

"Halfway sloshed when I got there," John replied. "She was ready to go, though. Suitcase was sitting by the door. I think she packed and then treated herself to a couple while she waited for me. But she was fine. Worried about Emmett. Seems too old for him—was she really a girlfriend?"

"Yeah, all the way back in high school. They've stayed in touch. Did she ask you about him?"

"Just whether I know him. I said yes, from lifeguarding."

"How's the aunt?"

"Fine. Not very far away, actually. Beverly Glen, couple of blocks north of Mulholland. They were curious. I told her on the way that she shouldn't say much, but she had it figured out."

"How do you mean?"

"She told them her plumbing was out, when she called them this morning. Pipes, or something. I was just a friend who gave her a ride. I think it was me they were curious about."

"Good," said Earl, relieved. "All right, now, I'm going to tell you boys a lot. This is not to be repeated, understand?"

They both agreed, so Earl continued. "Colonel Jordan's murder looked like a Japanese—oh, I don't know—ritual killing. A samurai sword was stuck in his belly, after he was shot. The FBI people think, or at least they say, it was a Japanese execution. Obvious reasons. The sword, of course, is one. Another reason is when it happened, just hours before Pearl Harbor was attacked. Also, Colonel Jordan had some very valuable, secret information about Japanese people in this area. Information about who really are spying for the Japanese government, but also about who is loyal to the United States. People who could spy on the spies."

"Jordan just knew all this?" John asked.

"No, it was in writing. A top secret FBI document. Had it in a file in his office at the university. We think."

"Sorry to interrupt," John said.

"Yeah. So, another factor is Colonel Jordan's article for *Time* magazine. Very alarming things about the Japanese military plans, and our own military plans, too. Anyway, in the investigation, which I'm involved in on an informal basis, let's say, we're trying to identify the killers. Obviously. The sword has engraving on it, and that's where you came in, Tim. I asked Tim to find out anything he could about the sword. Tell John what you found out."

"It wasn't a real Japanese army sword," said Tim. "It was probably a souvenir, and most likely from this one shop in Tijuana."

"Where Carson goes all the time!" John interjected.

"Where Carson went almost every day off last summer," Tim said. "You were at those parties he had after work sometimes. He was always showing us this crap he'd bought down there. Paintings, carvings, leather sandals, blankets, firecrackers—remember those things?—tequila, bullfight posters. Not to mention the pictures. Two women and a—"

"So," Earl went on, "as it happens, the Tijuana shop was closed down just a day or two after Pearl Harbor was bombed. No records, no owners, no former employees. All gone. But we're pretty sure the sword came from there, and that makes us a little curious about Carson. And then we just got lucky, you might say. A really big piece of information. Colonel Jordan was picked up from his house that afternoon, last time he was seen alive, in a cab. But none of the cab companies, none of their dispatchers, had any record of a call out to that address. That's when we went to visit Edna Sampson."

*   *   *   *

The green Chrysler turned left onto Wilshire. "When we knew Carson was out of town," Earl continued explaining, "we decided to have a look around his place. Not that I expected Tim to do it himself, but this was our chance."

John shot a glance at Tim. "You knew I was working last night, too, didn't you?"

"Yeah," Tim replied. "I was thinking I could find you on the beach if I needed help. I didn't think it would happen quite the way it did, though."

"Tim was looking for any one of several things," Earl said. "Something about the sword, the scabbard maybe, something from the Mexican shop. Or a document that looked like a list of Japanese names—what Colonel Jordan was supposed to have. Or the missing magazine article. Which is what he found."

"Barely," Tim said. "I was in there for a minute or maybe two when I found it. Then the shit hit the fan."

"So, who are the people who chased Tim?"

"Don't know," Earl said. "I just hope they didn't get a close look at him."

They pulled into the driveway. It was 2:30 PM on Friday, December 26. "What time does Mother get home?"

"Three, three fifteen," John answered.

"Let's relax a while," Earl said as they entered the house. "Tim, the pictures?"

"Yes, sir. In my bag here. He unzipped the duffel and pulled out three small photographs: one each of Alice and himself, school pictures, and one of his parents, seated side by side. Stiff, unsmiling. He also had an index card with a property description printed neatly in pencil.

"Perfect," said Earl, dropping the card and photos into his shirt pocket. "Excuse me while I make a call?"

The boys went outside. Earl made three telephone calls, then turned on the radio. The local news was reporting that the Santa Monica police were collecting radios and cameras from Japanese families. "This program, under the direction of the U.S. Department of Justice, is voluntary," said the announcer. "Local authorities report widespread cooperation, in Santa Monica and elsewhere. One Santa Monica officer, however, was saddened to confiscate a one-dollar box camera from a seven-year-old boy who had received it for Christmas. 'I felt like a heel,' the officer said. We now pause for this message."

He clicked off the radio and waited for Doris.

*   *   *   *

"Hi there," Doris said as she bent over to kiss him. He was on the telephone again, this time with his secretary.

"Where do you want me to leave the documents?" Maria asked.

"Hi, sweetheart," Earl said with his hand covering the mouthpiece. "Just give me a second here.

"Maria, just take them to the Golden Dragon Restaurant, on Broadway. You can leave them with Mr. Sun, the owner, in an envelope with my name on it. I'll pick it up there tonight. Leave early—soon as you've typed them. I'll see you Monday."

"All right."

He told Doris that they were going downtown, for dinner.

"When?"

"We need to leave as soon as we can."

"But it's only 3:30, love."

"We're going someplace else first. Let me explain on the way." He hugged her. "Please?"

The drive to Pasadena took an hour, which was barely enough time to explain.

*　　*　　*　　*

Doris flinched, squeezing Earl's arm, when they walked into Bud Fletcher's room. He lay in a bony heap under the blankets, and his skin was yellow-gray.

"Bud, you remember Doris."

Fletcher opened his eyes and smiled. "Of course," he whispered. "What a nice surprise. Move this up, will you?" He patted the bed.

Earl turned the bed crank, elevating Fletcher's head and shoulders. "Better?"

Fletcher nodded. "So I'm having guests at the ranch, eh?"

"I think we need to help these people, Bud. The Japanese kid has broken the case for us."

"Yeah," the older man rasped, "I agree completely. Like I told you on the phone, they should have a place to go. It will get ugly around here, and soon. Eleanor is taking care of it. She was in here just a while ago. Probably go stay at the ranch herself if her husband gets called up. The information is in that table over here. The drawer."

Earl opened the drawer and pulled out a single sheet of paper. Across the top were the words, "Fletcher Ranch—Nr. Austin, Texas." Below was a hand-drawn map and a few lines of driving directions. At the bottom was a short list of names and telephone numbers.

"There'll be work for 'em at the ranch if nothing else pans out," Fletcher said. "Takes about forty, forty-eight hours if you drive straight through. Just let Eleanor know when they're leaving." They watched him cough, his legs stiffening.

"I'll call Eleanor if there are any questions?"

"Yeah. Call her tomorrow. Just to let her know we talked." He coughed again, less violently. "FBI Tuesday, you said?"

"Right."

"Call me after, will you?"

"Yes sir. Maybe I'll stop by."

Doris opened her purse as soon as they left the room and pulled out a handkerchief. She dabbed at her eyes. "God, he looks like he's already dead."

"He's worse, every time I see him."

"Why is he doing this?" she asked. "For Tim's family, I mean."

They crossed the lobby and walked across the gravel to their car. "Colonel Jordan was a family friend, for one thing. Bud wants to do something good, I think, in Jordan's honor. And also I think he's a little disgusted with the crap he hears on the radio, Walter Lippman and all those people. He doesn't think everyone should be rounded up and sent away. He thinks if the government had been paying attention we'd know who's loyal and who isn't."

✳   ✳   ✳   ✳

"Mr. Brady," Sun said, "welcome, again."

"This is my wife Doris. This is Mr. Sun, the owner."

"Hello," she said.

"I am honored. This envelope was delivered for you a short while ago, Mr. Brady. Your table is ready, of course, but first," he took a step back, "if you will come with me."

They followed him through the room, past the kitchen, and into the office where Earl and Lindgren had dined in private nine days before. *An eternity,* Earl thought.

"Please," said Sun, pulling a chair away from his small desk. Doris sat, and Sun moved around to the other side. He looked at both of his visitors. "I assume we can talk about the subject of your call?"

"Yes," Earl replied. "Mrs. Brady knows everything."

"Very well. Unfortunately, there is a problem concerning one of the items we spoke about. The passports."

"I see."

"I am told it has become more difficult. Perhaps not impossible, but it could take a month or even longer."

Maybe that's better, Earl thought. *Save the pictures.* "Let's forget passports for the time being," he said.

"Birth certificates and driver's licenses can be obtained," Sun assured him. "I will simply need descriptions."

"Right. I can give you that, for all four people."

Sun pulled a pencil and a sheet of paper from his desk drawer. Earl described each of the Tanakas.

"One family, correct?" Sun asked.

"Yes."

"San Francisco?"

"What about it?"

"For places of birth and current address. Is San Francisco acceptable?"

"Oh, yes. Fine."

"We need a Chinese name," said Sun. He reached to a corner of his desk and pulled a small telephone directory toward himself. Then he pushed it toward Doris. "It could bring good luck if you picked."

She opened the thin cardboard-bound book. "How about Chung?" she said.

"Excellent," Sun replied. "May I suggest you and Mr. Brady enjoy dinner now?"

"When will these—"

"Within one hour."

"That's fast," Earl and Doris both exclaimed. Sun smiled. "I am so pleased to help. Colonel Jordan was a good man. Your husband, Mrs. Brady, is also a good man."

Earl gave an embarrassed half-smile. "I have one question," Sun said. "Perhaps it is not appropriate, but—do these people look Chinese?"

"Not exactly," said Earl, "but they'll pass, I think. Where they're going, I think they'll be just fine." He thought for a few seconds. "More important," Earl added, "if I can use your words to describe these people—we need them."

Sun nodded slowly. "Yes," he said. "You need them. I do understand."

The licenses and birth certificates arrived with the fortune cookies, less than an hour later. "They are in order," said Sun as he handed the envelope to Earl. "How was your dinner?"

*   *   *   *

After they were in the car, Earl pulled a small flashlight out of his glove compartment and took a look. "Amazing," he said. "What do you think?"

"They look real to me," said Doris. "What's in the other envelope, by the way?"

"Deeds," he replied. "Property deeds."

"Well," she sighed. "That gives us something to talk about on the ride home."

Thirty-Five

Saturday, by comparison, seemed routine. John Brady worked an uneventful eight-to-four shift, confirming as he signed out that Carson was still on the roster for Monday, December 29. Four to midnight, same as John. *That'll be interesting,* he thought.

Tim, exhausted, slept until ten and read magazines while listening to the radio for the rest of the day. Doris did laundry and played tennis. Earl, when he wasn't on the telephone, lounged with Tim. The radio in the background played music, news (*Life, Time,* and *Collier's*), and commercials.

His first call was to Fletcher's daughter.

"I'm on my way to see him now," Eleanor Berkson said.

"I won't keep you. Your father suggested I call you this morning. Just to tell you I have the map and all. And also, thanks. To both of you."

"Well, you let me know when the family is leaving for Texas. I can call ahead to Eddie. He's the caretaker and foreman. Daddy really wants to do this." Her voice rose to a tearful squeak at the end.

"I know," Earl said. "Give him my best."

He waited a *Life* and half a *Collier's* before placing a call to Edna Sampson. "I thought you were going to call last night," she complained.

I was, he thought, *but then I decided it would be better if you remembered some fraction of what we talked about.* "Sorry about that. I got pulled away on an emergency. Different case. I didn't get home until late. Must've been almost eleven. You all right there?"

"Yeah, it's fine. Anything else you can tell me?"

"Nothing new. You should plan on being there until sometime Wednesday."

"Wednesday? I thought you said three days."

"Careful," he said. "No need to get your aunt upset. It's plumbing, remember?"

"Yeah. This is expensive, though. Me being away from work so long."

"We'll make that up to you. There's a daily allowance, a per diem, for this sort of thing." It was getting easier and easier to make things up. "I'll call you Tuesday," he said.

He had almost fallen asleep on the sofa when the telephone rang. "Want me to get it?" Tim asked.

"No, I'll answer."

It was Lester Smith. "No luck on Carson's travel schedule," he said. "Zero."

"Could be he's on army transport flights," Earl said. "That's probably it. I'll look into that."

"I checked with Santa Monica Police," Smith said. "They did have a call about some shouting and a possible shot fired on Ocean Avenue, early Friday morning. No description, though. And there was nothing about the ... what shall we call it? The Idaho Avenue disturbance. That made me curious, so I went over there yesterday afternoon. Nobody home. It turns out Carson's landlord is out of town on a skiing trip for the holidays. Wish we'd known that. We probably could've walked right in there in broad daylight."

"Yeah. If, if, if. Who's Carson's landlord?"

"Let me see. I know his last name's Smith ... Winfield Smith."

"Any relation?"

"Don't I wish. What's next? FBI on this yet?"

"Nope. I called Gorman, but they're stalling. I meet with him Tuesday morning at ten thirty."

"Tuesday. That's a lot of bullshit," Smith muttered.

"I agree. But I have Tim staying here, and Edna's up in the hills, so I think we're covered for now."

"All right. Just let me know. You want me there Tuesday?"

"No, I don't think so. I might need you for something tomorrow, though."

*   *   *   *

Shortly after John was dropped off after work, the group convened in the kitchen.

"We need to visit Tim's family tomorrow," Earl announced. "Sometime. I guess it depends on what your shift is, John."

"Noon to eight," he said.

"Then we'll go down to Inglewood at ten in the morning, if that's all right with the Tanakas. Leave here at nine thirty or so, and we can drop John off at work by twelve. Call and make sure ten is all right, will you, Tim?"

"Yes, sir. Anything in particular? In case they ask."

"Plans. We need to talk about making plans. If Alice is there, let me talk to her."

She was. "Ten is fine," said Tim, holding the telephone away from his head. "Here's Alice."

Earl took the phone and sat down, motioning Tim beside him.

"Hello, Alice."

"Hello, Mr. Brady. Tim said you wanted to—"

"Yes. I think I'd better let you know what's on our agenda tomorrow. Then I'll let you and Tim decide what to say to your parents. Or, you can wait until tomorrow and let them hear it all from me."

"Yes."

*   *   *   *

Later that night, trying to sleep, Tim would go over, and over, what he had heard as he sat next to Earl Brady. My boss owns a large ranch in

Texas. The Hill Country. He was a dear friend of the man whose murder Tim has helped solve. Your family is invited to stay. The University of Texas. Jobs. The government is going to allow the Army Defense Command to have its way. All persons of Japanese descent will be removed from coastal areas. Yes, *all*. No, it isn't just the army pushing for this. Governor, mayors, state attorney general, they all agree. It's going to happen. You have a chance to stay ahead of this. Your house will be here when it's over. Dangerous for Tim. We don't know who, but somebody shot at him. Tuesday morning at the FBI. Extra documents if you get stopped on the way to Texas. You will live on a ranch. Your house will still be here when this is over.

Thirty-Six

The fog was burning off as the green Chrysler rolled to a stop in front of the Tanakas' house at 9:45 AM on Sunday, December 28. Alice walked out, alone, and was met by her brother halfway between the street and the front door. The three Bradys stood beside the car as Tim took Alice's hand. She nodded in Earl's direction and said, "Just a minute."

Tim and Alice walked halfway down the block, past three or four small houses. They stopped and faced each other, speaking quietly, for about two minutes, then returned to the nervous threesome standing on the sidewalk.

"Excuse us, please," said Alice, looking at all three. "I wanted to tell Tim a few things."

"Of course," Earl said. "I just wish—"

Tim interrupted. "Our parents are in agreement. Between what you know, Mr. Brady, and what Alice has been hearing ... we all understand that we should do this. The details are still not very clear, but ..."

"The details are exactly what we're here to talk about," Earl said.

"Please come in," Alice said.

They followed her into the small living room, to a dining table where Masako and Fumika Tanaka stood by their chairs. When everyone was seated, Mr. Tanaka spoke.

"Mr. Brady, we are thankful for your support." He appeared intent on saying more but stopped, unable to continue and unwilling to break down.

Earl decided to try a businesslike approach.

"Alice and I spoke last night. I believe she has given you the outline of our plans. This," he said as he unzipped a thin, leather briefcase he held on his lap, "is a map with driving directions." He slid it to the middle of the table. "Mr. Fletcher tells us that the journey is forty-eight hours, perhaps less, by automobile. If there are four drivers"—Fumika began shaking her head—"or three, it might be possible to go straight through. That would be up to you. When you reach Austin, Texas, as it says here, you should telephone ahead. One of Mr. Fletcher's employees will meet you near the turnoff to the ranch. There is a two-bedroom cabin for you on the property."

He pulled two more pieces of paper from the briefcase and placed them on the table. "These," he said, "are two deeds, called quitclaim deeds. As you can see, one deed transfers ownership of this house from Alice and Tim to Mrs. Brady. The other transfers ownership from her back to Alice and Tim. The plan is for both to be signed, and the first one recorded so that the public records will show this house owned by Mrs. Brady. The second deed restores ownership to Alice and Tim. It will be recorded whenever you believe it is advisable to do so."

Tim broke the long silence. "Our house will be here," he said, "when this is over."

Earl looked out the front window, then reached into his briefcase again. He was pulling out the envelope of false identifications when Doris nudged him. "He's here," she said. "I'll get the door."

"Perfect timing," Earl said. "This is Detective Lester Smith of the Los Angeles Police Department."

Doris led Smith to the table for handshakes, bows, and uneasy smiles.

"Detective Smith has been involved with Tim and me on the case. He is here for two reasons. First, to drive Alice, Tim, and Mrs. Brady to the real estate company where the detective's sister is employed, so that the deeds can be signed and notarized. That is, assuming we are all in agreement on the plan."

He looked around the table. There was no response of any kind for several seconds, until Alice spoke: "Yes."

"Then I can tell you the second reason I asked Detective Smith to join us. He lives in a very small apartment. If this house becomes vacant, he would like to lease it, until you return, with the rent payments forwarded to you in Texas."

"OK," Alice said.

"This envelope," Earl continued, "contains some documents that you probably will not need. As a precaution, however, on your journey, you should have them. Alice can perhaps—"

She came to Earl's rescue. "Right. I'll go over these later," she said, pulling the forgeries from Earl's quivering hand. Her parents appeared stunned. Earl looked at them, then at Doris, then at the floor.

Tim again: "We should talk about the timing of this." He looked at his parents and said something in Japanese. His mother nodded, closed her eyes, and leaned her head on her husband's shoulder.

"What do you think, Mr. Brady?" Tim asked. "When should we go?"

Earl looked at Smith. The detective responded by mouthing, "Now."

"I know this won't be easy," Earl said, leaning forward, "but I strongly recommend that you be on the road as early as possible tomorrow morning."

He had to keep talking, because nobody else was. Businesslike, or as close to it as he could manage, he said, "Mr. Tanaka, we should have you write a letter to your school principal. One of us will deliver it to him personally, tomorrow. The same for you, Alice, to the nursing school. We will obtain letters of recommendation for both of you. The Fletcher family is very prominent in Texas, and they are highly confident that everything will go smoothly. Alice can finish her nurse training in Austin, and Mr. Tanaka, you will be back in charge of a classroom soon. Very soon."

The Tanakas nodded. "We should go take care of the deeds, so we can start packing," said Alice.

"I'll come back to help tonight," John said. "I get off at eight."

They all stood. Smith said, "Mr. and Mrs. Tanaka, your son is a courageous young man. I will be here tomorrow morning to help you load the car and to follow you for the first hour or so. Make sure you get off to a safe start."

*   *   *   *

"You're getting off at eight?" Earl asked, stopping the Chrysler in front of lifeguard headquarters.

"Yeah," John answered. "I'll be dropped off at home. Can I take your car back down to Tim's tonight? I promised I'd help them pack up."

"We'll work something out. Don't forget to check the board again about Carson. See if you can find out if anybody's heard from him. Anything at all about his travel itinerary."

"Roger. I'll call up to the house if I hear anything."

*   *   *   *

Lester Smith, at that moment, was introducing his sister. "This is Mrs. Doris Brady, Alice Tanaka, Tim Tanaka. My sister, Anita. Thanks for coming over on a Sunday, Pinky."

"Pinky," she huffed. "It's nice to meet you all. I'll be polite and not use any of Lester's nicknames. Let's go in."

She led them up a set of outdoor stairs, then along a passageway to a door marked, "Bay City Escrow." She unlocked and opened the door, reaching in to switch on an overhead light. "Right over here," she said.

Five minutes later, the deeds were signed and notarized. Anita wrote on a notepad, then tore off the sheet and handed it to her brother. "Hall of Records, Temple Street."

"Yeah, I know where it is."

"Room 104. Recordings window. If you have any problems, ask for Mary Benedict and use my name. Remember, wait for them to give you the deed back with the date and stamp on it."

"Got it. We done?"

"We're done."

*   *   *   *

When the group returned to Inglewood, the elder Tanakas had finished writing letters to the principal of Venice High School and the owner of the Manchester Florist Shop. Smith took the letters.

"We'll be speaking with these people tomorrow," he promised. "Easy for me to say, but please don't worry. The recommendation letters are going to reach Mr. Fletcher's ranch about the same time you do."

Doris Brady nodded. "That's right," she said.

"I need to write my letter," Alice said, "but you and Mrs. Brady be on your way. I'll give it to you in the morning."

"Yeah," Smith replied. "What time can we get going, by the way?"

Alice and Tim looked at each other. Tim spoke in Japanese to his father, who gave a one-syllable response that sounded like "Aye."

"Six," Tim said. "We'll be ready to go at six."

"I'll take care of the letters," Doris said to Smith as they drove away. "You have enough to do tomorrow."

"Are you sure?"

"Yes. I know the principal of Venice High School, because he used to teach at Santa Monica. By the time I get through with him, Mr. Tanaka might be running the University of Texas."

Thirty-Seven

At 6:45 on Monday morning, John Brady collapsed into a chair in his parents' kitchen.

"They're off," he said, using a foot to push his knapsack under the table.

"Smith was there?" Earl asked.

"Yeah. They followed his car. Here's their house key," said John, tossing it onto the table.

"Good of you to help them pack. How much of it fit in?"

"Just clothes, really. Must be about fifteen boxes of things …"

"We'll get that shipped, by train. Want some toast?"

"Yeah. Then I'm going to bed."

"Don't forget to get to work a little early this afternoon, and call me. Remember, 'I'm at work' means Carson is there. 'Zero' means he isn't."

"Right. I won't forget."

✳   ✳   ✳   ✳

Earl was downtown and in his office at 7:45. It was a useful distraction, since he had stacks of paper to review. He returned phone calls, read arrest reports, drank coffee. At 8:30 he greeted Maria and went to a staff meeting. When he returned at 10:20, Smith was waiting.

"I led 'em out as far as Claremont," he said when they were alone, inside Earl's office. Smith slowly shook his head. "Hope we're right."

"Yeah. Thanks for doing that. Had to make them feel a little better."

"Tim and Alice are going to call your house sometime tonight," Smith said. "I gave them the gas coupons. They should be fine. Parents don't say much, do they?"

"No, but … their heads must be spinning. You have the deed?"

Smith pulled the document out of his jacket. Alice Tanaka and Tim Tanaka, grantors. Doris Osborne Brady, grantee. "That's it," Earl said. "Go ahead and take it over for recording today."

"Mrs. Grady has the other one, right?"

"Yeah, it's locked up."

"I was thinking," said Smith. "I should go out to Carson's place. See if our friend is back in town."

"Do that. Call me if you see anything. I need to get ready for my big meeting with the FBI. Meet you here tomorrow morning at 10:15. Out front."

As Smith left, Earl picked up the telephone to call Eleanor Berkson. The family left this morning, he told her, and would be calling tonight.

❋   ❋   ❋   ❋

It was 3:45 when John called.

"Zero." No Carson sightings.

"Mmm. Any explanation?"

"Bad weather, according to the message that came in," John replied.

"Delayed flight because of weather?"

"Yes."

"He's still in Washington, then?"

"So I hear. Tomorrow, maybe."

"Hmm. See you tonight."

He looked up to see Maria, standing across the desk from him. "Detective Smith wants you to call. This number," she said, showing him a slip of paper. "Shall I try it?"

"No, thanks. I'll do it." He didn't recognize the number.

On the first ring, "Smith."

"Where are you?"

"I stopped at the bowling alley to call you. I've been by the place twice, now. No sign of life."

"Carson was scratched from the lifeguard roster for today," Earl said. "There was a weather delay in Washington. He might be arriving tomorrow."

"All right, so I don't need to check again today."

"Not there, I guess." *We've got a couple of more places to look, though.* "You should go by Edna Sampson's apartment tonight, just to see if any lights are on. She told me Carson visits once in a while. I'll go to one other place tomorrow morning."

"Where?" Smith asked.

"In the … it's downtown."

"You gonna make me beat this information out of you?"

"OK, OK. Under the grandstand at the Olympic Swim Stadium. There's a coaches' office, in the locker room. Tim Tanaka gave me his keys. If they still work—"

"You can't go there alone," Smith interrupted. "What if he's there?"

"If I see anybody, I'll leave and call you. Promise."

"Right. Call me anyway, soon as you get to your office."

Thirty-Eight

The early morning drizzle had stopped when Earl parked his car on Menlo Avenue, near the back corner of the tall concrete grandstand. It was not quite 7:30.

As he rounded the corner and looked through the chain link fence, he saw steam rising from the pool. Tim's key opened the padlock on the gate behind the diving towers. Earl hooked the lock over a fence link and quietly shut the gate behind himself.

The locker room entrance, he knew, was opposite the pool's middle. He walked to it along the lower wall of the grandstand. He stopped at the door, and listened. Nothing. No lights were on inside, judging by the wire mesh opening across the top of the door.

He tried the second key, and could feel the bolt sliding back into the hollow metal door.

The tiled floor was dry. The high windows were bringing in enough light for Earl to see parallel rows of green lockers, several with their doors swung open. A varnished wood bench ran down the middle. He followed it to the end. On the right, Tim had said, were the toilets and showers; to the left, a trainer's room and the office.

The office door was locked. *I'll call the campus cop—what's his name? Brown. I'll call Brown this afternoon and—*

Earl heard a clanking sound. *The gate.* He froze, then hurried past the trainer's room and into the shower area. He went into a toilet stall and waited.

He could hear a key sliding into the entry door's lock. Then a shout: "Hello?"

Squeaking footsteps on the tile.

"Hello?"

The voice was now near the office. Earl listened to its door being unlocked, then crept out of the stall and looked around the shower room wall. The office door was standing open. A light came on inside the coaches' office, and Earl could hear the even clicks of a telephone being dialed. Earl moved, not breathing, to the end of the lockers. He slowly turned for the exit. He had taken several soft, crouching steps toward the door when he felt a hard object pressing against the back of his skull.

"Don't move. Hands on your head."

As Earl raised his arms, an old memory jumped him too. He was touring the coroner's office as a new prosecutor, required to watch the autopsy of a murder victim. Harsh lights, a steel table, a pair of chain-smoking, gloved men, sharp instruments. Butcher scales, and a scribbling stenographer. The body: a person who had thoughts the day before but was now an inert bag of labeled pieces. He remembered the bullet wound in Jordan's head. *Why did I do this?*

He had an urge to say something. "I was just looking," he offered.

"Shut up," said Emmett Carson, now holding the back of Earl's belt with one hand while still pushing the metal cylinder to his head. "Do not m-make another sound."

Carson nudged Earl forward. "Move," he growled. They walked past the lockers and were almost to the door when Earl spotted a small cardboard suitcase lying on the bench. He had another impulse to talk.

"Just get back in town?"

"J-just leaving," Carson said. Then he pressed it harder against Earl's head. "Now shut the f-fuck up."

Carson nearly lifted Earl off the floor as they went through the doorway. He turned Earl and pushed him toward the diving towers. They passed a grandstand stairway. Then Earl heard a different voice.

"Drop it, asshole," said Lester Smith. "This is a real gun I'm sticking in your ear, not some fucking scrap of pipe. Drop it and step back."

Earl stumbled away, and turned to see Smith aiming his pistol at Carson. "Get on the ground," Smith barked. Carson knelt; then Smith looked at Earl and grinned. "Saw your car outside," he said.

"I know better than this," Earl muttered. "Sorry."

"Don't mention it. Here, aim this gun at the piece of shit, and shoot him if he moves."

Earl took the pistol, and Smith quickly handcuffed Carson, then jerked him up to his feet. "I'm arresting you on suspicion of murder," he snarled into Carson's ear. The prisoner said nothing.

Earl pointed with his head at the locker room door, and made a suitcase-lifting motion for Smith. "Make it fast," Smith whispered.

The suitcase had no lock. Earl yanked a handful of wrinkled clothing from it, then saw something else. He only had to pull the first page halfway out of the envelope to recognize what it was.

He rejoined Smith on the pool deck, patting his left pants pocket as if to say, "Got it."

The three men trotted through the gate and around the corner to the street, Smith holding his pistol in one hand and Carson's elbow with the other. "Why are we running?" Earl asked.

Smith put a finger to his lips, then said, "Hurry up."

After Smith had shoved Carson into the back of his car, he said, "We know he's got friends. We gotta get the hell away from here. That's your car, right?"

"Yeah, but what are we—."

"Beat it, then. I'll lock him up and see you in a couple of hours."

Emmett Carson didn't say a word during the ten-minute ride to the downtown lockup. "Hold him for me," Smith told the jail cops. "He's a murder suspect. Emmett Carson. I'll come back this afternoon with the paperwork."

*   *   *   *

Smith's car was waiting when Earl and his secretary walked out of the Hall of Justice at 10:15. At the knock, Smith looked up from the *Los Angeles Times*, reached across, and pushed open the passenger door. "You all right?" he asked Earl.

"I'm fine. Do you have the deed?"

Smith pulled it from his jacket. "Here. Recorded yesterday. Your wife owns the house."

Earl turned and handed it to Maria. "Lock this in my evidence drawer, with the envelope I gave you this morning. I'll be back in a couple of hours, at the most."

Smith drove to a parking lot between the Olvera Street Plaza and the Federal Courthouse. He reported on his delivery of Carson to the downtown central jail.

"You got something to read, or work to do, in case this takes longer?" Earl asked.

"Newspaper, *Look* magazine. Yeah, I'm fine. You sure you're OK, after that little early morning adventure?" Smith was clearly enjoying himself.

"Enough," Earl said. "Here's something else you can read." Earl reached into the side pocket of his coat, then handed Smith the four pages of Jordan's article. "Don't lose this, it's evidence. Remember, if I don't call you, I'll just come to the restaurant when I'm finished."

"Yep. I'll be there."

"Don't eat too many *huevos rancheros*."

They set out from the parking lot in opposite directions. Walking south, Earl gazed at the massive stone box that was the U.S. Courthouse and tried to imagine the meeting he was about to attend. *I'm taking over the case, gentlemen. Relieving you of your command. You run a nice little operation here, but it's time to bring in—me. If you would be so kind as to turn over your files?*

He skipped up the granite steps and into the lobby, laughing to himself, the absurdity of it, then caught an elevator to the fifth floor. "They're expecting you," said the FBI receptionist as she examined Earl's DA badge. "Mr. O'Connor's office is room 508, down this way to your left."

O'Connor, he thought. *Good. They might be taking me seriously.* Gorman was standing at the door to O'Connor's office. "Good morning," he said, unsmiling, as they shook hands. "After you."

As he entered the office, Earl saw O'Connor, solemn-faced and standing behind a desk. Three brass-tacked leather visitor's chairs were arranged in an arc on the other side. Earl nodded to O'Connor, then heard something behind him. In a corner, a man was hanging a jacket on a wooden hat rack, his back to Earl. Then he turned around. "Good morning," Ted Lindgren said.

"This is a nice surprise," Earl said, shaking Lindgren's hand. "You didn't travel all this way just to see me, I hope."

Lindgren gave it away by shooting a glance at Gorman, then O'Connor. "Oh, no," he said, forcing a chuckle. "Just happened to be here, for the day. Feels like I live on these damn airplanes lately. Let's have a seat."

Gorman spoke first, stiffly. "Mr. Brady has told me that he has some new ideas on the Jordan murder."

With that, the three FBI agents sat in silence, looking at their visitor. *Your turn,* their expressions said.

Slowly, now. "I have a source of reliable information among the local Japanese residents. This goes back, oh, years. Long before this war. To make a long story short, because I know you fellows are busy, I've got at least one individual solidly linked to Jordan's murder. Physically linked, not just a say-so. I think there are others. I'd like to ask you to refer the case to LAPD or to my office directly. We can solve it."

Silence for at least ten seconds. "Or," O'Connor said, "you could give us what you've got. Right?"

Earl again paused. *Count to five.* "My sources probably won't talk to the FBI," he said. "Not bragging here, but it took time to cultivate these folks, you see? They're amateurs. Simple people. I'm afraid they'll just disappear if I even mention the FBI. No offense, gentlemen, it's just what's in their minds. They're skeptical about me, but they're downright afraid of you."

It was finally too much for Lindgren. "Can I talk to Mr. Brady privately?"

O'Connor glared at Earl. "That might be a good idea," he said. "Stay here and use my office if you want."

"I could use some fresh air," Earl said. "Out front?"

"Fine," Lindgren said. "We'll be back shortly. Give us twenty minutes or so."

They rode silently down in the elevator. Outside, they went to the bottom of the steps, then down Main Street, and sat on an empty bus bench.

"This is out of line, this referral back to LAPD," Lindgren finally said. "In a million years, it won't happen. You damn well know that. So, what are you up to?"

Earl took a deep breath. *Ask, don't answer.* "Have these notes of yours been recovered—by the FBI, that is?"

"No, I don't think so."

"I don't think so, either," Earl shot back. He let that sink in for a few seconds. "Here's my next question, Ted. Why did you have me interview Edna Sampson?"

Lindgren leaned back and folded his arms across his chest. A bus stopped. They waved the driver away.

"I didn't hear that," Lindgren said, pointing to his right ear. "Too noisy."

Earl Brady was losing patience. He decided to be more direct. "We've arrested Emmett Carson," he said.

"I know that."

Earl's entire body stiffened. "What do you mean, you know that?"

"We picked him up from the LAPD an hour ago."

"How? Why? This is—"

Lindgren put a hand on Earl's forearm. "We have him now, Earl. Just forget about it."

"Where is Emmett Carson?" Earl hissed.

"He's gone. Or on his way, anyhow. Mexico or South America. That's really all I can tell you."

"Well, he might be gone," Earl said, "but let me tell you something, Ted. Your Mr. Carson left a few things behind."

Lindgren folded his arms across his chest. "Such as?"

"That's really all I can tell you," Earl said.

Lindgren stood up. "Let's walk around the block," he said.

Bus engines, horns, whistles. Their conversation was half shouted.

I don't even know Carson. Somebody else was managing him. Things went too far.

Go on.

Brits have been doing public relations here for over a year.

So?

They just wanted the magazine article intercepted.

With a sword?

That was Carson's idea, but killing Jordan in the first place wasn't. Carson's friends got carried away. Maybe they misunderstood.

You could've stopped this.

If only I'd been here.

Edna Sampson?

Maybe I felt bad. Maybe I wanted you to catch the stupid bastard.

And you almost got somebody else killed.

I could help with that situation. The Japanese kid, I mean.

We did catch Carson. You just aren't letting us keep him.

That I can't help. Sorry.

Maybe I'm sorry too. About your career.

Does Carson know where my notes are?

He knows where they used to be.

✳   ✳   ✳   ✳

They had finished their conversation after one trip around the building; the second was for Earl to calm down. They stopped at the bottom of the courthouse steps.

"I should tell you," Earl said, "that I don't blame you for what happened."

"I hope not," Lindgren replied. "Can I trust you?"

"You'll have to. And vice versa."

"Right." Lindgren extended his hand, and they shook. "I think we understand each other. Good luck, Earl."

"Same to you. Give my regards to O'Connor and Gorman," said Earl as he turned to go. "Just tell 'em you talked some sense into me."

✳   ✳   ✳   ✳

It was just before noon when Earl ducked through the low doorway into La Golondrina. "Mr. Brady?" said Oscar. "Your friend is back here. This way."

"Jesus Christ," Smith whispered as Earl sat down. "I read that thing. Did Jordan know what he was talking about? Is that shit true?"

"Don't ask me," Earl said, opening a menu.

Smith scanned the room and then looked again at Earl, unconvinced. "Come on. Was he right?"

"I'm afraid so, mostly. Maybe it doesn't matter now."

"Bullshit. If we'd had more time to get ready—get into this war on our own terms—"

"Hey, listen … Lester. For our purposes, right here and now, it doesn't make much difference."

"Yeah, but … why would Jordan write this? Here, by the way. You better keep it."

Earl put the article in his pocket. "Different reasons. Mainly, you ask me, I think it was for his son. In the Philippines."

Smith nodded. "Mmm. Anyway, how was the meeting?"

"I think we're finished."

"We're … huh?"

"You and I are done with this case. Nothing left for you to do, except move into that nice little house and start paying rent." Earl handed the menu to a waitress. "*Carne asada con arroz. No frijoles.*"

Smith's face reddened. "Uh, same. With beans, though."

"Two Lucky Lagers," Earl said. "*Gracias.*"

"All right now," said Smith, leaning forward. "What the hell are you saying to me?"

"Carson is gone. He'll be sent off to South America someplace, to match wits against the Nazis."

"But he's a piece of—" Smith started to stand up.

"I know, I know," Earl interrupted, "but he's a valuable piece of shit. Sit back down, Lester. He's in their hands now. They need Carson. They can control him, with what they've got on him. It's perfect, in their minds. And it's been decided. Believe me, it's been decided. Carson's gone."

Smith was grinding his teeth.

"Hey, Lester," Earl said. "Look at it this way. The war won't last forever. If Carson survives—"

Smith interrupted Earl by pointing a finger at him. "That son of a bitch comes back here," he said slowly, "and he's all mine."

"There's no statute of limitations on murder," Earl offered.

"Yeah, well … maybe I'll get you involved and maybe I won't."

I didn't hear that, Earl started to say. He shrugged instead. Smith seemed to be calming down a little.

"Lindgren's going to help the Tanakas," Earl continued. "*Gracias*," he said to the waitress as the frosty brown bottles arrived.

Smith's expression had changed from angry to bewildered.

"What do you mean?"

"I made a deal. Made a little bargain with Lindgren."

Smith shook his head. "A bargain."

Earl took a gulp of beer. "Maybe that's not the right word," he said.

"Just tell me what the fuck you mean," Smith growled. "Please?"

"The Tanakas are better off staying away from here."

"I know that. I drove with 'em halfway out of California yesterday, remember?"

"Keep your voice down," Earl said. He looked both ways, as if to cross a street. "It isn't just Tim's involvement with us. Lindgren puts the chances of a mass removal order at ninety-nine percent. The way people are beating the drums, you know, the army, the governor, the mayor, all these opinion-makers—and more information about what happened before the attack in Hawaii. The pressure is rising."

"Where does this bargain come in? Your deal, or whatever you want to call it."

"The Tanakas are only going to be at Bud's ranch temporarily," Earl explained. "Then they're moving again, probably to Illinois. We'll know the details in a day or two."

"These plates are very hot," said the waitress.

"*Gracias*," Earl smiled as she scurried away. He looked around again, then turned back to Smith. "Tim Tanaka is going into the United States Navy. Great Lakes Naval Training Center, it's called. Just north of Chicago. He's going to teach recruits how to swim."

"I don't believe this," said Smith, poking his fork at the refried beans.

Earl swallowed another mouthful of beer. "His sister will go in, too. Navy nursing corps. Dad gets a teaching job, someplace."

Smith ate in silence for a minute, then looked up. "And the bargain is what? We just fold up?"

"That's right."

"I don't like this," Smith muttered.

"I don't like a lot of things," Earl said. "Let's eat lunch, and then we'll go over to my office."

*   *   *   *

"Actually," Earl said as Smith started his car, "we should go see Bud. Head out to Pasadena, on the parkway. It won't take long."

"What's he going to think about this—situation?"

"That's what I want to find out," Earl replied.

They drove in silence, through Chinatown to the parkway entrance. Then Smith spoke.

"You must know something," he pleaded, "about why Carson did this."

Earl didn't answer. He looked away, out his window at the passing sycamore and palm trees.

"You gotta know why Jordan was killed," Smith insisted, "and you gotta tell me. I think you owe me that."

Earl looked at Smith, who was facing ahead, gripping the steering wheel. "Don't you think?" Smith asked, gripping harder.

"I do owe you that, Lester. Promised Lindgren I wouldn't talk about it, but ... you just have to agree this stays between us. Agreed?"

"Right."

"Carson," Earl began, "has been supplying information to the FBI since about spring of last year. What he's done is use his Spanish contacts, and his language ability, to find out what the Spanish government spies are doing in Mexico."

"Wait a minute. What's the Spanish government got to do with anything?"

"They're on Germany's side. They're supporters of the Axis. And vice versa, if you know anything about the Spanish war. You remember, the one Carson dabbled in after the '36 Olympics."

"I remember."

"OK. Spain has been helping Germany and Japan. Big, big espionage networks in Mexico and in South America, where there are obviously a lot of Spanish but also large colonies of Japanese. Brazil, Chile, Argentina. Lots of recruiting over the last several years. A week after the Hawaii attacks, Spain agreed to spy in the United States for Japan. There are actually diplomatic communications, formal messages confirming it. We know, because our army people intercepted them."

Smith was shaking his head and muttering. "Jesus. Jesus."

"Even now, they're intercepting reports from the Spanish Embassy in Washington to Madrid, where they get forwarded right to Tokyo. Reports about convoys and other military stuff."

"And Carson?" Smith asked.

"Well, Carson will be in place, or whatever the right word is. The army and the navy and the FBI, they all think he can help. Has his network of contacts. They believe he can help catch some of the Spanish government spies. Working with opposition people who are trying to fight the Fascists any way they can."

"Did he really kill Jordan?"

"His friends did. He helped, though, no doubt about it."

"But what for?"

"Carson and his friends knew about the war plans, and they also knew about our government letting the plans out, into the papers. Just like Jordan knew. But see, Carson and his friends were happy about it— delighted. They *wanted* Japan to attack U.S. forces. That way, we'd have no choice. We'd have to go to war against Japan, and then we'd be at war against Germany, too."

"So," Smith interrupted, "Carson and his friends didn't like what was in Jordan's article?"

"That's why they grabbed him that day. They definitely didn't want public opinion to be against entering the war. They didn't want people to think America was being tricked into it by its own leaders."

"But everybody's furious about Japan," Smith said. "Jordan's article wouldn't have changed that, would it?"

"As it turned out, probably not. Nobody—not Jordan, not Carson, not Roosevelt—nobody thought the Japs would attack in Hawaii. Everyone figured the Philippines. Carson and his friends weren't sure the Philippines would be enough."

"Enough what?"

"Enough to piss off the American public," Earl said. "They were worried that a Japanese attack in some remote place like the Philippines wouldn't do it. They thought they would need something more to get public opinion worked up against Japan."

"Oh Jesus," Smith groaned. "So they stuck Jordan with that sword?"

"Yep."

"And it turned out they didn't really need to go to all that trouble," Smith said, shaking his head.

"That's right," Earl said. "The planes were on their way to Honolulu."

*   *   *   *

"Mr. Fletcher's daughter is with him," said the woman at the desk. "Let me go tell her you're here."

She shuffled around the counter and down the hallway. "Be prepared," Earl said softly to Smith. "He looks terrible. It's a little shocking."

Smith nodded. The woman waved them into the hall and stopped them part way to Fletcher's room. "Go on in," she said. "But try to keep it short."

"Yes, ma'am."

Eleanor Berkson, eyes red, shoulders drooped, met them outside the doorway. "This is Detective Smith," Earl whispered. "He knows your father. He's been working on this case."

"Hello," she said. "Go ahead; he'll be able to hear you. He might not open his eyes, but he'll squeeze your hand. He's excited, if you can call it that ... he's excited to see you."

"We'll make it fast."

"I'll be in the lobby if you need me."

Earl sat next to the bed and put his hand on Fletcher's and squeezed. "Bud. It's me."

The old man didn't open his eyes. He squeezed back and whispered, "Earl."

"Lester Smith is with me. He's been working on this, as you know."

Fletcher gave a small wave.

Earl leaned in close and talked, for about five minutes, stopping just twice to ask Fletcher if he understood. Both times, he nodded.

"That's it," said Earl, straightening but still holding Fletcher's hand. "I didn't think I had"—Fletcher squeezed, trying to interrupt—"any choice, unless"—Fletcher squeezed harder, and Earl stopped. Then Fletcher whispered, "One thing."

Earl bent down again, his ear just a few inches from Fletcher's mouth. Smith couldn't hear what the old man said. Only the reply: "Yes, sir. I suppose I should."

Earl stood and pointed to the door. "I'll see you tomorrow, or the day after, Bud. Eleanor will be back in just a minute. I'll—see you."

"What was that last thing?" Smith asked in the hallway.

"I'll tell you in the car. Let's say good-bye to Bud's daughter."

*   *   *   *

They pulled out of the driveway, onto the magnolia-lined Orange Grove Boulevard, where the Rose Parade should have been, two days later. Smith guided the car down the ramp to enter the parkway, then turned his head to his passenger. "Well?"

Earl rubbed his eyes. "Bud told me I should include John. 'Get your boy taken care of,' is what he said."

"Meaning you should—"

"Get John some help, from Lindgren. While he's at it."

"I'd feel better about it if you did," said Smith. "Yeah. Include John in the bargain. I'd feel better about this whole fucked-up deal if you could do that."

Earl sighed. He saw, just in his mind and only for a moment, his brother. At the water's edge, pant legs rolled, holding a small boy's hands. "So would I," he said.

Thirty-Nine

La Golondrina was observing St. Patrick's Day 1942 with green crepe-paper garlands, draped around the door and dropping from the ceiling beams. Earl looked at his watch: 12:15. Lester was late.

"Sorry, Earl," he said as he sat down. "I got delayed at the courthouse." Smith looked around. "This is a hell of a place to celebrate an Irish feast day."

"Got some news for you," Earl said.

"Please tell me Emmett Carson's back in town."

Earl smiled. "Sorry. But just in case he ever does come back I have the list, remember, and the magazine article. Locked up in my office. Especially the list. That's our trump card with Lindgren too."

The news, he told Smith, was that Jordan's son had survived, evacuated with General MacArthur from the Philippines. He was in Australia.

"That's great," Smith said. "But how are we ever gonna explain this to *him?*"

"We'll have to think about that. How's the house?" Earl waved to a waiter.

"It suits me fine," Smith said. "Mrs. Brady get the rent check?"

"Yep. Ah, beef enchiladas, *por favor*. Lucky Lager."

"Same here," said Smith. He leaned across the table. "Some goddamn deal with this Jap relocation, I'd say. Never seen anything like it. You were right about that."

"Yeah," Earl agreed. "Glad we got them out of here. That family, I mean."

"Everything working?"

"Perfect, so far. Tim and his sister got their orders, reporting next week, as a matter of fact. Parents are going to be staying at the ranch. They like it. Mr. Tanaka has a job at a school not too far away."

"John?"

"Back in college, full time, and I do mean full time. Supposed to be out in June of '43 with a degree and a navy commission. Then he can go to Intelligence if he wants."

"I'll drink to that, I guess," said Smith, lifting the beer bottle.

Forty

On a foggy June morning in 1942, Earl Brady showed his badge to a Coast Guard sentry at the entrance to Santa Monica pier. The young man excused himself—"Wait here, please"—and disappeared through a doorway several steps away.

"All right, sir," he said when he returned a moment later, "you may proceed. My instructions are fifteen minutes."

"Shouldn't even be that long," Earl said. He walked quickly past the wood sawhorses and through the gap in the burlap sandbags. In just a few minutes he was at the end of the pier. There was no wind and no horizon to mark the end of gray water or the beginning of gray sky.

"Are you sure?" Doris had asked, the night before.

"Not completely," he had answered. "But Colonel Jordan's dead, and so is Bud. The Tanakas are safe, and so is John if he wants to be. What's done is done. I don't see a reason to keep this, how it could do any good."

So he reached into his coat and pulled it out. The knotted sock held two pounds of lead fishing sinkers and four pages of onionskin paper. Jordan's article entered the water with a dull plop.

978-0-595-39886-7
0-595-39886-3

Printed in the United States
105279LV00003B/4/A

9 780595 398867